THE WARRIOR

WITH THE

PIERCED

HEART

Also by
Chris Bishop

The Shadow of the Raven Series:
Blood and Destiny
The Final Reckoning

THE WARRIOR
WITH THE
PIERCED
HEART

CHRIS BISHOP

RedDoor

Published by RedDoor
www.reddoorpublishing.com

© 2018 Chris Bishop

ISBN 978-1-910453-59-9

A CIP catalogue record for this book is available
from the British Library

Cover design: Patrick Knowles
www.patrickknowlesdesign.com

Map design: Joey Everett

Typesetting: Tutis Innovative E-Solutions Pte. Ltd

Printed and bound in Denmark by Nørhaven

For James and Abi

A glossary of some of the terms used in this story can be found at the back of the book

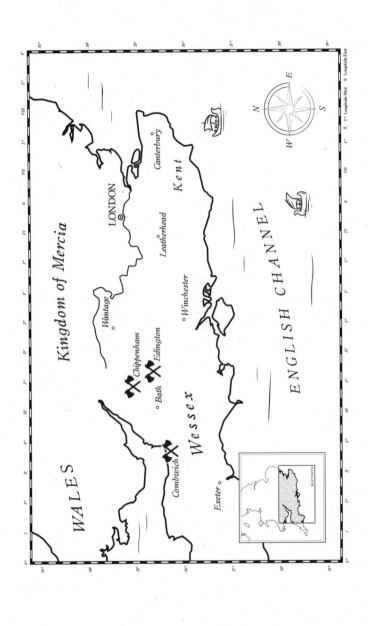

Our longest journey on this earth is from
the cradle to the grave
Fools and heroes complete it soonest

Prelude

Must my conscience be burdened for ever by all that transpired that first day after we left Chippenham? Am I to be blamed for all those who perished simply because I did as I was ordered? If so, then I must crave forgiveness even though I contend that I was not at fault – my only sin was one of undue haste and that I've freely acknowledged before God. Even though I might well have been counted among the number of those who were slain that fateful day, all that occurred still weighs heavy on my soul and thus I would now relate my account of those events – and all that followed – and will do so as faithfully as my memory allows.

You will recall that I, Matthew, christened Edward, third born son of the noble Saxon Edwulf, had forsaken my commitment to the Holy Church and declined the chance to become a warrior. Lord Alfred, in recognition of all I'd endured and achieved on his behalf, then offered to let me serve at his court as he sought to secure and restore his kingdom. He even agreed not to oppose my marriage to Emelda, the girl I loved, even though she was, in his eyes and that of many others, both a whore and the daughter of a traitor.

My first mission was to march ahead of Alfred's army and prepare for his triumphant entry into Exeter to mark his great victory at Edington. Thus, with an escort of a dozen men together with Edmund, the boy I'd offered to adopt and whose father my brother had slain, I set off across our still troubled land knowing full well that bands of restless Vikings still roamed free, armed and intent on vengeance. Even so, it should have been a journey of just five or perhaps six days but, as I was to find to my cost, in life the road you're given to travel is seldom what you wish for – and never what you expect.

Chapter One

Even as we left Chippenham things did not bode well for our journey. One member of my escort was unwell and had to turn back, little knowing that the pains in his belly would serve to save his life. The weather then turned against us so that we struggled through the wind and rain until forced to seek shelter, thereby losing several hours of precious daylight. Little wonder then that when I saw the chance to make up lost time I was tempted to take it.

Perhaps I should have known better than to make haste through such hostile terrain but I was far from being reckless. I sought only to ensure that we reached Exeter in time so, rather than skirt around the forest when we reached it, I ordered my men to follow a trail which led directly through it. The trail was wide with a small stream running beside it and trees steeped high on either side. I knew that these offered the perfect cover for an ambush and was prudent enough to order my men to keep their rank and walk side by side, each of them raising a shield so as to offer protection from both flanks. As Edmund carried no shield I gave him mine then shared the cover of those behind me, walking with them to make a less obvious target.

At first everything seemed as it should. There was no sign of any Vikings and I knew that such a large group of armed men had nothing to fear from robbers. Even so, we remained wary as we pushed on hard for the rest of that day hoping not to have to make our camp for the night whilst still within the forest. Perhaps in our haste we grew careless or perhaps we were just unlucky. Either way, we walked into the Viking trap like a linnet flying straight into the talons of an eagle.

It was Edmund's young eyes which saw them first and he at once drew his sword and raised it as high above his head as he could manage. I was not sure what had riled the boy but then caught sight of a glint of light as the rays of the setting sun struck the brightly burnished blade of a sword or perhaps a spearhead. I cannot say which but, like Edmund, I recognised at once what it meant. I turned to give the order to close up, but even before I could speak I was struck by an arrow which took me full in the chest. For a moment I remained standing, shocked by the sudden pain and by the sheer force of the strike. Then I staggered a few paces before falling, stunned and helpless. Although desperate to get up and relay my orders I found that I couldn't move for I was pinned to the ground like a beetle stranded on its back.

Had I breath enough to shout anything it would have been for the others to save themselves. In truth, there was nothing they could do to aid me, and, in any event, they reacted exactly as they were trained to do, turning to defend themselves back to back with their shields raised and their spears poised.

Thereafter all I could hear was the dreadful din of battle. I guessed that the Vikings had come down upon us in force. Men were shouting and calling as they locked in combat, some screaming in fear or from whatever madness they find in battle whilst others acknowledged their wounds with groans or shrill cries of pain and anguish. As I listened to all this I was surprised not to feel more pain but then recalled being told that the full agony of death comes only as the end draws nigh – as if some last, dreadful spasm is needed to force the soul to actually leave the body.

With my hand, I reached up and found the shaft of the arrow. I couldn't see it clearly as my vision was blurred but I could feel it well enough. There was blood from the wound but not as much as I expected, the arrow having blocked the flow of it. Even so, I judged that the arrowhead was embedded deeply enough, though I could not be sure exactly how far as part of the shaft had broken when I fell. From all I could tell it had pierced my heart or was so close to it as to make no difference; death would come as soon as it was pulled from my chest, or sooner. Certain that I could not survive the wound, I was tempted to pull it free myself and thereby hasten any final agony and be done with it; but to take my own life thus was against my Christian creed. In deference to my former calling as a novice monk I therefore lay back and prepared to endure what I was sure would follow.

During all that time the battle raged around me. I desperately wanted to see how my men fared but all I knew was that which I could hear. There was little comfort in that. Their screams seemed to echo from the trees and I knew that with such numbers set against them they would all be slain or taken soon enough. Even as I listened I kept seeing again that image of young Edmund with his sword held high and I prayed he would be spared even though I knew it was a futile hope; surely none would survive the blood fest which would follow such a crazed attack.

It was then, in what I thought to be my final moments, that my spirit seemed to leave my body. I found myself floating over the frenzied battle and looking down upon the slaughter.

What I saw saddened me beyond words, as my men were being slain and butchered. Like me, two of them had fallen to arrows as the Vikings attacked and they also lay dead or dying whilst the rest fought back against overwhelming odds. The Viking warriors numbered perhaps thirty or more and even having taken so few casualties seemed inclined to show no mercy. For them it was about vengeance, not stealing our supplies or looking for plunder, therefore only blood would serve to satisfy their cravings. Having split my small force, they had only to run the few survivors to ground to complete their slaughter. I watched as a man named Eagbert, whom I had chosen personally for the mission, ran towards the cover of the trees but was caught and skewered by spears from two sides at once. As he fell to his knees they twisted the shafts to increase his pain. Athelstan, another fine warrior, was slain with an axe blow to his forehead which all but cleaved his skull in two, whilst his brother, Aethelred, had been strung up against a tree and was being disembowelled, screaming as they pulled the entrails from his body.

I was helpless to assist but watched as the Viking warriors made themselves busy probing the bodies of the fallen with their swords and spear points to make certain that none still lived. Then I noticed that young Edmund had indeed been spared. I was at once grateful for that small mercy and could only assume that he had perhaps been recognised by one of his Viking kin.

Still looking down on them, I watched as the Vikings then started to strip the bodies, taking jewellery, weapons and anything else worth stealing. In my case they roughly turned my body over and removed my still sheathed sword – the one Edwin had given me and which had once belonged to our beloved father. They also took my birth ring, my gold crucifix and my purse before stripping away my fleece jerkin and my shoes to leave me naked but for my undershirt and leggings. They would have taken all except that my shirt had been soiled by blood and the leggings by the fact that I'd loosened my bowels as I fell.

I recall looking down on two men who were standing over me at that point, but they didn't finish me. Either they thought me dead already or reckoned that I couldn't hope to survive such a dreadful wound and would die more slowly if left for it to take its course. Instead, they kicked my ribs then spat in my face before leaving me to my fate.

* * * * *

I cannot now say how much of what I recall after that is true. Possibly it was just a dream or a manifestation of my tortured mind yet, if pressed, I would swear that I was engulfed in a pool of utter darkness through which I seemed to swim as though in the deep dark waters of a lake at night. There I saw the faces of many men I recognised but knew to have died, some of them many years before. Edwin was among them, as was my father, their arms waving as if to welcome me. I moved towards them, struggling to pull myself through the darkness, but, as I drew closer, I realised that they were not beckoning me as I'd thought, rather they were ushering me away, imploring me to turn back.

After that I seemed to wake. My limbs had grown cold and numb by then but the pain in my chest was much more intense. I shivered and convulsed in a way I'd seen dying men do and wondered how long it would take for me to die. I hoped it would be soon as all was quiet by then and I was probably the only one still living, the Vikings having gathered up their spoil and gone. Next would come the crows and the wolves and the other wild beasts of the forest intent upon feeding on the corpses which were still strewn across the battlefield. To be taken thus whilst still alive would test my faith to the limit. It was a terrible way to die and I had the means to avoid it by simply pulling the arrow from my chest.

As I lay there I recall that I could hear my own breathing, which was rasped and hoarse, sounding like a chain being drawn across a pebbled courtyard. I felt again for the shaft of the arrow and calmed myself when I found it, certain that when removed it would rip my heart from my breast so that death would then be instant. Thus reassured, I uttered a few short prayers before closing my eyes and prepared to surrender myself to God.

* * * * *

I awoke to find myself in a very strange place. It was not at all as I imagined either heaven or hell to be. In fact I gradually began to realise that it was nothing more than a cavern, open wide at the front and dimly lit with candles. There were many jars and pots wedged on to makeshift shelves formed within the fissures of the rock and others which had been placed upon the ground, several of them stacked one on top of the other. I was laying on a small cot, naked but covered with a single fur and with my head rested on a soft pillow that smelled of wild flowers, herbs and fresh cut bracken. I looked around and although too weak to move, gradually realised that I was not alone. My vision was still too blurred to see clearly beyond the fact that the person who was with me was a woman.

'W-where a-am I?' I managed, my voice not much more than a whisper as I struggled even to breathe.

She seemed to hear me and came across to feel my brow with her hand. 'You're with one who would help you,' she said softly.

I looked at her with eyes half closed. As such I could not make out her features.

'I am called Ingar,' she said as if knowing what I wanted to ask. 'I'm a healer and will restore you if you'll let me.'

As I stared up at her I realised that although still in pain, it was no longer quite as intense as it had been. 'H-how…?' I tried to ask, my voice failing before I could finish.

'Try to recall for yourself all that which has befallen you,' she urged. 'That's the only way you will fully restore your mind as once it was.'

As I thought back I did seem to remember a hooded figure who'd appeared from the darkness and gathered up what remained of me. 'The d-demon!' I blurted out, so terrified at the prospect that I reached out and grasped her wrist tightly with my hand.

She laughed aloud. 'There are no demons in this forest,' she assured me. 'Spirits perhaps, though all of them benevolent and kind. The man you saw was as mortal as you are and no more a sinner than any other. He meant you no harm but found you and gathered you on to a litter then brought you here to me.'

I realised that made more sense than my being carried off by demons and such like. 'B-but I d-died…' I stammered.

'Perhaps you did,' she said softly. 'Perhaps you died but the Gods saw fit to send you back to us. But we shall speak more of that when you're well.'

I reached up to touch the arrow as if to check it was still there, then shook my head thinking that if she meant to remove it I needed first to make my peace with God.

Once more she seemed to know what I was thinking. 'You must trust me,' she said. 'I have already given you something for your pain, but we must act before the wound festers.' So saying, she lit a small taper which was set in wax and floated in a bowl of clear liquid. She held it just above my chest and using her hand, wafted the fumes towards me. 'Breathe deeply,' she urged. 'Let the vapours take their course.'

'But this…this is p-pagan c-craft!' I said accusingly, then tried to push the bowl aside. As I did so another spasm of pain shot through my body. 'My God w-will not c-countenance t-this!' I protested, grimacing though, by then, too weak to stop her.

She placed her hand on my brow once more. 'Healing has no borders,' she said calmly. 'It is not confined to one God or another and my ways are those of the earth. They are the old ways, as much needed now as they ever were.'

'W-what are y-you?' I demanded, trying without success to raise myself up as a strange feeling of helplessness seemed to engulf me.

'As I told you, I am a healer as was my mother before me and her mother before that. I am neither a pagan nor a witch; I simply have the gift of the knowledge which was once shared by all. You must trust me in this, otherwise you will surely die before your time. And if you do that then you should know that your soul will never rest.'

I stared at the bowl, not sure what I should do but knowing that already the fumes were having an effect, making me feel distant and drowsy.

'Breathe deeply,' she urged again. 'For we must make all haste before your flesh cleaves to the shaft. Once it does the arrow cannot be removed cleanly.'

I had no choice but to do as she instructed for my will was no longer my own. As I lay my head back against the pillow I began to feel completely at ease as the fumes, which had a slightly sweet, almost sickly smell about them, seemed to fill my head and soothe my whole being. Then I began to drift into a strange trance during which, although awake, I felt an emptiness I can scarce explain. It was as though everything I saw was happening to someone else. Thus at ease, I watched as Ingar gently bathed the wound to cleanse it. Then, rubbing her hands together to warm them, she gently cupped them around the shaft of the arrow where it had entered my chest. As she closed her eyes she seemed to fall into a deep and intense contemplation before slowly but gently easing the arrow free using just her thumbs, stopping every few moments as if to rest. All I felt at that point was the intense heat from her hands as I watched as the arrow seemed to rise almost of its own accord from my chest until, at last, it was fully withdrawn.

When it was done she checked the bone arrowhead to ensure no splinters had been left within, then she wiped away the blood from my chest before applying some sort of balm. That done, she sealed the wound with beeswax, firmly pressing it into the hole made by the arrow before allowing me to fall into a deep and much-needed sleep.

Chapter Two

I cannot say how long I slept though I recall a few waking moments during which I watched this strange woman as she went about her work. She was certainly very striking to look at, being tall and slender and with long red hair that reached almost to her waist. Unlike most women she made no attempt to conceal it with a cap, nor even a shawl, but rather she let it hang loose and free. She wore a long white shift which was tied at the waist with a girdle on which had been embroidered the shape of many serpents, all of them entwined so that it was hard to tell where one began and another ended. She also wore a thin but richly patterned torc around her neck that I took to be of gold. All this I noticed between fitful bouts of sleep during which I endured many terrible dreams about all the men who had died on my account. Often I would wake sweating and full of remorse, sometimes even weeping but, mercifully, on such occasions Ingar never allowed me to remain awake for long before wafting yet more of her soothing vapours towards me.

When awake, I would sometimes watch her as she busied herself with her herbs and potions, working at a low stone slab which seemed to have been skilfully hewn from a single rock and had many strange symbols carved into the sides. It looked to be too big to have been hauled there by human hands but must have at least been moved to that position, being so well set just outside the entrance to the cavern in what looked to be a small clearing within the forest. Sometimes I could hear her singing softly under her breath but mostly she worked there in silence.

Although still weak, I was aware that during this time many people came to visit her – or perhaps they came to see me as they would always enter the cavern and peer at me as I lay there. I would pretend to be asleep when they came lest they ask me about my wound and how I came by it, for there was nothing I could say to explain why I was still alive.

For what seemed like several weeks Ingar continued to tend to my needs, unashamedly washing down my naked body even though we were alone. Few women would have risked their reputation in such a way, but she seemed to pay it no mind. Instead, she gradually allowed me to remain awake for longer and longer each day and, once my wound started to heal, we would sometimes talk.

'So,' she asked me on one such occasion, 'tell me all that you now recall.'

I told her about floating free from my body and looking down upon the frenzied battle, then about seeing people I knew to have died before me who were sending me away.

She nodded as though she understood all that. 'It explains much,' she assured me. 'It also shows that it was not your time to die, perhaps because your destiny is yet to be fulfilled.'

'Then why do I feel such guilt at having been the only one to survive?' I asked.

'The Gods saw fit to spare you,' she said. 'Be grateful for that.'

I glanced down at the wound and shook my head. 'I sometimes wish I had died along with all the others.'

'You cannot mean that. Life is a precious gift for which you should give thanks to whatever God you worship. It should never be willed away nor taken lightly.'

'But I feel it's wrong that I alone should have survived when all the others perished on a mission which I selfishly undertook for my own advancement.'

She said nothing for a moment and I feared I'd offended her.

'I am truly grateful for all you've done to heal me,' I added, hoping to make amends. 'I will of course repay you when I can. You must tell me what you most need. I am not without means and…'

She smiled at me then lifted the blanket to cover my shoulders. 'There are ways you can repay me but not as you think. As for the guilt you feel for the loss of your friends, I can say only that it will ease with time. But Matthew, hear me in this, although the wound to your chest may seem to heal, it will one day claim your life, of that you can be certain. The years you have left are what we call "the given years" and you should use them as best you may.'

I tried not to listen to her warning, not wanting to hear what she was saying even though I feared she was right given that I still felt much weakened by the wound. Instead, I told her of my life; of how I'd once been a novice monk but had then followed the path of a warrior, proudly fighting at Lord Alfred's side. I also told her of Emelda and of how I longed to return to her as soon as I was healed.

Although I was still not strong enough to rise unaided at that point, Ingar would sometimes help me to walk outside the cavern, supporting me about the waist as I strove to manage even a few uncertain steps.

During all this time she continued to tend my wound each day, wiping away any secretion then applying more balm to soothe it and reduce the bruising until, at last, it did indeed begin to heal. She also gave me a bowl of gruel each day, feeding me from a spoon until I was able to manage for myself. As well as the gruel, she bade me sit up and drink deeply from a flask of strange amber liquid that had an acrid smell and which tasted warm and salty. Once past the smell, it was palatable enough and although she refused to say what it was, she assured me that it would make me stronger. With these ministrations I eventually recovered enough to stand unaided and even managed to get up and walk a little, at first just shuffling as far as the stone slab and back, then gradually going further. One day I was surprised to discover a small pool at the very edge of the clearing which I'd not been able to see from my cot. I assumed she used it for water and for washing.

'It's called The Bloody Pool,' she informed me when I asked her about it. 'It's named for those nights when the waters take on the light of the moon which turns them almost crimson. It's said that it marks the place of a terrible massacre in which many innocent people died. The slaughter was so great that their blood filled a hollow in the ground and thus the pool was formed.'

I confess I was doubtful but didn't press her further.

By then I'd recovered enough to spend most of each day fully conscious and free from sleep, though I still needed to rest and remained morose and troubled by all that had happened to my men. One evening, as I lay in my cot, I saw Ingar walk outside. I swung my legs to the floor intending to join her but only went as far as the entrance to the cavern.

Not knowing I was watching, she moved towards the pool where she unfastened the girdle she wore around her waist then opened her shift and let it fall from her shoulders so that she stood naked in the moonlight. I couldn't help but stare at her body which was pale but also rounded and full, her breasts heavy and her limbs long and slender. She then waded into the pool and there bathed herself. When she'd finished, she emerged and walked, wet and still naked, to stand beside the stone slab. I had initially taken this to be some form of work bench where she mixed her cures and potions, but that night all had been cleared away and instead she had placed several curious items upon it as though they were deserving of reverence. These items included some animal skulls and a large piece of rock which contained a prominent vein of quartz. In the centre of all that she'd placed a gnarled and twisted piece of wood which formed the easily recognisable shape of a naked woman standing with her arms uplifted. The wood had not been carved into shape, of that I was certain; rather it had grown that way of its own accord. Anyway, she stood there for some moments with her head bowed, then raised her own hands as if reaching upwards thereby imitating the wooden figure whilst bathing in the glow of the moon. When she had done, she quietly began to dress herself.

'What were you doing?' I asked, having returned to my cot before she came back. Her own cot was in a corner which she had screened with a richly embroidered drape.

She smiled and came across to stand beside me, seemingly unembarrassed to learn that I'd seen her. 'I'm aligning the cycle of my bleedings with the passage of the moon,' she said simply.

I knew little of such matters so said nothing, even when she did the same thing again every night after that for the next four or five days.

Then one night she came into the cavern without having performed her ritual. She snuffed out all the candles then came over to me and sniffed my wound as she sometimes did and seemed satisfied that it was indeed healing well. A dry scab had formed by then and she saw no cause to disturb it. Instead, she gave me a different potion which she bade me drink. This was quite unlike anything she had ever offered me before and tasted so bitter that I shuddered as I drank it. Having done so, I lay back on my cot in the darkness and gradually realised that whatever the elixir was it was having a very strange effect on me. All my senses seemed to come alive and my vision became as sharp as any sword. It was as though whatever it was had seeped deep into my bones and was gradually taking over my very being. Seeming pleased at this, Ingar helped me from the cot. My legs were still shaky, but she led me gently outside where it was dark but for a few torches which seemed to flicker and set their light dancing on the trees that surrounded us. As I watched and marvelled at the brightness of those lights, I was suddenly aware that many people had gathered in the shadows beyond the slab but had stayed close to the edge of the forest as though afraid of drawing too close. I could see none of them clearly but those I could make out were all wearing masks or strange headgear that seemed to represent all the beasts of the forest – stags, foxes, bears, wolves and such like, all with skins and furs draped across their shoulders. Even as I stared at them I seemed unaware of my own nakedness as Ingar led me to the pool where she too undressed. To my amazement, the waters had indeed taken on the colour of blood or, if not quite that, they were imbued with something like it. Perhaps it was a trick of my mind, but I confess that at that point my head was filled with strange thoughts that seemed to tumble around inside it. Having bathed together, she then led me to the slab where she gently guided me to sit then made me lie back upon the cold hard stone.

At this, those watching us began stamping their feet or beating the trees with staves. At first it was just a slow, repetitive beat like that of a distant drum but, as it gradually quickened, they began a strange rhythmic chant that seemed to invoke and possess me until my whole body could not help but move in unison with it. As it did so, I was suddenly aware that all my manly impulses were beginning to stir, so much so that I could scarce control myself. It was as though my blood had become heated from within and wanted only to explode from my being.

I'll never know what was in the potion she gave me to drink that night but, by then, it had taken over my whole body. I recall staring longingly at her nakedness, every sinew of my being needing to possess her to the extent that when she knelt astride me all was quickly accomplished. Like a willing slave, I entered her with so much impatience that all it took was a few moments for me satisfy my longing.

In my defence, I did try to resist her and pull myself away, but she held me fast with her long fingers, gripping me so hard that her fingernails broke the skin on my back and left large red wheals upon it. It was all so intoxicating that, moments later, I entered her again. In fact three times we were united that night until, fully sated, I finally lay back exhausted.

* * * * *

My dreams that night were as vivid as any I can ever recall, though, as I began to wake, I remembered very little about them except that they contained some strange visitations. These reminded me of the Holy saints and martyrs and, for some reason, included my old abbot, Father Constantine, who seemed to be watching me disapprovingly. I also recalled seeing young Edmund with his sword raised as we were attacked but realised that was my conscience berating me for having led him and the others into a trap. I shook those unholy images from my mind and crossed myself in the hope of redemption.

Once fully awake I was distraught and could scarce believe what had transpired the previous night. My first thought was to seek solace in prayer, repenting the fact that I'd allowed myself to be used for some pagan ritual. Even though I'd not committed the sin of my own accord I knew that it would not sit well with my faith and that I would need to do penance for it. Not only that, but in failing to resist the temptations of the flesh I'd betrayed my unspoken oath to Emelda; not knowingly it was true, but once started I'd been as willing as when first I lay with her. And not just once, but three times in all.

As I gently eased myself from the cot I found that I was dressed in my undershirt and leggings once more, except that they'd been cleaned and mended. I knelt beside the cot and began to pray though struggled to find the words I needed in order to make my peace with God and thereby ease my troubled conscience.

Seeing me awake and finding me on my knees, Ingar came and offered me water. 'You have committed no sin,' she assured me. 'It was the destiny about which I told you. The reason you were sent back from the afterlife.'

'How can such an act as that be my destiny?' I demanded, still angry as much at myself as I was with her. 'I've betrayed my faith and the woman I love!'

'You have betrayed no one. What was done was a course set by a hand much higher than either yours or mine. Remember what I told you about the given years and how you should use your time with purpose? Well, it was ordained that I would one day conceive a girl child and that she would inherit great and mystical knowledge, combining my own powers of healing with those of a man who even death could not hold. You are such a man.'

For a moment I was too stunned to say anything. 'Who foretold such a thing!' I demanded.

'Think no more on this,' she said, helping me to my feet. 'All that has transpired between us is simply a part of your destiny and mine. And the fruit of our loins will be of great import, you'll see, for she'll have such powers of healing as may benefit all.'

'You cannot be sure that you've conceived a child from our union, much less that it will be a girl!' I chided her.

Ingar smiled. 'You'd be surprised what is given for me to know.'

'Even if what you say is true you must realise that I cannot stay to help you raise a child,' I protested. 'As I told you, my duty is to Lord Alfred himself and besides, I'm promised to another and—'

She put her fingers to my lips to stop me saying more. 'Matthew, you have no further part to play in this. When you're strong enough you can return to your woman and think no more upon the events which have happened here, for I have taken all I need of you. Our Earth Mother is a divine provider and she will amply supply whatever else is needed for me to raise our daughter in her ways, as did my mother and her mother before that. Now, let me examine your wound. I fear that all your exertions last night may have taken their toll.'

'My wound is fine,' I snapped, still angry at having been used by her.

She looked at me for a moment then went to pick up an apple and a knife which she held up for me to see. 'Matthew, think of this apple as your heart,' she said, then used the knife to cut it with barely enough pressure to do more than scratch the skin. 'This mark shows how the arrow I eased from your chest grazed your heart. If you watch you will see how in time even that slight wound will cause this fruit to rot from within. And so it is with you. Your wound will never fully heal and will one day kill you, just as surely as the small cut in this apple will cause this fruit to wither.'

'But surely the wound will heal in time?' I said.

She shook her head. 'No, Matthew. You're dying,' she said coldly. 'You have the given years but they will last only as long as your fate allows.' With that, she helped me to lie back on my cot where she untied my undershirt and gently opened it to reveal my chest. Normally an arrow wound would be livid and scarred, not just from the impact but also from where a knife had been used to dig out the arrowhead intact, making it much larger than that which had been inflicted. The scars from that were always puckered and swollen, even when fully healed, but mine was not much more than a large blemish, albeit still covered by a crusted scab. That was beginning to bleed again but she wiped away the blood then applied a balm, which she later told me comprised of wild garlic, onions, wine and salt, all of which had been left to brew in a copper cauldron for several days. That she assured me would counter any risk of infection. When that was done she also applied some of the balm to the wheals on my back which had been caused by her nails as she gripped me so hard during our union.

I began to realise that whatever her convictions, Ingar was as truly committed to her craft as any priest and more skilled than any healer I had ever come across – even at the Abbey where some monks took it upon themselves to make a study of medicines and cures. 'Is this the same balm that you used to heal the wound when the arrow was removed?' I asked.

'No, I used a small amount of comfrey,' she said. 'It was ground fine and mixed to form a paste with other herbs and the bark of a particular tree that grows beside the stream.'

'And you didn't stitch the wound to close it?'

She shook her head. 'There was no need. Although it was deep, because I was able to draw the arrow so cleanly all I needed was beeswax to seal it, nothing more.'

'You are truly a gifted healer,' I admitted. 'But such craft is forbidden by my faith. You had no right to…'

'Perhaps, but then my calling would not allow me to watch you die when you could be saved.'

'But surely these are dark arts of one form or another and therefore the hand of the Devil lies within them?'

'I'm no witch if that's what you mean. As I've told you, I'm a healer. I use only that which the good Earth Mother has provided. I have no spells or incantations and I promise you

21

that neither your God nor any other was called upon to help in my ministrations.'

'Yet you drugged me with your potions to have your way with me.'

'That much is true. As I said, it was your destiny. Mine was to ensure you could fulfil it. Besides, you said you wanted to repay me and in this way you've bestowed a gift more precious than any you could ever imagine.'

'So what was in the strange amber potion that you made me drink each day and which you said would make me stronger?'

She laughed. 'I didn't make you. But if you would know what it was then I will say only that it is the true elixir of life.'

'There's no such thing!' I protested.

'Oh, believe me there is, though few would deign to taste it.'

'Why, what is it?'

She laughed again. 'It is that which the fool wastes each day but of which the wise man drinks his fill,' she said teasingly.

We Saxons loved a riddle but this was one I couldn't solve at first, however hard I tried. Then it dawned on me what it was. 'Are you saying that I drank my own piss!' I said aloud.

'Not just your own. Yours was bloody and had traces of pus within it so I gave you some of mine as well, albeit mixed with herbs to sweeten it.'

'Then you've surely poisoned my guts!'

'No, what I've given you has helped to make you well. As I've said, it's your wound that will kill you in time, not my remedies. In fact I'm surprised that you survived the exertions of our coupling as, with your destiny fulfilled, there is no reason why you should live any longer. You must surely have the heart of a warrior or perhaps the Gods have yet more in mind for you to accomplish. Whatever the truth of it, be warned that even you cannot endure such a wound for ever. Remember the apple and how I showed you that even the slightest graze can cause it to rot and then to wither from within.'

* * * * *

Ingar tended me well for several more days after that and under her care my strength gradually returned, though I still worried that in doing so she was damaging her reputation.

'I've tended men before and often in intimate ways,' she chided me as if to justify her actions. 'There's no shame in healing the wounded nor in tending the sick, for sickness and disease are as much a part of nature as are we all. Besides, you cannot be more intimate than to share what we have shared. As for being alone with you, my calling requires me to live apart from others, free from the distractions of heart and mind so that I might concentrate on all that's needed for my craft. All my forebears did as much and I see no cause for me to depart from that.'

'But what of all the people who came to watch what we did that night?'

'They are those who will benefit most from my healing. They know how important it is for me to give birth to a daughter who will one day continue my maternal line and thereby preserve the craft of my forebears. You may not recall, but even before that night many of them called to visit you, curious to see a man who has returned from the dead. So much so that they even have a name for you.'

'What is it?' I asked intrigued.

She laughed as though not sure whether she should tell me. 'They call you "the warrior with the pierced heart",' she managed at last. 'And your reputation has spread so far that you are now a legend in these parts.'

'But I didn't die!' I protested. 'As you well know, the arrow somehow missed my heart, albeit not by much.'

'To their eyes you did but were then sent back to fulfil your destiny, just as I've said. They and I truly believe that to be so. But whatever the way of it, remember these are but simple folk who still fear the old ways as much as they do the new.'

'Then you shouldn't let them believe such nonsense! They would be better served in looking to their priests for comfort, not witchcraft or pagan rites.'

'They do. They go to your Church to find solace and to beg forgiveness for their sins as they have little enough in this world and hope for better in the one to come. Prayers and confession are the only way they know to secure repentance for their souls, but to cure their mortal aches and pains they come to me and I provide the remedies they need. Such an arrangement works well enough and besides, they'll find no succour for whatever ails them any other way.'

I found it hard to accept what she was saying. If true, it meant that for them their religion and their Church were just a means to an end. That was at odds with all my training as a novice monk in which I'd been persuaded that there was nothing more powerful than prayer and that worship and dedication to God needed to bleed from every fibre of our being. Yet I had to admit that Ingar impressed me greatly, not least because she seemed so at one with her world, something

24

I and others I'd known, be they warriors or monks, never seemed able to achieve.

'You should not be too quick to judge the old ways nor even other beliefs,' she once chided me. 'I've met people of many different faiths. They may not admit it but most simply view the same God but from a different place.'

'But what of those like the Vikings who have many Gods?' I asked.

She shrugged. 'Perhaps there are many Gods, or perhaps there is just one who has many different guises. Few of us can say for certain except perhaps those who, like you, have died and returned to us.'

'But you know that's not what happened!' I protested. 'True I was close to death, but to claim that I've risen from the grave is blasphemy!'

'Your faith runs deep,' she mused. 'I wonder whether you were right to leave your precious Church?'

Those words troubled me as the guilt I felt for all my many sins, particularly that of having led my men to their deaths, still weighed so heavy on my conscience that I feared I was beginning to doubt my faith. 'So, what of you? Which Gods do you fear most?' I asked.

She shook her head. 'I fear none. All I need for my comfort and protection is here, in the forest and in everything you see. The Earth Mother provides for me and spares me as any mother should.'

'Ah, but not everything in nature is benevolent,' I tried, thinking of some of the herbs I'd seen or heard of which could poison or cause great pain.

She nodded wisely. 'It's true that nature offers some things which can cause terrible torment or suffering and, in some cases, bring even death. But look again Matthew and you'll see that she always provides a remedy for each. For example, the dock leaf grows beside the nettle and will assuage its sting. It is the knowledge of these remedies which is the calling of all true healers, myself included.'

'Then there are no miracles or magic potions? Is that what you're saying?'

'Your Church relies on miracles and strange happenings which defy all logic but there are none in nature, save the miracle of life itself.'

As part of our discussion I reminded her that I stood to become a counsellor to Lord Alfred himself. 'Once restored I shall of course make proper provision for you and our child,' I said as if that might please her.

She seemed not to care about such things. 'Have you understood so little of what I've told you?' she said. 'I neither ask nor want anything from you save that which you have given.'

I had to admit that I'd never met anyone so complete in herself and so at one with her beliefs. Yet my Christian faith would not accept that I could leave her if she was with child. But that was another decision fate would make on my behalf for there was nothing I could have done about all that was to follow.

Chapter Three

I was not sure how long it had been since I'd left Chippenham but at least several months had passed as the days were noticeably longer. Knowing this, I realised it was unlikely that anyone would still be looking for me. Alfred would surely have despatched a small group of men to discover what had become of me and my escort, but the search party would have first needed to return to Chippenham to retrace our steps from there. As they couldn't be sure which route we'd taken, it would have been several days at least before they found what was left of my party – a group of by then rotting bodies, stripped of anything of value and no doubt ravaged by crows and wild beasts. I therefore had to assume they would be unable to tell one man from another and, though they would bury them all, they would not know for certain whether I was to be counted among the ranks of the fallen.

In the end they would have returned to Alfred with the dreadful news that the party had been attacked and that all but two bodies had been recovered and buried. After that there was nothing they could do save to assume that the two who were missing had either been taken by the Vikings for slaves or that their remains had been dragged off by wolves.

I knew Lord Alfred well enough to know that he would be deeply saddened by that news, but I also knew that whatever his regard for me, he could ill afford to have his men waste more time looking for bodies at a time when so much needed to be done within his realm. It was therefore up to me to find my own way back to Chippenham – and thereby to Emelda – as soon as I was strong enough to travel.

Meanwhile my wound had all but healed visibly, the scab having fully crusted and fallen away to reveal a bright pink scar where the skin had regrown to seal it. Ingar assured me that I still needed to rest as much as I could to allow the flesh to fully knit together within, sternly reminding me of her prediction that the wound would one day kill me. It was whilst she was applying yet more of her precious balm one morning that I suddenly had the strangest sense of foreboding; a feeling so intense that it made me shudder.

'What's wrong?' she said, stopping what she was doing and allowing me to sit up and listen to the sounds of the forest.

There was little to be heard. A light breeze lifted the boughs of the trees but that caused barely a whisper. Then something scurried through the undergrowth near the edge of the clearing but, whatever it was, it seemed to present no cause for concern. Yet despite this we both knew that something was wrong as all seemed much too quiet. Even the birds had stopped singing.

'I think someone has just stepped across my grave,' I said, trying to make light of it.

'You heard something, didn't you?' she pressed.

I shook my head. 'No, it was more like something I sensed. Something which has aroused all my instincts as a

28

warrior.' In truth, I doubted whether after all I'd been through those instincts still survived but there was no denying that something had awakened them. Then, for no obvious reason, I seemed to know exactly what it was.

'Hide yourself!' I ordered, getting up and looking about for something that would serve as a weapon. We were in my world then, not hers, and I wasn't about to let either of us be taken without a fight. 'Gather what you can and go!' I urged, almost pushing her aside.

Bemused, she got up and quickly started to gather up her things. 'Matthew, be careful!' she warned. 'Remember your wound!'

'Just go!' I ordered, meaning to follow her. 'We can hide in the forest until it's safe to return.'

I'd never before seen her look frightened but, as she ran towards the trees, she was plainly terrified, all the more so because she had scarce reached them before the raiders appeared.

There were seven or eight of them, all armed and looking ready for a fight. Having not made good my own escape, I seized a stout broom from the corner of the cavern, broke off the end with my foot and thus turned it into a useful staff, the only viable weapon I had. I then went outside to confront the intruders.

They were indeed a motley group. As they blundered into the clearing they were no doubt expecting anyone who had heard them coming to have fled. On seeing me they laughed as one of them stepped forward with his axe poised, not thinking that a boy armed with nothing more than a broken broomstick would give him much trouble. Hence, he was surprised as I drove the end of the stick straight into his face with all the force I could manage. He was already spitting blood and teeth as he reeled away but I gave him no chance to recover. Instead, I struck him again across the back of the neck and he went down hard. As he lay there, moaning as he endured his pain, the second one to try my hand got similar treatment. I dodged his blow and struck him full in the belly, winding him before breaking the stick across his back.

By then the raiders realised what they were up against. They'd thought me an easy target and therefore not allowed me due respect. Two of them had already paid the price for that and the others were not about to make the same mistake.

What they didn't know was that I was all but spent. Although what was left of the splintered broomstick might have been sharp enough to serve as a weapon, so much exertion seemed to have sapped every morsel of strength from my body. Worse still, my wound throbbed as if I'd torn the parts of it inside which were so newly healed and I began to feel dizzy and lightheaded. Empty and exhausted, I dropped first to my knees then fell and lay face down on the ground.

The raiders were quick to seize upon my weakness. Two of them grabbed me and roughly turned me over. As they did so I could hear Ingar's prophecy ringing in my ears 'that wound will surely kill you'. It was not the way I'd expected it to happen but by rendering me helpless I was certain that it was indeed about to cost me my life.

I lay there, staring up at the raiders, so fearful of what I was sure would follow that I almost forgot to breathe. Yet, strangely, although they had overcome me, it seemed they were not intent on blood. Instead, they lifted me up by my arms then half carried, half dragged me over to the stone slab.

Roughly sweeping aside all the items Ingar had placed upon it, they pressed me back against the stone and then bound my hands in front so that I had no chance of escape. Little did they know that I barely had the strength to stand, never mind defend myself again. At that one of them roughly looked me over, forcing open my mouth as if to check my teeth then tipping back my head and staring hard into my eyes. Satisfied, he let me be, no doubt distracted by Ingar as two of his comrades dragged her struggling and kicking from her hiding place.

Unable to believe their good luck at finding such an attractive prize, they started to abuse her, ripping the torc from her neck and tearing at her clothes until one of their number stopped them. He was a big ox of a man, not tall but with a full belly and a mass of tangled yellow hair that hung lank and loose about his shoulders. Whilst I can't be certain of what he said to the others it was clear that he wanted Ingar for himself. As he seized her none there seemed inclined to argue. Instead, Ingar was made to stand beside me where she was also bound then, together, we watched in silence as they ransacked her home and rifled through her few belongings.

* * * * *

When they'd finished rummaging through Ingar's cavern there was little left that wasn't spoiled or broken. Even the pots which she'd filled with her precious herbs and potions had been smashed, but still the raiders found nothing worth stealing except the wooden figure of the naked woman which had once had pride of place on Ingar's altar and which they seemed to find amusing. That they despoiled and insulted with lewd gestures and no doubt some very crude comments.

Disgruntled at finding so little spoil, they marched us both off into the forest. I was still dressed in just my undershirt and leggings and with not even any shoes on my feet whereas Ingar's modesty was barely preserved by the torn shift she had hastily secured with her girdle.

I can recall little of where they took us beyond the fact that we were led deeper into the forest, following what looked to be a freshly cut path – presumably one they'd cleared on their way to find the cavern. I remember thinking that as their path led directly to it they must have known exactly where it was, suggesting someone had betrayed its location. In any event, we had only a short way to go before we arrived at a makeshift camp where two of their number waited, having been left to guard six other prisoners who were all securely bound together with a long rope, forming a file of miserable and dejected men.

With my hands still tied, I was added to this line. As the rope was secured around my neck I noticed that the others all had rips and tears in their tunics which revealed livid wheals to their backs, no doubt caused by the cruel lash of a whip. Though none of them made any attempt to introduce themselves by name, I glanced at those on either side of me. The first was dressed in the habit of a monk and who I later learned answered to the name of Brother Benedict. He was a willowy figure, so tall and slender that I thought he might sway and bend in the wind. The crown of his head had been shaved into a tonsure as a sign of his devotion but he wore no crucifix, his having no doubt been taken. The other man was of stouter build, being short but with broad shoulders and thick-set arms which suggested he was used to hard labour. His hair was cropped close and he had the shadow of a silver beard, indicating he was older than he at first appeared. Still, he looked as though he could handle himself well enough, so I judged him to be a useful ally if we had a chance to escape, though from all I could see at that time there was little hope of that.

Ingar was taken directly to another man who had been laid out on a litter and covered over with furs. It was then I realised that it was her they'd come for, not me. Having heard of her healing skills they needed her to tend one of their own, presumably a man of some importance.

Ingar seemed to know at once what was expected of her. With her bonds untied, she knelt beside the litter then lifted back the furs to examine the man's wound. What she saw seemed to startle even her. I learned later that he had a deep wound to his side, probably from an axe. Ingar told me that even as she looked at him she knew he was beyond saving but, undeterred, she bathed the wound then tried to tell them that she required herbs which could be gathered from the forest. They couldn't understand what she was saying and, by a cruel twist of fate, had destroyed the very remedies their chieftain needed. It was then that the stout fellow next to me was dragged over and made to translate for them. When he explained what she was saying, Ingar was taken off under guard to search for what was required.

Whilst Ingar was away our bonds were checked and we were all made to sit on the ground to wait, though we were offered neither food nor water.

At length Ingar returned and set about her ministrations, cleansing the man's wound again and then examining it even more closely. I could see she was worried. She mixed a poultice by crushing whatever herbs she'd gathered and pressed it into the wound directly before stitching the flesh to seal it. She also mixed some form of elixir with which she wetted his lips, though he seemed too badly wounded to actually drink it.

With that she got up as if to say she'd done all she could. The raiders seemed to understand but instead of dragging her back to join us, they took her to tend the two men I'd struck when they attacked us. They were both complaining about their wounds. One was still bleeding from his jaw and the other kept stretching himself as if to relieve the pain in his back.

'It looks as though you gave a good account of yourself, boy,' said the stout fellow who sat next to me. He quietly introduced himself as Aelred, though seemed reluctant to say why or how he came to be there.

'So what do they want with us?' I asked, knowing I was not going to like the answer. 'They could have easily killed me back there but brought us both here instead.'

'Pah! Don't get your hopes up!' warned Aelred. 'They've spared you for a reason.'

'Why, what's to become of us?'

He gave a snort of derision. 'Think of these bastards as being like alchemists; except it's human flesh they turn into gold, not base metal.'

At first I wasn't sure what he meant, then suddenly it dawned on me. 'You mean they're slavers!' I said, horrified at the prospect and recalling how my elder brother and my sister had both endured a similar fate.

'Aye, slavers. They're probably taking us to the coast where they'll sell us to others who'll then carry us abroad. After that, as like as not you'll wish they had killed you back there. Life will be brutal but, God willing, mercifully short.'

'Surely there's none here who could fetch enough to be worth their while?' I queried, looking at the miserable group of men. Most looked to be too old or frail to be of any value and none appeared to be of noble worth such as might command a ransom.

'Don't worry about that. They'll soon round up a few more to add to our number along the way.'

It was no wonder they hadn't killed me. As slavers, I was worth more to them alive than dead, particularly if they realised who I was. 'But you seem to speak their tongue,' I said, having seen him translate for them when they spoke to Ingar.

'A bit,' he admitted. 'I once lived near the coast and we sometimes traded with their kind when they needed food or fresh water after many days at sea. For that they let us be. When this lot caught up with me a week ago I thought to trade with them in the same way. I soon realised my mistake and, when they turned on me, I, like a fool, tried to make a fight of it.'

'What of the others here?' I asked.

He cast his eye over the other prisoners. All were bruised and dirty, having clearly been beaten into submission and with all the fight knocked out of them. Most were so dejected that it seemed they hardly dared to even look at us, never mind speak. Even Brother Benedict just hung his head in sorrow and seemed to be forever at prayer, though whether that was for his safe deliverance or for his mortal soul I couldn't say.

'Most of this lot are all long past making any attempt to resist,' explained Aelred. 'The poor wretches just suffer in silence and have scarce said two words to each other in all the time I've been here. I don't reckon they'll put up much of a fight even if we get the chance.'

'The monk looks as though he could still be resilient enough,' I said.

Aelred laughed. 'That pious fool is all for turning the other cheek,' he mocked. 'He'll not stand in our way but don't count on him helping much if it comes to a fight.'

'So what's to be done?'

'Nothing. At least, not unless the chance arises. Until then just keep your head down and your mouth shut. And try not to rile the bastards.'

Meanwhile the Vikings had set Ingar to help them pull a broken tooth from the man I'd struck in the face. It was clear from his cries that he was in considerable pain from where they'd tugged at a piece of twine which they'd first wound around what was left of the tooth, taking turns to yank it as hard as they could whilst others restrained him. Ingar eased them aside and gently persuaded the man to open his mouth wide enough for her to see the tooth properly. She then took a small twig which she placed in his jaw to keep it open as she reached inside and deftly pushed and then twisted the tooth with her bare fingers. The man writhed and tried to curse as she did this, but the tooth came free so quickly and so easily that we were all stunned into silence.

'Why would she help them?' I asked.

'I don't know, but if she can distract the bastards long enough that might give us a chance to escape,' said Aelred.

'And if not?' I asked.

He looked at me long and hard. 'If not, our fate will depend on what we're worth. Those of us that fetch a goodly price will be sold readily enough, those that don't will be killed. They might keep me alive because I speak their tongue but when that's no longer needed they'll not waste any more time on me.'

'And what about Ingar?' I asked.

'They'll use her skills of healing to cure that poor sod over there,' he said pointing towards the litter. 'After that who knows? Most likely they'll abuse her and she'll end up bloated with the bastard child of some warrior whose name she'll never know and who'll she'll never see again. Either that or she'll die riddled with the pox. That just leaves you.'

'Me?' I asked. 'Why am I any different?'

He pointed to my chest. 'When they see that scar they'll not reckon you've a day's work left in you so will save themselves the trouble of feeding you. If I were you I'd tie your undershirt tight and try to hide it as best you can, unless that is you'd rather die now and get it over with.'

Concealing the scar was going to be easier said than done given that my hands were still tied. As I did what I could Aelred saw the scar more fully and was plainly shocked.

'How the hell did you survive a wound like that!' he asked.

'Ingar tended me,' I said. 'She saved my life with her potions and goodness knows what else, though I don't know how she managed it.'

'Holy Mother of God! Do you not see what she is?'

'What do you mean? She's a healer. A good one I grant you, but nothing more.'

'She's a Celt, that's what she is,' he said as if that explained everything. 'Therefore as like as not she's some sort of sorceress or a witch.'

It was only then that I realised he was right. The symbols on her girdle and on the sides of the stone altar, not to mention others I'd noticed daubed on the rock face outside the cavern, were indeed of Celtic design. It also explained her flame red hair and the torc she'd worn around her neck. 'She's not a witch,' I assured him. 'She practises the old ways, that's all.'

Aelred sneered. 'Then she's a witch. They're strange folk, the Celts. I've heard that the women sleep with women and the men sleep with sheep.'

I laughed but wondered whether he would dare to say such a thing if he came across a Celt in battle. Edwin had once told me that he'd rather confront three Viking warriors than face a single Celt who was roused and intent upon a quarrel.

'Well, at least if they think you're some sort of warrior you might fare better than the rest of us.'

'What do you mean?' I asked.

'I mean that if she can't heal that poor sod over there they'll give you a sword and set you upon him so that he dies fighting and thereby earns his place in Valhalla,' explained Aelred.

'But he's half dead already! What kind of contest would that be?'

'Don't worry, it won't be a fair fight. They'll as like tie your legs together first or beat you near senseless before you start.'

'And if I kill him?'

'That's what they want you to do, but if I were you I wouldn't. You'll get a much quicker death if you let him get the better of you – and probably a much cleaner one as well.'

'So is he their chieftain?' I asked.

Aelred shrugged. 'More than that,' he said. 'He's their Jarl. For what it's worth he's called Knut or something like it.'

With that, seeing that one of the Vikings was coming over I quickly finished trying to conceal my scar, but he was not so easily fooled. He all but ripped open my undershirt again to fully reveal my chest. For a moment he stood staring at it, then called others over as well.

As they clustered around me they all seemed strangely quiet, then one of them started shouting at me. I couldn't understand a word he said but it was clear that he was growing angry, peering directly into my face and leaning in so close that I could smell his stinking breath.

'He wants to know your name,' said Aelred.

I had assumed as much but knew better than to tell him; instead, I just stared back at him. In the end the man went away again and seemed to be discussing my fate with the others.

'Would you believe they're actually afraid of you?' said Aelred who seemed to find that amusing. 'Be grateful for it, boy. It seems they've heard a rumour that you're the one they call the warrior with the pierced heart or something. They've also heard that you're supposed to have returned from the dead and, because of that, are afraid to kill you in case they offend their Gods by returning you to them before your time.'

'Why? I'm as mortal as you are!'

'Because they're superstitious heathens, that's why. Their whole creed speaks of warriors who live for ever in Valhalla, so one that comes back from there is treated with awe and respect. Remember, they fear the dead far more than they do the living.'

'But I didn't die!' I protested.

'Well, with a wound like that you should have.'

'So what will they do with me?'

Aelred shrugged. 'I don't know. But I'd guess that your reputation will pretty much seal your fate. I reckon they'll use you so that Knut can earn his place in Valhalla. Either that or they might keep you in the hope that you bring them luck. If that's so and they find you're not the talisman they take you for, I wouldn't want to suffer whatever cruel plans they devise for sending you back to whatever hell you've come from.'

Chapter Four

Had I not been weakened by my wound, I was certain I would have killed at least three of the slavers before being taken. To me they looked to be nothing more than a band of wastrels. None of them had much in the way of war gear and all were roughly dressed in skins and furs with just a few amulets on their arms which I assumed was their personal wealth. Of the two who had remained at the camp, one was a hunchback and the other had but one hand, having presumably lost the other whilst fighting. Such was a fairly common wound in battle but men who'd suffered thus tended not to fight again for fear of losing the other hand as well!

The camp was a temporary one; a base where they could keep their prisoners secure whilst they looked for Ingar in the hope that she would have the skill to heal their Jarl. Despite this, from all I'd seen I was certain he would die within days and was surprised they hadn't put him to the sword to relieve his misery. However, whatever respect they had for him didn't stop them moving on as, having had Ingar do what she could for him, they wasted no time before setting off again. Two men led the way with the line of captives, yoked together by the neck and with their hands tied, following in single file. Aelred and I were set to lugging the litter on which Knut still lay, for which purpose our hands were freed but we were still roped together lest we tried to escape. Two more Vikings brought up the rear of the column, together with the hunchback who was leading a mule on which they'd placed all their belongings, including pots and pans, plus a few weapons, some provisions and a small sack containing their meagre hoard of spoil. All the others stayed close beside the captives ready to beat or cajole any who looked to be lagging behind. One of them wielded a stout leather whip for that very purpose and, still feeling weak from my wound, I was struck several times in a futile attempt to make me walk faster. In fact it served only to slow me down, but I was obliged to keep moving for fear that if I couldn't keep up or seemed to be finding the burden of carrying the litter too hard, they would kill me where I fell. I was also anxious to be on hand to help poor Ingar, though how I thought to achieve that I cannot say.

At length we left the forest and after travelling some distance without even a brief rest, reached a place where they planned to spend the night. It was actually a circle of ragged and weathered standing stones set atop a grassy mound, too small to be called a hill but high enough at least to give a good view of anyone who approached, be they friend or foe. The stones were of a kind which were erected long before our time and usually marked the site of a burial ground or possibly a single grave and as such were considered sacred. Doubtless the circle also served as a place of refuge in times of danger and would have originally been encircled with some sort of ditch or fortification to keep it secure and make it easy to defend. The stones themselves reminded me of a group of old men, each bowed in reverence towards a much taller stone in the centre. Whatever their purpose, when Ingar saw them she looked hesitant about entering the circle and protested loudly. In the end she had no choice but was first taken under guard to fetch water from a small stream which meandered through the vale below. When she returned she was set to preparing food for us all.

During this time Brother Benedict still kept himself to himself, saying little except in prayer and focusing instead on remaining alive. He seemed anxious not to align himself with anyone who looked as though they might cause trouble and that, I assume, included me. I therefore sat with Aelred.

'She's lucky,' he said as we assessed our position. 'The fat one over there is their chieftain now and he's claimed your woman for himself. You may not like it but believe me that's good news for her as she'll only have one of them to abuse her.'

'She's not my woman,' I said simply, though I knew he was right even though I doubted it would make much difference in the end. The man would tire of Ingar sooner or later and then she would no doubt be passed between the others like so much baggage.

'Don't even think to cross him,' warned Aelred. 'He kills without warning, does that one. What's more, he takes pleasure in it. Only the other day he was in a foul mood and slew a captive for no good cause, cutting him down where he stood and not even bothering to bury him. I doubt the poor wretch even knew what he'd done wrong.'

'That doesn't make much sense,' I said quietly. 'If they plan to sell us surely they should keep as many of us alive as they can?'

'Perhaps,' said Aelred. 'But these rogues haven't the sense they were born with! So just do as I say for now and keep your head down and save your strength for when we get our chance to escape.'

'Much good would that do me,' I said ruefully. 'Because of my wound I seem to tire too quickly to do much in the way of fighting. That's why I was so easily taken.'

As we waited to be fed, Ingar looked at Knut's wound once more. She had taken to giving him something to ease his pain so that he lay quietly enough, barely moving and with his eyes half closed. Yet even from where I sat I could see that he was none the better for having been carried along on the litter for much of the day. The wound itself was still raw and bleeding and, as Ingar sniffed it, I could tell from the look on her face that he was not long for our world, despite her ministrations.

'They'll finish him sooner or later,' warned Aelred. 'So you'd best be ready. They want to be about their business of collecting more slaves and he's just slowing them down.'

I'd already resolved what I would do when the time came. They would no doubt release my bonds and give me some sort of weapon which, once I'd sent Knut to Valhalla, I would use to send at least a few more of them to follow in his footsteps. I knew that with my own wound I couldn't hope to kill them all but decided it was better to die fighting than to be sold as a slave.

* * * * *

Supper for us that night was just stale bread and water, whilst the Vikings drank mead and gnawed on legs of cold mutton. Afterwards they set two guards whilst the rest settled down to sleep. Ingar was clearly expected to share the new chieftain's blanket and knew better than to resist. He took her roughly several times that night but she made no complaint, preferring to suffer in silence rather than endure a beating which she knew would be the punishment if she failed to please him.

In the morning, with her bonds left untied, Ingar went once more to the stream to wash herself. Once cleansed, she brought us yet more stale bread, water and a few half-chewed bones left over from the night before. I managed to speak with her briefly, saying I was sorry for all she'd endured.

'Better to suffer the groping of one than of them all,' she reasoned.

'But if you are with child as you've said, then surely you can no longer be certain as to who is the father?'

She managed a smile. 'Don't worry, Matthew, all remains as I told you. Your daughter is safe enough, for it was foretold that I would bear the children of two men, not just one. They would share my womb and be born as twins, yet they would be as different as night and day.'

I knew so little about such matters that I wasn't even sure whether it was possible for a woman to conceive the children of different men at the same time, but I accepted what she said. 'So will you endure his attentions or will you…?'

She didn't let me finish. 'What you're thinking is not an option for me,' she said firmly. 'I'm pledged to be a healer so could not consider taking my own life, much less that of my unborn children.'

I actually meant to suggest that she use her skills to kill the chieftain, not take her own life, but then realised the answer would have been the same. 'If you have your chance you should take it,' I said, noting that her hands had not been retied and thinking of the freedom she had in being allowed to go down to the stream, albeit never without a guard.

She hurriedly inspected my wound. 'Don't worry,' she advised. 'I doubt you were sent back from the dead only to die in bondage. Your chance to free yourself will therefore surely come, so just be ready and be sure not to waste it. Until then be patient and compliant. Whilst your wound seems to have settled always keep in mind what I told you – that if you abuse it your heart may well burst within your breast.'

* * * * *

I assumed that the plan would be to remain at the stone circle for a few days to give Knut a chance to heal but early the next morning a man I hadn't seen before arrived at the camp and went straight to speak with the chieftain. Whatever news he bore seemed to cause great excitement among the slavers.

'What's happening?' I asked Aelred.

'That bastard who has just arrived is one of their spies. They sent him out a few days back to look for possible targets and it seems he's found some sort of settlement nearby. I assume they're planning to raid it.'

'But he's a Saxon!' I said, not sure that he was. He wore Saxon garb right enough but his clothes could well have been stolen to serve as a disguise.

'So who better to send out on a mission like that? And don't look so shocked, boy. There are as many traitors in these parts as there are fleas on a dog's back.'

'What are they saying now?' I asked.

'It sounds like they're going to strike today.'

'But surely they're not that stupid! If they had any sense they'd wait till dawn and take the place when all are still abed?' I protested.

'These fools strike when best it suits them. After all, it's likely to be some humble farmstead not a garrison full of warriors, so the people who live there won't put up much of a fight. Sacking that will barely delay them beyond the time it takes to round up the poor wretches and add them to our number.'

'So what can we do?'

'Nothing,' he said looking at me strangely. 'That's their fate and it's not our problem. But don't worry about them, worry about yourself. If they take more captives they'll soon have enough to be worth selling and so your fate and mine will have got just a little bit closer.'

With that we were all ordered to stand. One of the Vikings said something to Aelred, who then translated for the rest of us. 'He said we're to follow quietly. If anyone makes so much as a sound, he'll slit their throat.'

A few moments later we moved off, the captives still yoked together and with Aelred and I struggling to carry the litter on which Knut still lay. He looked to be sleeping though I suspect Ingar had given him more of whatever she used to keep him subdued.

Two men were detailed to keep guard over us as we travelled whilst the rest of the slavers moved on ahead. Aelred whispered that it might be the time for him and me to make our move. Although not armed, he was right that we stood a good chance of taking both men whilst the rest of the guards

47

were so far off, but I glanced back at him and shook my head. 'Only if they come close enough,' I hissed. 'If they stay back they'll have too much time to ready themselves before we can get our hands around their throats.' He knew I was right and besides, in such open ground we wouldn't get far even if we did manage to make a run for it given that we were still bound together by the rope about our necks.

Our path took us across an open heath of softly rolling hills, parts of which were so low lying that the ground there was often too wet to tread upon. The landscape beyond looked very damp and marshy and I wondered why anyone would live there. It was also dreadfully exposed, with precious little shelter from the wind and rain. At first I could see no sign of any settlement then, tucked beyond a slight rise, we came upon a cluster of seven or eight buildings which relied upon the lie of the land to protect them without even a fence or a ditch. In fact they had no defences at all apart from a small stream to one side and what looked to be a sizeable marsh of tall reeds to the rear.

'What in God's name do they do for a living here?' muttered Aelred.

There was no sign of any livestock and the ground was surely too wet for crops, so it had to be something they made. When I looked more closely I could see that one of the buildings was some sort of workshop, though there was no sign of a forge or a kiln. Three men and two women were working there but I couldn't say for certain what it was they were doing. Beside it was another much smaller building which looked to be some sort of mill. It had a wheel which was turned by the flow of the stream but much too slowly to serve any obvious purpose. When I looked at the damp soil I wondered whether it contained some minerals or other deposits which had some use in making metals or perhaps pottery, but it remained a mystery.

All the other buildings were obviously homes which, although not much more than hovels, looked to have been freshly thatched with reeds, presumably taken from the fringes of the marsh. Smoke was rising from one of the buildings suggesting it was occupied and I could hear the voices of children playing somewhere in the distance.

Meanwhile we were made to sit with the hunchback and the one-handed man to guard us whilst the other slavers edged close enough to peer down at the settlement and formed their plan of attack, carefully keeping themselves from view.

It occurred to me that if they had the nerve they could just walk in and take their prisoners without the need for blood to be spilled at all. With the marsh behind them, the people there would have nowhere to go except into the reeds from where they could be easily rounded up and taken. It was this that led me to realise that our captors were quite unlike raiders. They were of the lowest order, deserters and outcasts, second sons and probably those convicted of crimes, who had come together to trade in human misery. Certainly they were not warriors, but probably all the more dangerous for that.

At the chieftain's word, the raiding party began creeping closer using whatever cover they could find to keep themselves from being seen.

'We should try to warn them!' I whispered to Aelred, but he only scowled.

'They'll all be slaughtered if we don't!' I pressed.

With that he turned to look at me. 'And we'll be slaughtered if we do! Is that what you want? To die like a dog for no reason? They'll kill you in an instant and then still butcher all the people in that settlement down there as well!'

At that the raiders stood up and surged forward, quickening their pace as they made their assault. Then, once they reached the first of the buildings, they began screaming and shouting as they charged headlong into the settlement.

I can only imagine what sheer terror the people who dwelt there felt when they saw the Vikings coming down upon them. Most tried to run or hide, gathering up their children and possessions and scurrying towards the reeds where they hoped they might be safe. Some of them did try to make a fight of it. The first of them came out armed with nothing more than a long-handled scythe and, before being cut down, he managed to seriously wound one of the raiders in the belly but otherwise sold his life cheaply. The next to confront them was a young woman who had left it too late to run. She held a small knife but looked so frightened that I believed she was more likely to take her own life than that of one of the attackers. She was quickly overpowered, knocked to the ground then beaten with a stick where she lay. Meanwhile two of the other slavers lit a torch and threw it into the building which looked to be occupied. The dry thatch was like tinder so the building was quickly engulfed in flames. It was not long before two women rushed out, their clothes and hair blazing as they tried to roll themselves on the ground to douse the flames.

The two slavers just stepped aside and laughed as they watched them die in agony.

By that time two men had emerged from the workshop, both armed – one with a short-handled hammer and the other with a wood axe. At first they looked defiant but seeing that all hope of resistance was futile, the one with the hammer gave himself up whilst the other ran.

Within no time at all the slavers had swarmed through the entire settlement wreaking havoc. They paid no mind to the carnage they inflicted, seeming to revel in all the blood and destruction they'd wrought. In the end they'd taken just five prisoners – three men and two women, all of whom were hustled into a group and prodded harshly with sticks and spears until they knelt in compliance, the women sobbing as they anticipated their fate. Even so, the slavers were careless of their prize, allowing several others to escape from the settlement, including the children who, clearly terrified, could be heard screaming as they ran desperately seeking whatever cover they could find within the reeds. Surprisingly, it seemed that the slavers could not be bothered to follow them, having presumably secured enough new prisoners to satisfy their needs.

As I watched the raid I realised that the bloodshed had been unnecessary and wanton, the poor folk who lived there having had no proper means by which to defend themselves. Although incensed by the needless brutality of it all, I was grateful that at least the children had escaped, even though many of them would be orphans.

Once the slaughter was complete, the Vikings burned all the other buildings having first searched them for whatever they thought might be of some value. It didn't amount to much – just some tools and a handful of brooches. Aelred asked whether we might be allowed to bury the dead and have Brother Benedict say a few words for their souls, but the slavers just laughed when he suggested it. Instead, we were forced to leave their bodies to rot where they lay and their souls in want of salvation.

Chapter Five

Having completed their slaughter, the slavers forced us to join them in what was left of the settlement, making us sit amid the still smouldering ruins whilst they collected up their meagre booty. It was hard to believe that so much carnage had been wrought in so short a time and for so little profit.

'They're animals,' said Aelred as we watched the new slaves being secured and added to our number. The two women were screaming and struggling against the prospect of their fate, but both were quickly silenced by a brutal fist. The men put up less of a fight, having no doubt realised that, for them, the punishment for resistance was almost certainly death. As he waited to be bound, one of them did try to intervene with the plight of the women. He made a brave but futile attempt to push past two of the slavers but was knocked to the ground and then kicked and beaten into submission before being dragged across to join the rest of us.

Eventually the women were taken to one side. One of them was much younger than the other being not much more than a girl of perhaps sixteen years of age. She was also quite pretty despite some severe bruises to her face and the slavers soon began to argue over which of them would have her first.

'They're worse than animals,' I said to Aelred.

'What do you mean?'

'I mean they've killed almost as many as they've taken. Good warriors would have surrounded the settlement and captured everyone alive and thus increased their profit. These fools prefer to satisfy their lust for blood before thinking of their purse.'

'Oh, and how would a boy like you know about such things?' said Aelred, surprised at my logic.

I was tempted to tell him about my life as a warrior but decided to say nothing. Instead, I pointed to several of the Vikings who'd been wounded. 'At least some of them were made to pay for their butchery,' I observed.

One of the Vikings was seriously injured with a wound to his stomach which had been inflicted by the man with the scythe. Two others had cuts which were probably not serious but needed attention. Once again Ingar seemed willing to help them and, as it appeared to have been decided that we'd remain there for the night, went off, accompanied by one of the slavers, to look for the roots and herbs she'd need for her ministrations.

'They'll finish off that poor bastard with the stomach wound if he can't march come morning,' observed Aelred almost gleefully. 'That'll be one less for us to deal with when the time comes.'

I was surprised given that they'd carried Knut so far without ending his misery. Surely one more wounded man would make little difference to their progress?

'Knut is a Jarl and therefore to kill him would be a crime for which they might well be called to account,' explained Aelred who seemed to know what I was thinking. 'The other man is just another warrior for whom death is to be expected. Besides, few men will survive a wound to the gut and I'll tell you something else, it's a slow and very painful way to die.'

'Who would know if they killed them both?' I asked.

'They would,' said Aelred firmly. 'They'll have sworn a sacred oath of allegiance to their Jarl and will not deign to break it. As for the other poor sod, they owe him nothing so won't risk him slowing them down. Besides, reducing their numbers means a larger share of the loot for the rest of them.'

In the meantime, the Vikings began sifting through the pile of booty they'd secured. Even this showed them to be miserly and mean as they quarrelled over trinkets that were all but worthless yet had cost the lives of so many.

After she'd done what she could for the wounded, Ingar brought us some water.

'Are you all right?' I asked.

'What do you mean am I all right?' she snapped, no doubt angered at having been forced to witness so much pointless slaughter. 'I've been raped and groped like a common whore and must now pretend to lie willingly with a man who stinks like a dog's arse and whose rancid breath is so sharp it could cut through iron! And you ask if I'm all right!'

One of the new prisoners urged us to be quiet. 'Sssh! They'll surely kill us all if they hear you!' he insisted.

'Kill us?' laughed Aelred. 'That's the least of our worries! In fact killing us would be a mercy given what's in store for us!'

The man was suddenly quiet.

'Why in God's name do you still help them,' asked Aelred almost accusingly. 'Tending to their Jarl is one thing if it's to curry favour with him but you should let the other bastards die so there's fewer of them for us to deal with when the time comes to free ourselves!'

'I'm a healer. It's not my way to leave men to suffer. Matthew here is testament to that.'

'Pah!' said Aelred. 'Let them all bleed out! And the more pain they suffer in the process the better so far as I'm concerned.'

I realised that, unintentionally, Ingar had now mentioned my name but it hardly seemed to matter. 'The one who has taken over from Knut and claimed you now seems to be their chieftain. Do you yet know what he's called?' I asked.

She gave a little laugh, perhaps feeling better for having vented her anger. 'His name is Ljot, but I call him Ljot the large. He seems flattered by that but it's a reference to the size of his belly, not his manhood.'

Both Aelred and I enjoyed the joke, as did several others who heard it.

'Will you be able to help us?' I asked, wondering whether her scruples would allow her to deal with her abuser as he deserved.

'Help you with what?' she asked.

'With our plan to escape. If you could but…'

'Matthew don't even think of trying to escape. You're not yet strong enough and you know full well that these men will kill you just for trying.'

* * * * *

As was bound to happen, the slavers soon turned their attention to the two women they'd taken as captives. The younger of the two had been knocked to the ground when the slavers first attacked; the other was possibly her mother or more likely an aunt who'd stayed to help her and thus been taken as well. The girl had been hauled roughly to one side where three of the slavers began to taunt her, pushing and shoving her as they each tried to force themselves upon her, revelling in the fact that she screamed in terror at the prospect of what she must have known would follow. The older woman tried to intervene, but the slavers had no interest in her and, given that she was too old to have much value either as a slave or as a whore, one of the men pushed her back hard against a tree and bound her to it.

The three men began to get more and more impatient with their victim. Eventually they pushed her to the ground where they forced her to drink strong mead from a bowl then beat her several times before stripping away her clothes. Then, when she was all but naked, they took turns to rape her. When they had done with her they just left her where she lay, sobbing bitterly.

The older woman pleaded to be allowed to help the girl, but the slavers just laughed. When she persisted one of them cruelly struck her with the flat of an axe, lashing out wildly and hitting her so hard that she slumped back against the tree, killed outright.

'Bastards!' I said as we watched all this, powerless to help.

Aelred looked at me as though I was mad. 'What did you think they'd do?'

'They didn't have to kill the older woman!' I said. 'If they've no use for her they should have let her go.'

'I'd say she's the lucky one,' he said simply.

'What do you mean?' I asked.

'I mean that they've spared the younger one for a purpose.'

'You mean to sell as a slave?'

'Only if she lives that long. Most likely they mean to abuse her again and again. So what would you prefer if you were her? To die quickly like her friend or to be abused by them until they tire of you then kill you anyway just for the hell of it?'

I knew he was right, just as I knew that I could no longer stand by and watch what they were doing. I looked around the makeshift camp but quickly realised just how bleak our position had become. The older woman's body was bound to the tree, the rope securing her to it still tied around her waist; the girl who had been raped was still on the ground sobbing and all the other captives were sitting in silence dreading whatever fate lay in store for them. Even Ingar, who had been forced to witness the rape with a knife pressed to her throat lest she try to intervene, seemed to accept that there was nothing to be done.

When the slavers settled down after their exertions, Ingar was allowed to tend the girl, though there was little even she could do except to help her dress as best she could given that all her clothes were torn. That done, she walked the girl towards the stream so she could at least wash herself, then soothed her and tended to her bruises. As they returned Ingar stopped to speak with me.

'I'll do what's needed,' she said simply, having clearly seen enough to persuade her to help us, despite her convictions.

'Have you a plan in mind?' I asked.

'There is a way,' she said simply. 'Just hold yourselves ready. Whilst gathering herbs and roots I found all I shall need to give you your chance for freedom. Just remember that the next time you're given food eat only the gruel and any dry bread,' she advised. 'Pass the word to the others and, when the time comes, do exactly as I say. All being well I shall pass you a blade with which to cut your bonds. Free yourselves then get as far from here as you can. And Matthew, don't try anything heroic. Just remember that your wound is not yet healed within and will not stand too much exertion.'

'What about you?'

'Have no concern on my account,' she said. 'That fool Ljot is arrogant enough to think that I lay with him for my own pleasure and am so enamoured of his vile carcass that I'll not even try to escape. Because of that I'm now left unbound. But don't worry, I'll not leave until I've freed you all.'

'And you'll then come with us?' I asked hopefully.

'No, I shall return to the forest where I'm more at home and where they'll not find me again however hard they try. You, on the other hand, must rest. You know what to drink to make yourself stronger?'

It was my turn to scoff.

'Do it,' she said firmly. 'But remember, find somewhere safe and lie low there for at least two weeks to give your wound a chance to fully mend within. And do nothing to exert yourself for two weeks after that.'

* * * * *

Later that day Ingar lay beside Ljot, playfully offering him morsels of food and gently caressing and teasing him. He was more interested in resting at that time but Ingar made it clear that she was keen to keep his company, as if whetting his appetite for the night ahead. Given it was all just a ploy on her part, I can only say that she played it well, seeming both compliant and eager. It appeared that her ruse was not to control him but rather to let him think that he was controlling her. We could only hope that she knew what she was doing as any chance we had for freedom depended upon it.

During this time all the new captives sat either in silence or sobbing quietly to themselves, probably regretting not having opted for death when they had the chance.

Meanwhile the slavers seemed intent on playing some sort of board game, gambling and arguing, so much so that it seemed to absorb them fully. So engrossed were they that they failed to notice someone creeping towards us. Whoever he was, he was at pains to use the bank of the small stream as cover in order to get as close to us as he could. Aelred and I had both seen him and wondered why he was so intent on joining us. We half hoped that he was with others come to free us but, as he showed himself more fully, we realised he was just a young boy of no more than eight or nine years of age. Not only that, but he was clearly alone.

By then, one of the new captives had seen the boy as well. As soon as he did he became very upset and tried desperately to usher the lad away. But the boy was having none of it. Instead, he broke his cover and ran towards us, boldly brandishing a small knife with which he clearly meant to cut our bonds. Unfortunately he didn't get far. He hadn't seen the hunchback who, for whatever reason, seemed disinterested in the game the others were playing and was instead resting in the longer grass and idly making a whistle from a short length of reed. As soon as he saw the boy, he leaped to his feet then rushed across to seize him so roughly that the poor lad was lifted up then slammed down hard upon the ground.

As the boy lay there, stunned and clearly harmed, the hunchback kicked him brutally in the face so that blood spurted from his mouth and nose. Then the Viking picked up the knife the lad had been carrying and examined the blade.

For a moment it was not clear what would happen next but, unbeknown to me, one of the new captives was father to the boy. I heard him cry out in desperation, but the hunchback merely looked back at him, grinning as though he relished what he was about to do. The other slavers had, by that time, realised what was afoot and went across to watch. As they roared their encouragement, the hunchback dragged the boy to his feet again, gripping him by the nape of his neck so tightly that I feared he would kill the lad with his bare hands. In the end he almost threw the youngster down once more then set about him with a stick.

As the thrashing continued, the boy's father was up on his feet shouting at the hunchback to stop but the more he shouted the more severe the beating became. The man called him the son of a whore and a coward, but the Viking didn't understand a word he was saying and, even when it was clear that the boy was unconscious, continued striking him without mercy. Then, when he'd finished, he strode towards us, clearly intending to beat the boy's father as well.

I thought at first that others sitting close to the man might rise to his defence, perhaps overpowering the hunchback or even killing him. It would have made little difference to our plight but at least it would have been something. Instead, they just sat there as the man was dragged across and made to kneel beside his bruised and bloodied son.

By some miracle the lad was still alive, but only just. As the man wept, one of the other slavers drew a knife from his belt, clearly intending to slit both their throats. It was at that point that Ingar intervened, getting to her feet and screaming at Ljot, ordering him to stop the slaughter. Her tongue was as sharp as any knife though I doubt he understood a word she said. More likely he was thinking of his profit, but we were all relieved to see that, on his orders, both father and son were spared. Ingar was not allowed to tend the boy and instead he and his father were each given a few more brutal kicks before being dragged back to be bound with the rest of us.

* * * * *

Most of the captives spent what was left of the day in silence, any thoughts of escape having been settled by the brutality inflicted on the man and his brave son.

Meanwhile the girl was still weeping as she tried to come to terms with all that had befallen her. It was therefore left to Ingar to prepare the food on her own as well as tend those with wounds, including Knut who, from what I could see, was all but dead by then. Certainly he didn't move or make any sound other than a low moaning as he endured his pain.

The Vikings were set to enjoy a veritable feast from what had been taken from the stores at the settlement whilst we, as usual, were expected to share very little of what was on offer.

'So you're called Matthew?' asked Aelred as we waited to be fed.

There seemed no point in hiding my true identity any further. 'Yes, but I was christened Edward,' I explained. 'My father was an Ealdorman and friend to Lord Alfred himself.'

'So why did you change your name if you're from such good Saxon stock? And how the hell did you end up here?'

'I was destined for the Church but got caught up in the battle at Chippenham. I was therefore one of the few who went with Alfred into hiding and became a warrior.'

'A warrior! But you're not much more than a boy!'

'That's as may be, but I proved myself and even commanded part of Alfred's army at Edington. Besides, I had a good teacher. My brother was one of the greatest Saxon warriors of our time. His name was Lord Edwin, son of Edwulf.'

Aelred clearly knew of Edwin's fame and looked impressed. 'No wonder you kept your name a secret! If these bastards learn who you are they'll tear you limb from limb! And that only after they've boiled your flesh in oil!'

'I know it. So say nothing. Just be ready to follow when I make my move. I made a poor fist of it last time, but I will prevail if I get the chance. Either that or I'll die trying.'

'And do you think that woman of yours can do anything to help us?'

'As I've told you, Ingar is not my woman.'

'Well, I wish she was mine. Though by the time Ljot is done with her she won't be worth having as she'll no doubt be riddled with the pox!'

Later, Ingar brought us food. She said nothing as she passed it round but then no words were needed – the look on her face told me that the time had come for her to act.

The food didn't amount to much, it was just some thin gruel which we all ate hungrily enough considering how little we'd been given over the previous few days. We also shared some stale bread which helped to swell our bellies. Meanwhile as our captors waited to gorge themselves on roasted pig, they drank so much mead that I thought Ingar's plan was to get them drunk but, as soon became clear, she had an even darker scheme in mind.

Among the food on offer she'd mixed some mushrooms she'd gathered whilst searching for what she needed to tend the men's wounds. The Vikings seemed to favour mushrooms and all ate them greedily as the meat was being cooked, picking out the most succulent and gorging on them like sweetmeats or pastries. It therefore didn't take long for Ingar's plan to take effect.

One by one the slavers started to complain of feeling unwell and several of them began to vomit. Within no time at all it was clear they'd been poisoned by Ingar but, even if they realised that, they were all too busy retching their guts out to punish her. Yet, as was her way, Ingar tried to comfort them, encouraging them to vomit freely or to allow their bowels to loosen to ease their pain. Even so, their sufferings gradually grew worse as they began to endure all manner of torments – clutching their stomachs as their bowels rumbled and their bellies ached. I'd seen men endure less pain from wounds they'd received on the battlefield though, to my discredit, I couldn't find it in myself to feel any compassion for their suffering.

Seeing her ploy work so well, Ingar seized a knife from one of the Vikings who was too ill to protest, then came across to where we all waited. 'Is your freedom reward enough for what I took from you?' she asked pointedly.

'You owe me nothing,' I managed, impatient to be free. 'You healed my wound and if you now free me whatever account there was between us is settled in full.'

She nodded as if accepting that, then handed me the knife.

Once I'd cut myself free I passed the blade to Aelred then began rubbing my neck and wrists where the coarse rope had chaffed the skin. 'What in God's name have you done to them?' I asked looking round at the slavers, all of whom were in agony.

'I did nothing in God's name,' she assured me. 'But as I told you, the Earth Mother has ways enough of her own.'

I must have looked puzzled. I knew she had the skill to poison them but was certain it would be against her creed as a healer to actually kill them.

Having freed himself, Aelred passed the knife to the next man. As others waited for their turn Ingar explained what she'd done. 'The mushrooms I fed them were yellow stainers,' she said. 'I sometimes use the smallest piece to purge the gut. These greedy fools have eaten a hundred times that amount and more. There is a remedy, but they'll have to find it for themselves.'

'Don't worry, we'll not leave them to suffer long,' Aelred assured her.

He was right about that. Even as Ingar calmly walked away from the ruined settlement we set about the Vikings, seizing their weapons and wreaking such revenge as would have put even their kinfolk to shame. I went first to Ljot who was, by then, on his back clutching his stomach as the gripes wreaked their way through his whole body. I picked up his sword and, as he looked up at me, drove the blade into his already aching guts. Rasping and choking, he turned to one side, his whole body shaking. There was never any hope that he'd survive that but, partly for Ingar's sake and also as a way of venting my own anger, I let him suffer. Then something from my Christian conscience prompted me to show some mercy. I realised that the vengeance I sought was for my men who'd been slain that day in the forest and for which I alone was responsible, not him. Thus I plunged the sword into him again with so much force that he died even before I could withdraw the blade, choking on his own blood and vomit.

I turned and looked for Ingar. 'Now we're even,' I shouted as loudly as I could in the hope that she might hear me. 'I've repaid you for freeing us by doing that which you couldn't do yourself.' Unfortunately she was already much too far away.

Killing Ljot reminded me of how wretched I felt after killing the unarmed warrior during the battle at Chippenham and the merchant Sweyn – and even after slaying the traitor Cedric. Such slaughter did not sit well with me even though I knew that in all cases I'd had good cause. Therefore even though I knew I should help to finish off the rest of the slavers, it was not something I relished. I resolved to start by killing Knut but, when I went to him, I was relieved to find that he was dead already, having died from his infected wound at last. After that I just watched as others did the rest of the killing for me.

Once freed, the girl who'd been raped set about one of her tormentors with particular venom, repeatedly stabbing him in a frenzy of blood lust as she took her revenge. The other captives were less vindictive but offered no mercy as they slit the slavers' throats or sliced open their aching bellies. Soon all the Vikings lay dead or were in the throes of dying.

* * * * *

'What now?' asked Aelred.

I was surprised that with the slavers dead all the captives seemed to be looking to me to lead them. 'You have your freedom,' I said loud enough for all to hear. 'Why waste it?'

Four of the original captives took me at my word and left, but Brother Benedict remained with me, seemingly intent on helping those from the ruined settlement. Meanwhile Aelred busied himself stealing what he could of the Vikings' booty and taking a few amulets and rings from the bodies as if that might be some recompense for all the insults and ill treatment he'd suffered at their hands. 'Don't you want a share of this?' he asked.

I held up Ljot's sword and said that I had all I needed and that he was welcome to the rest. The sword was not a particularly fine one, the blade having been used to hack and slash indifferently rather than as was intended. Still, it was better than nothing. In any event, the slavers' booty didn't amount to much as they'd only raided a few poor farmsteads where there was little in the way of silver or jewels to be had. Ingar's torc was probably one of the most valuable items and that she'd recovered before she left.

Some of those from the settlement who'd managed to escape when the slavers first attacked then emerged from hiding in the reeds. They included a man I later learned was engaged to be wed to the girl who'd been so ill used. Still struggling to preserve her modesty, she wandered towards her betrothed and held up her bloodied hands as if to show that she had defended his honour and avenged her own. For a moment he seemed not to know what to do, but then went to her and wrapped his cloak around her. I thought they would be reconciled but, as they embraced, he slid a knife he was holding gently and quietly into her belly. She gasped as she pulled away from him and looked down at the wound but otherwise made no complaint as she slipped to the ground, seemingly grateful to him for having ended her plight. He knelt beside her as she died, weeping as he cradled her head on his lap. Then he took the knife and used it to sever his own wrists so that they lay together, reunited in death.

Even though it was getting dark, the others who were from the raided settlement started laying out their dead, intending to bury them the next day.

'So what will you do now?' asked Aelred looking pleased with himself as he spotted another ring and set about cutting off the dead man's finger to retrieve it.

'Nothing,' I said firmly. 'My wound pains me again and, as Ingar advised, I need to rest.'

'Then what?' he demanded, looking bemused.

'Then I shall return to Chippenham and there repent my many sins. I assume Lord Alfred will by now have gone back to his royal Vill there and I would join him to reclaim my former life. I have treasure enough so will marry the woman I love, raise children and serve my King. What else is there for a Saxon warrior to do in time of peace?'

Aelred shrugged. 'Then I'd best come with you. From all I've seen and heard of you you've a nose for trouble and are going to need someone to keep an eye on you.'

I didn't agree as, by that time, I was certain I could look out for myself. But I did need someone to watch over and provide for me whilst I recovered. Besides, I had come to like Aelred. 'What of your family? Are you not anxious to return to them?'

Aelred laughed. 'I've a sour-faced wife who has a mother with a tongue as sharp as flint. Why the hell would I want to find them again?'

'What about your children or your parents?'

'My parents passed away many years ago and I never had any children, though I have a sister and two nephews I should like to see again one day.'

'So when did you last see your wife?' I asked, hoping to learn a little more about him.

He shrugged. 'Several years at least. Like I said, I once lived near the sea where we had no cause to fear the raiders. Even so, we were obliged to serve in the fyrd and were one day forced to help a settlement nearby which had no such alliance. I fell during the battle and was left for dead. When I came round I found that everyone had gone so, seizing my chance, I went to the forests where I joined others who, like me, had grown weary of working land we didn't own and for a master who treated us like dirt.'

I should have reproached him but I could see he had a point. 'What part did you play in the fyrd?' I asked.

He grinned, clearly remembering it with no small amount of pride. 'I was a spearman, and a good one,' he boasted. 'I had no problem with that but when we weren't fighting I resented slaving behind a plough for days on end or reaping corn that would feed some other man's family. Thus when I got the chance to leave I took it and have never given any mind to going back.'

I looked at Brother Benedict who had thus far remained silent. 'And what of you good Brother?'

'God has answered my prayers and seen fit to spare me,' he said solemnly. 'I would therefore return to my abbot if I can and there give proper thanks for my deliverance. The trouble is I've no idea which way to go and would therefore travel with you if you'll have me.'

I sat and rested on a fallen log for a moment, leaning forward against the hilt of Ljot's sword to support my weary body. 'There's just one problem with that,' I admitted. 'I've no idea which way to go either.'

Aelred came and stood beside me. 'All we have to do is retrace our steps,' he advised.

'I didn't pay much mind to the route we came by,' I admitted, knowing that was a grave error on my part. 'As best I can tell we've been travelling roughly south, which does make sense as the slavers would have been headed for the coast.'

Aelred agreed. 'So, we should head north and hopefully find a road which leads to Chippenham from there,' he suggested.

'Actually, it's easier than that,' I said. 'All we have to do is find a large settlement. Once we do, I can insist on speaking to their Ealdorman and ask him to send word to Lord Alfred who will then despatch an escort to see us safely home. But first I must find a place to rest for, as Ingar said, this wound will surely be the death of me if I don't.'

Chapter Six

Having done what they could to protect their dead from wild beasts, the survivors from the settlement sat together in a small group and ate the roasted pig which Ingar had been cooking for the slavers.

As I kept my distance, unwilling to intrude on their sorrow, Aelred came across to join me and swung a heavy sack he was carrying from his shoulder.

'What's in there?' I asked. 'More booty?'

He shook his head. 'No, I couldn't find much worth taking,' he said. 'This is a gift from the other captives.'

As he opened the sack I saw that it contained what remained of a small pig which had been butchered to the extent that one of the rear haunches was missing, but it was otherwise intact. 'That's very generous,' I said.

'The Vikings slaughtered all their stock,' explained Aelred. 'They butchered swine, chickens and even their goat. All that flesh will rot long before they can eat it, so they offered us this for helping them. I reckon there's enough here to feed us for three days at least.'

'Did you find out what they did here for a living?' I asked, still curious to know.

He gave a little laugh. 'I gather they used the reeds from the marsh to weave baskets. Once dried and split, the ones which grow here are said to be ideal for that.'

'And that was enough to keep them all?'

'So they say. One of them was particularly skilled and could turn out some really fine work.'

'So where is he now?' I asked.

Aelred pointed to where all the bodies lay. 'It seems the good Lord has a fancy for a new basket. It's all a bloody waste if you ask me.'

I nodded my agreement knowing that skills like that took a lifetime to fully master yet could be lost to a single stroke of a sword or sweep of an axe.

In the meantime, Brother Benedict had spent yet more time in prayer, kneeling with his hands held high and clasped together as he thanked God for his deliverance. 'So my friends, where to?' he asked when at last he came to join us. He seemed more cheerful than I'd ever seen him before, clearly relieved that his ordeal was over. Either that or perhaps his prayers had helped to lift his spirits. The thought reminded me that it had been a long time since I'd prayed in earnest. It was something I was finding hard to do given that I still blamed myself for the loss of my men and felt I was not deserving of absolution or forgiveness. I decided it was a matter I would discuss with Brother Benedict if and when the chance arose.

'Well, we can't stay here,' said Aelred. 'Those dead Vikings will soon start to stink like hell.'

'You're right but it's too late to go anywhere now,' I said. 'We'll have to risk staying here tonight then leave tomorrow.'

'Aye. We could then go back to the mound with the standing stones and rest up there for a while.'

'No, it's too exposed there,' I warned. 'We'll be safer in the forest.'

Brother Benedict looked worried. 'But surely there are even more dangers in the forest,' he said.

'Yes but at least we won't starve,' said Aelred pointing to the sack. 'This should suffice for a while unless, that is, you have any objection to eating pig meat. When that's gone we can hunt and fish until Matthew here is fit enough to start the journey to Chippenham.'

* * * * *

We settled down to a very uncomfortable night sleeping on the damp ground with the bodies of the dead slavers not far from us. As we feared, they quickly attracted all manner of scavengers, so we stayed close together, sharing the comfort of a fire which we hoped would keep the wild beasts at bay.

As we listened to the scavengers gorging on the bodies, we found we were none of us inclined to sleep. Instead, we lay there, gazing up at the sky which seemed to be all but full of stars. 'Is that not strange?' mused Brother Benedict.

'What now?' groaned Aelred.

'I was just wondering whether if the sun and moon both move around the earth as we're told they do, does the sky not do the same?'

'Of course it does. Why would you think it doesn't?' I reasoned. 'It must move for it always looks different every time you look at it.'

'It only looks different because the clouds move,' said Aelred. 'You can actually see them sailing across the sky if you look, sometimes even at night.'

'That's true,' said Brother Benedict. 'But do they all move as one?'

For a moment we were all silent, not so much troubled by the question as by our own ignorance of such matters.

'Well,' said Aelred, 'one thing's for sure. The sky will still be there in the morning whether it's moved or not. And that will come around all too quickly for my liking as I'm sorely tired and need all the sleep I can get. That's if you'll both shut up long enough to let me.'

* * * * *

Aelred was right, the sky was indeed there the next morning, but we had far too much to do to waste more time looking at it. Before leaving, I recovered the sheath for Ljot's sword then removed a stiff leather jerkin from one of the other dead Vikings. Although too big for me, I felt it would serve as useful protection if we were attacked again. I also found some shoes and proper leggings which, though far from clean, were better than nothing.

Aelred's weapon of choice was a spear with which he professed to have some skill, whereas Brother Benedict decided that to bear arms was against his calling so made do with a stout staff instead. 'Whilst permitted to join battle, the Holy Church forbids us to spill blood,' he told us.

'So that means you can fight but you're not allowed to win!' sneered Aelred. 'What the hell is the point of that?'

'We can win,' explained Brother Benedict. 'We just can't draw blood. That's why Holy men who go into battle carry a club or a stave.'

'That's very noble, that is,' teased Aelred. 'Because of your vows you won't kill a man cleanly, but you'll happily beat his brains out with a lump of wood instead.'

The remark was lost on the good brother who, by then, had strapped what we needed from the Vikings' effects to their mule along with Aelred's small stash of booty. Although not tethered, the beast had not strayed far from the ruined settlement, perhaps having been as fearful of the scavengers in the night as we had. The items he chose included various pots and pans, some loaves of stale bread, a rind of hard cheese and what remained of the flagon of mead. To this we added the carcass of the pig to save carrying it and some other weapons and a shield Aelred thought might be needed.

Whilst we were preparing to leave, the survivors from the settlement started to bury their dead and, when they'd finished, Brother Benedict stood beside each grave and although not ordained, offered prayers for the souls of the fallen. That done, the survivors gathered up all they could find that had been stolen from them and left. There was no point in them staying as their homes had been destroyed and little remained that was worth saving. Also, I fancy the place held too many sharp memories for them to settle there again. None of them said very much beyond thanking me for freeing them even though I tried to explain that Ingar had done far more to help than I had. Whatever the truth of that, I knew they would struggle to rebuild their lives given all they'd been through. We watched them file away, all looking dejected though no doubt grateful to be alive.

The father and his son who had been so cruelly beaten went with them, the young boy hobbling whilst leaning on his father for support. He still looked to be in much pain and I feared that at the very least he had several broken ribs and was surely bruised and bloodied well beyond reckoning.

'So where will they all go now?' asked Aelred as we watched them leave.

'I imagine they'll just get as far from here as they can,' I said ruefully.

'Well, I just hope they find somewhere they can protect more readily next time.'

I considered that for a moment, then shrugged. 'A fence or ditch would have made no difference to what happened here. What they needed was warning of the attack to give them time to hide themselves and their belongings. No settlement could expect to see off a raid unaided, particularly if it was a band of warriors who attacked them not just a few miserable slavers.'

Once they'd gone we also left and started out by wending our way northwards. As we went, it occurred to me that we were indeed a very strange group. Led by me, a wounded warrior with no real war gear apart from an old sword, plus Aelred of whom I knew little and Brother Benedict who was a monk without even a crucifix or a bible. I wondered what anyone seeing us would make of such a motley band.

When we eventually reached the forest, we found a wide path which we assumed was some sort of track used by carts as it was deeply rutted on either side. It was plain enough to follow and we decided that if it was used by merchants or traders it was probably the safest route to take. Also, if we were lucky enough to meet any of them along the way they could well be relied upon for directions.

We followed the track for most of the day as it weaved its way between tall stands of pine and fir until, eventually, we came across a small glade just to one side of the track where there was also a wide, fast flowing stream of crystal clear water. It looked to be the ideal place to make our camp.

I knew very little about Aelred's past, but it soon became clear that he'd learned much during his time hiding in the forests and, using those skills, he quickly built a crude shelter from branches and covered it with bracken to keep out the worst of the weather.

Brother Benedict gathered firewood and it didn't take Aelred long to get the fire going and to build a makeshift spit. I was worried that a fire in the forest might attract unwelcome attention but said nothing as, like the others, I relished the prospect of a hot meal. Instead, I watched as Aelred and Brother Benedict set about roasting the remains of the small pig. Then, leaving Aelred to finish cooking our supper, Brother Benedict came to tend my wounds. He first bathed my feet which were raw and bleeding from having travelled so far without shoes. He then mixed some sort of poultice and applied it to the cuts quite liberally, saying that he was sure it would help them to heal more quickly. I'd also suffered a wheal across my back inflicted by a cruel lash of the whip and that he soothed as well, tactfully not mentioning the marks which Ingar had inflicted during our union. That done, he examined the wound to my chest.

'Who tended this?' he asked, looking worried.

'The woman Ingar,' I said.

'Then she was truly a gifted healer. You surely should not have survived this wound. The arrow must have lodged so close to your heart that it's a miracle she didn't tear that out when she removed it.'

I told him how she'd done it without probing or prising the arrow free and he seemed much impressed. He then said something which surprised me greatly.

'Some pagan healers have a remarkable gift,' he admitted. 'Sometimes I think we could learn so much from them if we would simply open our minds to what they tell us. The Church relies too much upon the written text of the scriptures and thereby fails to see the full extent of God's great bounty.'

It was a brave thing for a monk to admit, being a heresy given that the Church would not countenance anything that was not overtly Christian – miracle cures wrought by Christ and by the Holy saints being the only exceptions. 'She was indeed a very remarkable woman,' I agreed, but decided to say no more about all that had transpired between us.

Brother Benedict bathed the wound but admitted he lacked the skill to do much more. In the end he simply took some of the fat from the roasting pig, allowed it to cool and then spread it on my chest. 'It's a remedy we have to help the skin to heal more quickly,' he advised. 'We also need to mix some broth to make you stronger.'

I told him of Ingar's advice about drinking my own piss and he found that very amusing.

'I think you'll find my broth more palatable,' he said laughing. 'And every bit as effective. But if it's piss you want then you're most welcome to some of mine!'

Aelred joined in the joke. 'Is that like Holy water?' he asked.

'No,' said Brother Benedict. 'But perhaps it will be even more effective if we mix in some of yours as well.'

'Ah,' said Aelred. 'But that would mean that we all need to piss at the same time lest some of it gets too cold for Matthew to enjoy fully!'

Their humour did much to lift my spirits and I took it all in good part knowing it was a sign of just how relieved they both were to be alive after our ordeal. I chose not to tell them that being just three men alone in the forest meant that the dangers were far from over as I could see they needed time to rest and recover almost as much as I did.

** * * * *

That night we all ate well, feasting on the roasted pig and drinking a goodly portion of what was left of the mead. As we settled down to sleep it occurred to me that we should have set a guard – not only against the prospect of thieves or robbers but also in the hope of seeing a merchant from whom we could ask directions. In the end I decided we were all too tired. Aelred, however, seemed wide awake.

'Shall I tell you the story of a small man who lived in a land of giants?' he announced.

Brother Benedict groaned but then turned over. 'There are no such things as giants,' he complained, clearly preferring to sleep. 'The good Lord made only creatures of grace and beauty.'

'Well, he made you!' joked Aelred. 'And I don't see much grace and beauty in your long, skinny hide!'

'He made us all in his own image,' replied Brother Benedict emphatically. 'The Holy Bible tells us so.'

'Ah, but it doesn't say that he made us all the same size!' retorted Aelred. 'For all you know he made a few giants.

After all, midgets are common enough so why not giants as well?'

Brother Benedict groaned again. 'All right,' he managed. 'Let's hear the story and then perhaps we can all get some sleep.'

Undeterred, Aelred sat up and warmed his hands against the fire. 'Well, if you don't like giants, just think of them as being very tall people,' he conceded. 'But our hero was not as tall as all the others who lived in that place. In fact Hereric, for that was his name, was only about half the height of everyone else who lived there. His story goes something like this…'

'Hereric was regarded by everyone as being all but useless as a warrior as he was much too small to fight in the shield wall. Some men would have been glad to be excused from serving in the fyrd but not Hereric. He would have willingly taken his turn but, as everyone else was so much taller, there was just no place for him to stand. Whenever he did attend the training sessions he was always the one everyone picked on so, not only did he get a beating, but he also became very unpopular when he was knocked down leaving those who stood on either side of him in the shield wall open and exposed. So instead Hereric was always given the standard to carry, which, of course, is the worst job of all.'

'Why is that the worst job of all?' asked Brother Benedict who clearly knew nothing of battles and combat.

'Standard bearers are targeted by everyone,' I explained. 'They seldom survive a battle hence the job is always given to the man you can most readily afford to lose.'

'Exactly,' continued Aelred.

'Despite this, Hereric practised with the spear whenever he could, honing his skills until he was actually quite good with it but even so, he was still not allowed to fight with the rest of the fyrd. Then, one day, the Shire was attacked by a very fierce Viking war band and everyone quickly retreated behind the palisade. Once all were safely inside they promptly secured the gates.

'The Ealdorman, a man named Trounhere, was a wise fellow and realised they were unlikely to beat off the attackers. Surrender seemed impossible so he sent a runner to the next Shire asking for help and reinforcements. That meant all he had to do was delay matters long enough for help to arrive.

'The Viking warlord came forward and shouted up to the Saxons, challenging them to come out and fight. The challenge was a serious dent to Trounhere's pride, so the Ealdorman had to think of something quickly. "Why should we waste our time fighting puny warriors like you?" he shouted back. The men under his charge were horrified – the Vikings certainly didn't look puny and they saw no cause to rile them any more than was needed.

'The warlord raised his axe and shook it at the Ealdorman defiantly.

'Trounhere laughed, trying to appear bolder than he felt. "So, who is your strongest warrior?" he demanded.

'The warlord knew the answer to that and called for a man named Grendon to step forward.

'Trounhere had thought he would be able to buy enough time for the reinforcements to arrive by challenging the chieftain's champion to a fight but, when he saw Grendon, he quickly realised his mistake. What stood before them was truly the fiercest warrior they'd ever seen. Not only did Grendon stand as tall as a tree, he also looked to be as strong as an ox and carried a huge battleaxe that most men would have struggled just to lift, never mind wield in battle. The Ealdorman turned to his men. "I need a volunteer to fight this ogre," he said. "Who will be my champion?"

'Even when Trounhere offered a heavy purse of silver to any man who would answer Grendon's challenge, none of his men seemed prepared to go up against such a fearsome warrior, knowing that to do so would mean certain death.

'"Someone has to fight him," insisted the Ealdorman. "We need to buy enough time for help to get here."

'Still there was utter silence until a small voice at the back spoke up. "I'll fight him," said Hereric.

'At first everyone laughed but Trounhere quickly realised that he didn't seem to have any other choice. "Very well," he agreed. "The only trouble is I don't think we have any war gear small enough to fit you."

"I don't need a mail vest or a helmet," said Hereric. "Just my trusty spear and a seax. That way I can move about more freely."

'The Ealdorman looked surprised. "You do realise he'll kill you if he catches you?" he said to Hereric, stating the obvious.

'The little warrior nodded. "Yes my Lord, but at least I'll die doing something useful for a change rather than standing around waving the banner in the air. And I'll do my best to last as long as I can," he promised.

'The Ealdorman returned to the Viking warlord. "My champion will meet with yours at dawn tomorrow," he yelled. "But on one condition."

"What is it?" demanded the Viking.

"If my champion slays yours you will depart this Shire and swear never to return."

"First let me see your champion," demanded the warlord wondering who could possibly be brave or foolish enough to take on Grendon.

'With that, Hereric scrambled up on to the top of the palisade to show himself but had to stand on tiptoes just so the raiders could actually see him.

'The warlord laughed so much when he saw him that he almost fell off his horse. Still laughing, he agreed at once,

84

knowing that Grendon had never been beaten by anyone and wasn't likely to fall to such a puny little maggot.

'That night Hereric was treated like a hero. He sat beside Trounhere at supper and everyone came to shake his hand knowing they'd probably never see him again and regretting having been so unkind to him over the years. "Hereric has more guts than the rest of you put together," declared the Ealdorman. "It's such a pity that he'll die, but we are all very grateful to him."

'At dawn the next day the Ealdorman ordered the gates to be opened. As Hereric prepared to meet his doom he turned and gave one last wave to his new friends, then stepped forward bravely to meet his fate.

'"What's this?" roared Grendon, who was resplendent in all his war gear. "He's so small and puny I can barely see him!"

'Hereric stood up as tall as he could, which wasn't really very tall, but he was seemingly unafraid. "And you're so big and clumsy that I'm worried you'll trip and fall directly on to my spear," he shouted in reply. His friends were delighted with his response and all cheered loudly.

'"I don't need a weapon to kill the likes of you," said Grendon. "I'll simply squash you with my foot." With that he raised his huge axe and brought it down on Hereric with so much force that the poor little man barely had time to step aside. As he did so, the axe hit the ground so hard

that the earth seemed to shudder under the weight of it. But Hereric didn't hesitate even for a moment. Instead, as Grendon struggled to recover his heavy axe, he ran straight past him so that he was then standing behind the giant.

'Having shouldered the axe once more, Grendon wasn't quite sure where Hereric had gone. Then he looked around and, seeing him, turned and struck again. Once more Hereric dodged the blow and ran past the giant. This went on for some time until Grendon realised what Hereric was trying to do – and what's more, it was working! Having to keep wielding such a heavy axe whilst wearing all that war gear was making the giant very weary indeed, so much so that he realised he had to end the fight before he became too tired to carry on. He decided that to do this he needed to catch Hereric out and finish him off either by flattening him with the axe or, better still, using it to slice him in two. Thus the next time he only pretended to strike but, before letting the axe fall, he turned to face the other way where he was sure Hereric would soon appear. That was his big mistake! Hereric was ready for him and instead of running past him, stayed exactly where he was. Realising he'd been tricked, Grendon tried to turn again but Hereric was much too quick for him. Whilst the giant's back was still turned, he drove his spear home, thrusting it hard and deep into Grendon's thigh, which was the only part of the giant which was exposed and which he could reach with ease.

'At first it was as though Grendon didn't know what had happened. Groaning with the pain, he managed to keep to

86

his feet but then gradually started to sway before dropping his axe and sinking to his knees, quite unable to stand any longer as blood pulsed from his wound.

'Hereric went up to him and, for the first time, was able to almost look the giant straight in the eyes – but he didn't waste much time on that. Instead, he walked around to stand behind Grendon then, whilst the giant was still on his knees and quite unable to move, reached up and swiftly cut his throat with the seax.

'Grendon fell forward and lay face down on the ground and Hereric stood with one foot on his back and held his bloody weapon aloft. "I claim victory," he shouted and all the Saxons cheered and cheered.

"'There," said Trounhere, "your champion cannot defeat even our smallest warrior. If I were you I'd honour your pledge and go to pillage elsewhere. If you don't I'll send my other warriors to fight you and you can guess what will happen then!"

'Being more than a little troubled by the way things had turned out, the warlord simply rode away, shaking his head and looking very bemused. Needless to say, after that although Hereric was still too small to serve in the shield wall he was always given a very special place to stand in any battle, right next to the Ealdorman as his personal bodyguard. With such an important role, from that day onwards the little man in the land of giants stood very tall indeed .'

'That's a meaningless story,' said Brother Benedict, who by that time was also wide awake. 'It's just like the story of David and Goliath from the Bible.'

'It's not,' said Aelred, a little disappointed. 'It serves to show that even small warriors can play an important part in a battle. You just have to use their skills as best you can.'

It was usual for we Saxons to debate the meaning of any story for a long time after it had been told, teasing out whatever lessons could be derived from it. On that occasion I was much too tired to argue the point. 'Well next time you can tell us one of your stories,' I said to Brother Benedict. 'Then we can discuss them both. But for now, can we please get some sleep?'

Chapter Seven

We remained in the glade for several weeks during which time I came to realise just how different my two companions were, not only from me but also from each other.

For example, Brother Benedict seemed not of our world. Like the monks I'd known at the Abbey, he spent much of each day at his devotions. He seemed to care little for his own earthly needs beyond that of food and sleep, instead concentrating on his due in the next world. That said, he was a good cook so took it upon himself to gather roots and herbs from the forest with which to flavour our meals. He also persuaded me to join him for a few moments of quiet contemplation each day, saying that it would serve to soothe my troubled soul and thereby help me to make my peace with God.

At first I resisted, saying that I didn't deserve forgiveness.

'Is that because you fear that God has forsaken you?' asked the goodly Brother.

I said I thought not. Rather that I was being justly punished for my many sins. 'I should have perished with the rest of my men,' I explained. 'Therefore I must now endure whatever hardships he sends my way.'

Brother Benedict assured me that was not the way of it. 'God does not punish,' he said. 'It's you who are punishing yourself for something which could not be helped. It's good that you should feel remorse but it's hardly your fault that you survived when others didn't.'

What he said was of some comfort and, as the days passed, I did begin to feel better. I also felt stronger and less troubled by my wound given that I was allowed to rest and required to do nothing more than light tasks such as gathering firewood or tending to the fire itself.

It was therefore left to Aelred to provide everything else we needed and though that seemed unfair, he offered no complaint. He was clearly an accomplished woodsman, not only building the makeshift hut in which we sheltered but also providing food for our bellies by employing all the skills of a poacher. It was not surprising that he hadn't mentioned this before as the punishment for poaching fish and game, particularly on lands belonging to an Ealdorman or the King, was severe.

In truth, Aelred was not a hunter in the way that Rufus had been during those dark days at Athelney. He lacked any natural skills and, in any event, he had no bow. Even so, he more than managed to provide for us all. In fact he seldom came back empty handed, catching fowls such as wood pigeons and even song birds by setting an ingenious trap. Basically, he would tempt the birds down to feed by scattering some crumbs of stale bread on the ground, usually beside a bush or at the base of a tree. He then pulled a thin length of twisted wool from his tunic, unwound it and then threaded it through some more crumbs to form a sort of necklace. This he placed among the other crumbs and then simply waited. The birds found the food quickly enough and sooner or later one of them pecked at a crumb which was attached to the thread. Unable to spit it out, the greedy bird simply swallowed it and, because of the thread, had no choice but to swallow the next crumb as well. Once started, the poor thing could not help but keep swallowing crumbs until its crop was so full that it choked.

He also fashioned a long thin basket which he wove from some pliable twigs taken from a willow that grew close beside the stream. It had two chambers joined by a narrow neck and, once baited with dead fish, he placed it in the stream to catch eels. Its design was such that once inside the trap the eels found it difficult to get out so could be simply lifted from the water – though then killing them was easier said than done as they seemed to keep slithering and writhing even once their heads had been cut off! Even more difficult than killing them was skinning them. It involved removing the skin in a single piece, pulling it off like a sleeve whilst the rest was securely pinned to a tree. The eels then needed to be hung up to ensure that all the blood drained out of them as Aelred said it was like a poisonous bile that, if swallowed, would rot the gut.

All this was very effective, but it was his manner of catching small trout which impressed me most. He would lay on the bank alongside the stream and watch until a fish came into view. As was their way, a trout would spend a short time catching insects and the like which were carried to it on the flow, then dart back to its lie under the bank for some brief respite from the current. Aelred would simply watch and, when the time was right, slip his hand into the water beside the bank and wait for the trout to return, keeping so still you might have thought him dead. In fact he seemed to go into a sort of trance as he waited, often for some considerable time. But the wait was always worth it as, when the trout returned, he was ready. Slowly and carefully he would work his hand towards the fish, taking great care not to alarm it. His touch was then like silk, so smooth that the fish seemed hardly to notice as he began very gently stroking its belly. Gradually, Aelred would work his way along the underside of the fish, soothing and brushing it with just the very tip of his finger. Either the fish found this movement comforting or perhaps mistook it for the current gently flowing past it but, either way, it seldom made any attempt to swim off. Then, when he judged the moment to be right, Aelred would hook the fish up and out of the river to land somewhere on the bank. He never tried to grasp it; he simply pushed it up and out of the water. So accomplished was he that we dined regularly on fresh trout. They were not large fish but when smoked over the fire they tasted as good as any I'd ever eaten.

Thus all in all we fared well enough and I have to say that I look back on those few weeks in the forest as the happiest of my life. Not only was it one of the few times that I felt safe and rested, I had also come to enjoy the company of both men, even regarding them as friends. That said, I was still anxious to return to Chippenham as soon as I could, not only to seek counsel from my old abbot but also to resume my position as one of Alfred's advisers and, with his blessing, to wed Emelda. Thus as soon as I felt able to travel I announced that it was time for us to move on.

'Are you sure you're yet well enough?' asked Brother Benedict one night as we sat around the fire having eaten our fill.

I said that I was though, in truth, that was not the case – I had simply persuaded myself that I would have the chance to rest along the way or, better still, once we reached

Chippenham. In particular, I was struggling to sleep well at that time being troubled by a frequent dream in which I saw my men being butchered and young Edmund running straight into the hands of the Vikings with his sword held high – images which troubled me greatly. Even more worrying was that I still felt an occasional pain deep within my chest if I exerted myself. It was enough to cause me to sit down and rest for a while, though seemed to pass quickly enough. Anxious not to let them press me too hard on this, I reminded Brother Benedict that he'd also promised to tell us a story.

'Please, not one of your pious tales about saints and martyrs,' pleaded Aelred teasingly.

Brother Benedict took the jibe in good part. 'I was going to tell you about St Kevin,' he said.

'I've never heard of him,' said Aelred.

I laughed as I knew the story well enough. 'St Kevin was a hermit,' I explained. 'He was also a monk and a very devout man who loved all things God created.'

'Ah,' said Aelred. 'Then he and I have something in common because I love all the things that God created as well, particularly women!'

'I think Matthew was referring to St Kevin's love of animals and birds,' suggested Brother Benedict.

'Well, I like animals and birds,' teased Aelred light-heartedly. 'Particularly the ones I can eat.'

Brother Benedict shook his head in dismay. 'Do you want to hear about St Kevin or not?' he asked.

Aelred shrugged. 'Not really. But I have a feeling you're going to tell me anyway.'

'Well, St Kevin was a very pious monk who liked to pray with his arms outstretched on either side of him, thereby opening up his heart to God. One day, whilst praying thus, a blackbird settled on the open palm of his hand. Kevin was so deep in his devotions that he didn't notice it was there and spent so long at prayer that by the time he did the bird had built its nest. Kevin didn't want to disturb the bird so kept his hand stretched out and even allowed the bird to lay its eggs in the nest and then for the young birds to hatch and finally fledge.'

'Then what happened?' asked Aelred.

'Well, when people realised how much Kevin truly loved and cared for all God's creations it was said that his way with them was like a mirror reflecting all the glories of heaven, so they made him a saint.'

'What, just for not killing a blackbird?'

'That's not the point,' I said. 'The story urges us to value all living things.'

'That's right,' said Brother Benedict. 'And it reminds us to respect everything the good Lord has created.'

Aelred seemed unimpressed. 'Well I've never knowingly killed a blackbird, except the ones I wanted to eat. So perhaps they'll make me a saint as well.'

I laughed. 'I think you'll find you have to do a bit more than that. For one thing you'd need to cleanse your soul and, in your case, I fear it would take a priest so long just to hear your confession that even one as patient as St Kevin would give up long before you were done!'

Although we were all in such good spirits and getting along surprisingly well, the other two were also anxious to return to their respective lives. Therefore, having seen no sign of any merchants travelling along the track, I resolved that I'd rested long enough and that we should go in search of a settlement where we might seek assistance.

'They'll be obliged to help us,' I explained. 'As I said, I'm of noble blood so they can't refuse to lend what aid they can.'

'That's if they believe you are who you say,' cautioned Aelred. 'You look more like some wretched beggar than a person of "noble worth".'

It was a point well made. After all I'd endured there was little that might suggest my true identity as everything of value had been stolen, including my birth ring and my father's sword, both of which would have counted for something. 'All we can do is try,' I said. 'Worst way we'll have to settle for directions and then find our own way back to Chippenham or, at least, to somewhere where I'm known or can be recognised.'

We packed our few belongings onto the mule the next day then cleared away all we'd constructed within the glade so as to leave no trace of our having been there. Aelred was keen we should do that as we'd partaken freely of all the forest had to offer. As he reminded us, that was, in itself, a serious crime for which we could well be called to account.

That done, we set off without further delay, following the track which had led us there but continuing northwards until it left the forest. I was confident that we would quickly come across a settlement where I could expect to be welcomed and restored. Certainly I had no inkling of all the troubles which lay in store for us, but then I should have known that it's from ignorance and undue confidence that there comes the quickest fall.

* * * * *

The first settlement we came to after leaving the forest was actually a large one. It comprised at least thirteen homesteads which had gathered together where the road crossed a wide but shallow river. The river provided some measure of protection but there was also a tall fence with a pair of stout gates to the front which, although ajar, could no doubt be quickly closed against an attack.

As we approached our spirits rose as it seemed likely that such a large settlement would include someone, perhaps a headman or even a thane, who could get word to Lord Alfred. At the very least they would be able to give us directions to Chippenham. As we were bearing arms, I resolved to go straight to whoever commanded there and explain our position. Whilst he would be obliged to help us, he would doubtless require something in return as indeed he was entitled to do.

Although not quite an Ealdorman, my being from a noble family should have made things easier for us but I was aware that not having a first name derived from that of my father might make people suspicious. Therefore as we approached the settlement we let Brother Benedict lead the way whilst Aelred and I followed a few paces behind, me with my sword sheathed and Aelred with his spear lowered. Even so, I was not surprised to find a man come forward to greet us armed with a somewhat rustic axe.

'I'm known as Matthew,' I said out loud as we drew near enough for him to hear. 'I was christened Edward and am the third born son of Lord Edwulf who was a counsellor to Lord Alfred himself. My friends and I require only—' He didn't let me finish. Instead, he summoned others to come out from the settlement and stand at the entrance, thereby fully barring any access to the gates.

'We come as friends,' I tried, realising something was wrong. 'As I said I'm Matthew and—'

'We know full well who you be and you're not welcome here!' he bellowed, still keeping his distance.

For a moment I couldn't believe what I was hearing. 'But we're honest Saxons. I want only to pass word to your Lord seeking his permission to cross his land whilst bearing arms. That and for him to send word to Lord Alfred of our coming.'

'I also know what you be and if I was you I'd not risk another step.'

I looked across and saw that three men had positioned themselves just outside the gates, their bows raised and drawn ready to shoot. 'Who are you to deny me my Saxon rights?' I demanded. 'Who is it that you think I am?'

The headman looked at me suspiciously. 'You are that there warrior with the pierced heart we've heard tell of, are you not? If you dispute that, then open your shirt and prove it so.'

'What's that to do with anything? It's true that I was wounded in the service of our King, but I offer no threat to the lives of you or your families.'

'No, not to our lives. Not with these odds against you, you can be sure of that! But you would steal our very souls if we let you. For is it not true that you died and returned from the dead? That you plucked out your own heart when you withdrew the arrow that killed you but never put it back!'

'What, are you saying that I no longer have a heart?' I said, incredulous that he could even think such a thing. 'If so, then feel my breast, for it beats within as does that of any man. How could I live and breathe without it?'

'The Devil looks after his own,' said the man, then crossed himself.

'So what are you looking at? A ghost? Believe me I'm as mortal as the next man. If you doubt that then loose your arrows and you'll see that I bleed and die as easily as any other. But beware, in killing me you'll incur the displeasure of your King.'

'We was warned that you'd try to trick us,' said the headman. 'It's said that you're set upon snaring the souls of men for Lucifer himself, which is why he sent you back from hell. And we'll have no truck with that here. So leave or we'll send you back to him!'

'You would refuse aid to your fellow Saxons even though I've told you who I am?'

'I don't care who you are but do know full well what you are!' he said.

'I told you, I am Matthew, christened Edward, the son of Lord Edwulf and I serve our King.'

'You serve the Devil most likely! And you expect me to believe that you're of noble birth, yet you travel half naked and in rags. What's more, you fare no better than those wretches who travel with you! So what do you take me for? A fool?'

Brother Benedict came to stand beside me. 'This man is no servant of the Devil,' he said.

The headman scoffed. 'There speaks a man of God who has not the commitment to his faith to even wear a cross about his neck.'

'You do not need to wear a cross to do God's work,' replied Brother Benedict boldly. 'But you should know that all we owned was stolen when we were taken captive by Viking slavers.'

'We've heard tell of that as well. It's said they released him because even they feared to kill him. What's more, he consorted with pagans, rutting with them like an animal in the forest.'

'None of this is true!' I protested, carefully ignoring the last point for I was certain there was no way I could explain what had transpired between Ingar and myself.

'Pah! I hear the Devil's voice in every lie you tell. You should repent your evil and look to repair your soul to God, not trouble simple folk like us who seek only to follow the path of righteousness.'

'I think it better that we leave,' whispered Aelred. 'You may have a body that can't be slain but I'm a mere mortal and have no wish for them to prove it so.'

'That's right, you should leave whilst you can,' said the man having clearly overheard what Aelred said. 'Either that or I'll have your worthless carcass flayed wide open. Then maybe we shall see your wicked soul for ourselves!'

The group by the gate were looking very unsettled at that point and I could sense that their mood was growing darker. 'We'll leave,' I said solemnly, having decided that nothing I could say would be believed. 'But Lord Alfred shall hear of this for in refusing us you have betrayed your Saxon heritage.'

With that we turned and left.

* * * * *

Once safely away from the settlement we stopped to decide what best to do.

'It seems you've become something of a legend,' said Aelred having clearly taken no offence at having been turned away. Perhaps he was used to it, which reminded me that I still knew very little about his past life beyond that which I'd assumed and the few words he'd said on the matter.

'It's my fault,' I told them. 'I'm being punished for the many sins I've committed. There's no call for you both to suffer with me.'

Brother Benedict shook his head. 'That's not the way of it,' he explained. 'These are simple folk who have not fully forsaken their ancient beliefs but rather they've welded them to their Christian faith. Thus they are all too ready to believe the rumours and superstitions they hear tell of. Don't judge them too harshly for that for they have so little in this world that they'll do anything they can to protect their souls in the next.'

I nodded knowingly. 'What you say is true,' I admitted. 'Although less committed to my calling than you are, from all I learned as a novice at the Abbey I know that such doubts and fears are rooted deep in their beliefs. That being so, we cannot hope to explain the truth of our position even if we get close enough for them to listen. Therefore I see little point in trying and our best course is to continue in the hope of finding another settlement where we may be received more warmly. Failing that we'll have to find our own way to Chippenham.'

'You were once a monk!' said Aelred. 'Christ, is there anything you haven't done? For one so young you've already lived and done more than many men who've lived three times as long as you!'

I could see he had a point. 'Yes, but when I abandoned my calling I did so because I thought God had shown me a path he wanted me to follow; a path I willingly trod though it has nearly cost me my life several times at least. Now it seems he's spared me again, so I'm bound to wonder what else he has in store for me.' Even as I spoke I realised that as

I hadn't actually renounced my calling before leaving to fulfil Alfred's orders I was, in essence, still bound by my vows. I had only been a novice so hadn't fully pledged myself to the Church but still the thought troubled me, particularly as I hadn't offered prayers for my redemption even though the list of my sins seemed to grow longer by the day.

'It's of no matter,' said Brother Benedict when I mentioned this. 'God knows what's in your heart. No amount of mumblings or pleadings will change things and besides, God cannot answer everyone's prayers at once because what suits one man will not be right for another. And remember, if you pray only to make things better for yourself you are not acknowledging God, you are seeking help with whatever burden you carry, something you should manage for yourself.'

It was an intriguing point but one I'd never really considered. 'If that's so, then why should we bother to pray at all?' I asked.

'You should pray to give thanks for his providence, not to trouble him with pleas to improve your lot in life or to deliver you from harm. So confess your sins and thank him for his bounty. That's all he asks of you.'

'But you prayed almost constantly whilst we were held captive by the slavers,' I pointed out.

"I admit it. I was weak and very frightened at the time,' said Brother Benedict. 'Yet in my heart I knew it was wrong. Even so, the good Lord saw fit to hear my prayers and doubtless will hear yours when you're ready.'

'Then are prayers not enough to gain forgiveness for our transgressions?'

'No, confession is the time for that. But don't expect to bargain with the Lord for your sins to be set off against some act of piety. Only fools believe they can barter or buy their way into heaven.'

'Yet the Church would have us pay for redemption.'

'Don't look to me in that regard for I'm not ordained. But my order has no truck with men seeking to ease their conscience with silver. It demands instead that we perform some act of contrition that is of benefit to others but offers no advantage to ourselves. I shall do as much if and when the chance arises.'

'So what of me?' I asked. 'What must I do to assuage my many sins?'

Brother Benedict looked at me kindly then placed his hand on my shoulder. 'Your soul is deeply troubled, I know. But you must first find it in your heart to forgive yourself. To do that I've found that it sometimes helps to share your burden in confidence with others.'

'There's much I should confess,' I admitted. 'I caused many men to die on my account and that troubles me daily. I've also killed men with my own hand, albeit mostly with good cause, and, as you know, I lay with Ingar as part of a pagan ritual. Not of my own accord you understand, but I did so willingly enough. In doing so I not only betrayed my faith but also the unspoken promise I gave to the woman I love.'

'Huh! That I should be so lucky!' said Aelred, who seemed to find it all amusing. 'I'd have willingly traded my soul to lay with a woman like that!'

'I had no choice,' I explained. 'She drugged me with some potent brew so that I became consumed with lust. She later told me that she'd conceived a child, though I cannot say how she knew that so soon after our union.'

'Such things are beyond my understanding,' admitted Brother Benedict. 'Therefore there's little I can offer by way of guidance except to say that if you sinned against your will I cannot see how that will weigh heavily upon your soul.'

'It's true that I was not fully conscious, though as I've said, I was willing enough at the time.'

'I bet you were!' mocked Aelred. 'Anyway, what difference can it make now? She's gone and as like as not any child she carries could be from that bastard Ljot.'

I decided to let the matter rest there and instead concentrate on looking for another settlement. At least that might speed our return and I could then take further counsel from my old abbot. I could also speak with Alfred to explain how my men came to be lost and make my confession to Emelda and beg for her forgiveness for having thus betrayed her. Given that she had been a whore and thereby lain with many men, any contrition I felt for what had transpired between Ingar and myself may sound strange, but the truth is that Emelda's sins were not of her making whereas my betrayal of her was something for which I felt I was, at least in part, to blame.

Chapter Eight

We were all three of us unusually quiet that night as we ate our supper. We'd set our camp at what we judged to be a safe distance from the settlement in case the people there felt the need to drive us off still further. I have to say that it did not sit well with me that we should be regarded as outcasts, though neither of the others seemed to see it as a slight.

'So, tell us about this woman of yours,' said Aelred, breaking the silence. 'The one you say you've betrayed.'

I was not sure how best to answer. 'I've not actually asked for her hand in marriage,' I explained. 'But it is…understood between us that we'll wed.'

'Which means that you've bedded her but not actually committed to taking her to wife,' he teased knowingly.

I said nothing.

'I'll wager she's the daughter of a rich Saxon Lord or some fat merchant.'

How could I tell him that her father was a traitor and that she'd been forced to become a whore, as was her mother? As I thought about that I began to realise why Alfred had such misgivings about the match. Ordinary people like Aelred would find it very strange for a person in my position to marry someone so far beneath my station.

'At least tell us her name?' pressed Aelred.

'She's called Emelda,' I replied.

'And judging by your taste in women, I bet the fair Emelda is a real looker, am I right?'

I couldn't resist a smile. I was thinking back to when I first saw her that night at her father's camp when most of the men barely gave her a second glance. Although never beautiful, not like my mother or my sister, she was pretty enough to my eyes but then she let herself go once Alfred had decreed her fate. 'She provided much comfort in the difficult days at Athelney,' I managed.

'I bet she did!' mocked Aelred. 'Just like Ingar provided comfort as you recovered from your wound.'

'It wasn't like that,' I assured them.

Aelred just laughed and said something like 'it never is', although I didn't hear him properly. Brother Benedict on the other hand said a great deal more albeit in far fewer words.

'I'm not sure what your abbot would say about how you have consorted with these women. I know you mean to renounce your vows, but they are still relevant until you do.'

Those few words touched upon many of the things which troubled me. Not least of which was how my faith, which had once been so important to me, had become neglected. It was as though it had died when the arrow struck and perhaps grazed that part of my heart in which I carried my love for the Holy Church. 'My intentions towards Emelda remain unchanged,' I said, not absolutely certain that was still true. 'Besides, there was much at the time which might mitigate my sin. I can't say more, but believe me that's so. As for Ingar, as I've said, that was not of my doing.'

Brother Benedict just looked at me for a moment then nodded wisely as though he'd said all that was needed.

'I just hope I get to commit a few more sins worth mitigating before I die,' said Aelred, still laughing. 'Or even just get to bed a few more women if it comes to that.'

* * * * *

'How's your wound?' asked Aelred as we rose the next day and started on our way.

I hesitated before replying. 'It pains me less, but I sometimes find it hard to catch my breath and still seem to tire too easily.'

'Perhaps you should have rested longer,' suggested Brother Benedict.

'There'll be time for that once we're safely back at Chippenham,' I reasoned. 'That of course assumes Alfred has returned there. He may have moved on to Winchester by now from where he could more readily govern his realm.'

Aelred stopped in his tracks. 'God's truth, Matthew, we can't keep chasing across the Shires looking for him!'

'We'll learn more as we go,' I assured him. 'Failing that, once we reach Chippenham we can send word to him from there.'

'That's if anyone will actually speak to us!'

We had come to what looked to be an old Roman road, still paved and lined with stones but in need of much repair. We thought it might lead eventually to Chippenham – or at least to some other significant settlement. After all, no one ever took the trouble to build a road to nowhere. We therefore followed it and our hopes were raised still further when we came across a signpost which actually named Chippenham but which pointed towards the east. If true, it meant we'd been travelling in the wrong direction.

'It's probably a shortcut,' suggested Brother Benedict.

'More likely it's some fool's idea of a joke,' said Aelred. 'Chippenham can't possibly lie to the east unless someone has turned the whole world around whilst we've been away!'

I doubted that either of them was right. Given that so few people could read, it was unusual to find a signpost of any sort except at very important crossroads, which certainly that wasn't. In fact the route to the east was nothing more than a rough track so to me it was obvious that the sign had been placed there by someone who was anxious we should not reach wherever the road was headed. With that thought in mind, I decided we should continue as we were.

We had not gone far when we came across a flock of about two dozen sheep. I looked around to see who was minding them but could see no one. I knew it was unlikely that a shepherd would leave such a large flock untended so called out aloud.

'Show yourself!' I ordered. 'We come in peace and mean no harm to you or your flock.'

There was no immediate answer. 'Well,' said Aelred, loud enough for anyone nearby to hear, 'if these are "wild" sheep we shall dine on roast mutton tonight and for many days to come.'

With that a man appeared from behind a small clump of bushes beside the road. Having shown himself, the shepherd kept his distance, holding his sling in one hand. Shepherds spent much of their time living rough and were very good at avoiding robbers or bands of Vikings. They were often expert shots with the sling, able to loose a handful of stones so quickly and with such precision that few men would take them on. In fact even when carrying a sword or a spear, it was foolhardy to face a skilled man armed with a sling as they could fell you with a single shot before you could get close enough to strike.

'We mean you no harm,' I said again to reassure him. 'We've escaped from Viking slavers and are wending our way home. I am called Matthew, christened Edward and son of—'

'I know full well who you be,' he said gruffly. 'Word has reached even the likes of me.'

I was not sure how to respond.

'I'll have no truck with you, so be gone,' he warned. 'I want none of your tricks or your evil doings here.'

'We have no tricks,' I said, growing angry. 'And if you know who we are you will also know that we are good Christian souls in need of aid.'

'I'll not give succour to the servants of the Devil,' he said roundly.

It was Aelred who replied. 'Who the hell do you take us to be?' he demanded.

The shepherd hesitated before replying. Instead, he walked a few paces forward, still holding his sling as though ready to use it at any moment and also to show that he was not afraid of us. 'He's that there warrior with the pierced heart,' he said pointing at me accusingly. 'A man sent back from the dead to serve the Devil's hand and trap men's souls.'

'That's superstitious crap!' said Aelred. 'He's as mortal as any other man and bleeds as easily.'

'It's true,' I added. 'I was sorely wounded but was healed, though I am still troubled by the injury.'

'Healed by what?' challenged the shepherd. 'By fornicating with witches and pagans from what I hear of it.'

I couldn't deny that so said nothing more, but Brother Benedict was not done with the man.

'My son, I am a Holy man as you see. As committed to the Church by my vows as I am by my love for God. Therefore trust me when I say that this man is not as you think and your Christian duty is to help him as you would help any other of God's children. Remember our Lord's teachings about the good Samaritan?'

This seemed to unnerve the shepherd. 'What is it you want of me?' he demanded.

'I'm a warrior in the service of Lord Alfred and would return to him as quickly as I may. That's my sworn duty and, to fulfil it, I need only to know which way we must travel to reach him.'

'Do you think I'd tell you that even if I knew?' sneered the shepherd. 'To bring the servant of Satan down upon Lord Alfred and betray him thus would be treason for which they'd have my head in an instant!'

'Do you not think that if I were truly who you say I am I would need to ask a shepherd for directions?'

That seemed to puzzle him. 'What do I know of such things? My task is to mind these sheep, not meddle in things which are far removed from my station. Now be gone with you, and if your greedy friend here so much as touches one of my sheep I'll send you all to hell. And this time you'll not come back, be assured of that.'

* * * * *

'What are we going to do now?' asked Aelred. 'It seems your fame has spread so far and wide that there are none who will even talk to us, never mind help us.'

'I fear you're right,' I said. 'I think that signpost back there had been placed and turned on purpose in the hope of sending us off on the wrong road.'

'Nothing like being made to feel welcome!' said Aelred. 'Chippenham can be but a few days from here, but we can't just walk on aimlessly hoping we might stumble across it by chance.'

He was right, for none of the route we had travelled thus far looked even vaguely familiar. That being so, we had no choice but to press on along the road and hope that by travelling north we were at least headed in the right direction.

At length we reached another settlement, but it wasn't Chippenham. It comprised a small Vill with a Hall and numerous other homes and outbuildings, all well protected and surrounded by fertile fields. By then it was raining hard so we all went to ask for shelter.

The man who greeted us was a short, stocky fellow who walked with a limp. It was clear that he was every bit as worried by our presence as was the shepherd and those at the other settlement we'd visited.

'I've trouble enough!' he shouted as soon as we drew near. 'You keep your distance or I'll loose my dogs on you. They won't care much whether your flesh is that of the living or the dead.'

'This is madness,' I explained – or rather I tried to. 'I was wounded and then healed. There's no pagan craft involved and nor am I returned from the dead, whatever others say.'

He still didn't look convinced. 'Everyone knows the truth of it, for rumour travels faster than fire in these parts. If you're hungry, I'll leave food for you, but you're not welcome under my roof.'

There seemed no point in arguing as his mind was set.

'We need nothing from you,' I replied. 'We seek only directions that we might return to Chippenham.'

He raised the stick he was using as a crutch and pointed to the Roman road we'd been following. 'Continue as you've come,' he said. 'But if you're as mortal as you say you are I wouldn't tarry here any longer than you need to. There are rumours that a Viking warband is abroad and you'd not want to fall foul of them.'

We were grateful for the information so thanked him and continued on our way.

'So, just to add to our problems, do we now have to be wary of a Viking warband as well?' asked Brother Benedict.

'No, he was probably referring to the slavers we've already killed,' mused Aelred.

'I doubt it,' I reasoned. 'It's been several weeks at least since we killed them and in any event, they could never be described as a warband. They were just a few rogues and outcasts who'd sunk so low as to become traders in human flesh and misery.' Even as I spoke it occurred to me that whilst that was so, it could well be that the man was referring to the warband which had attacked my escort. After all, we couldn't by then be all that far from where that attack had taken place. If so, it meant there was a band of hardened warriors to contend with, not just a few fools who could be so easily tricked as the slavers had been by Ingar. I decided not to mention this to the others given that we already had problems enough to be going on with.

We decided to take shelter from the rain under the canopy of a large tree. Everything was too wet for us to light a fire but once out of the rain we were comfortable enough and decided to wait out the weather.

'That farmer back there looked to be doing well for himself,' observed Aelred.

It hadn't occurred to me at the time but when I thought about it I could see he was right. 'He was not high born,' I acknowledged. 'Perhaps he earned his freedom in battle which might explain the injury to his leg.'

'What? And he was given land as well?' said Aelred.

'Maybe he earned enough spoil to better himself. Either way he's prospered in these difficult times and we should think well of him for that.'

'It's always the same,' said Aelred woefully. 'Those that have land fare well enough whilst those that labour for them starve. The price of grain is now so high that it's well beyond the purse of ordinary folk and only fills the bellies of those rich enough to afford it.'

Brother Benedict nodded knowingly. 'That's as maybe,' he said. 'But the price is so high because so many men have died in these wasteful wars with the Vikings and there are now too few left to work the fields and bring in the harvest.'

All of that was new to me. As the son of a wealthy family such matters were beyond me, but I had begun to see how hard life had become for so many. 'Well. the wars are now over and Alfred will soon put things to right,' I said weakly. Even as I spoke I was not sure how he could do that but decided to say no more. Instead, I tried to sleep, grateful for a chance to rest.

* * * * *

The following morning was much brighter, so we pressed on until we found ourselves in open country.

It was truly beautiful there, with softly rolling hills steeped in lush grass and with meadows filled with flowers. It was from this that I realised just how much time had passed, for it had been early spring when I left Chippenham on Alfred's mission and now the summer was fully underway.

In the far distance we could see a column of smoke rising from beyond what looked to be a small hill. There was nothing to suggest anything sinister such as a raid, so we ventured closer, reaching it just before dusk.

What we found there was another small farmstead of five or perhaps six families working together and probably enjoying a good living from such rich pastures. They had built their homes on the northern slopes of the hill and surrounded them with a stout wicker fence. Three men and a boy were busy repairing the defences whilst the women hastily carried bundles of clothes or blankets from their homes as if trying to hide them in the small wood which was but a short way from their stockade. It was clear that they'd also driven their stock into a holding pen within the trees where they hoped it wouldn't be noticed, something which struck me at once as being a futile gesture.

We had no intention of asking anything of them except directions but, from all we'd seen, even that was more than most people were prepared to offer.

'You should remain here,' said Aelred. 'It looks to me as though they've already heard we may be coming and are seeking to hide from us as best they can. No doubt they've heard the same rumours as those at all the other places we've been to.'

I hated the prospect of being feared, even unjustly, but what Aelred said made sense. So, as a precaution, we sent Brother Benedict in alone whilst we waited half hidden some fifty paces from where they were working. From there we could clearly see all that was going on.

As he was not bearing arms it was easy for Brother Benedict to approach but, as soon as he appeared, those mending the fence stopped work and stared at him.

'What can we do for you good Brother?' demanded one of them who looked to be older than the others. His manner was amiable enough though not especially welcoming.

Brother Benedict raised his hands. 'God has seen fit to give me all I need,' he said cheerily. 'But I fear I'm lost. Can you show me the path whereby I might return to Chippenham and thence rejoin my order?'

The man looked surprised. 'Chippenham, you say? Then you're still a good long way from home with yet two days' journey ahead of you at least. And unless God has given you the power to smite heathens with your bare hands you're sadly lacking what you'll need to get there.'

Brother Benedict was bemused. 'He has safely brought me thus far,' he said. 'But what is it that troubles you so?'

The man put down his tools and went across to explain. 'What worries us is that there are raiders coming. So far they've evaded the fyrd at every turn and already looted farmsteads nearby. We fear we may be next. If the good Lord was set upon helping us he'd have sent us a dozen warriors, not a monk.'

'So what will you do?'

The man looked at him as though the answer was obvious. 'We'll defend our homes as best we can,' he said simply. 'We'll bury all that which we value most then hide our stock in the woods yonder. You're welcome to stay with us if you've a mind to.'

'How many of them?' asked Brother Benedict.

The man shrugged. 'At least thirty by all accounts. Maybe more. All of them thirsting for blood if the places they've already looted are anything to go by.'

'Then surely you cannot hope to hold them! You'd be best advised to hide yourselves as well. Homes can be rebuilt and crops regrown but once slain your life is lost for ever, at least as far as this world is concerned.'

'So speaks a man of God with no home or family to protect.' With that he walked away to continue working on the fence.

Brother Benedict recounted all this when he returned to us. It explained why they were so busy, though it was obvious to me that even once repaired, the fence would count for nothing when the raiders attacked, particularly if it was the band I'd already encountered. What's more, even if we could persuade them to hide, they'd need to find somewhere more remote and less obvious than the small wood which, being so close to their homes, was the first place the raiders would look.

'What do you think?' asked Aelred.

'I think that if they stay here they're all as good as dead,' I said.

Aelred seemed to think about that before he answered. 'Well, we can either go down and die with them or we can get as far away from here as we can. I know which I'd prefer to do.'

'I can't stand by and watch these helpless folks be slaughtered,' I said. 'But there's no need for you both to stay as well.'

Aelred looked surprised. 'You'll be killed for certain if you join them!' he warned.

'So? Apparently, I've died before and it doesn't seem to have done me much harm.'

'That's all very well for you,' he teased. 'I'm not so keen on finding out whether I share your little trick of coming back from the dead!'

'Be that as it may, this is my chance to restore my damaged reputation and try to make amends for all those who were slain whilst under my command. Either way, if I can save a few Saxon lives folk might start seeing me in a better light.'

'Is that wise?' asked Brother Benedict. 'When I asked for directions they said we are but a few days' march from Chippenham. It would be a pity to get yourself killed when so close to home. Surely we should hurry there and fetch others to help us?'

'Aye,' said Aelred. 'Or maybe the fyrd will yet get here in time to see the bastards off. Either way, what difference will it make if you stay?'

'Even so, it's my duty to help them if I can,' I said.

Aelred didn't look keen on the idea of staying but neither did he seem inclined to leave without me. 'Then I suppose that if I'm to look after you I'll have to stay as well.'

Aelred had boasted several times that few men could handle a spear as well as he could. If he'd acquired that skill by serving with the fyrd then that was to the good. I'd seen many men trained in that way though it seldom produced any who could be described as warriors. Thus I wasn't sure how much help he'd be and didn't want him to risk his life for no purpose.

Meanwhile Brother Benedict seemed to have decided to stay as well. 'My duty is to tend the souls of these good people,' he said bravely. 'That is the penance God requires of me to make amends for my weakness whilst a captive of the slavers. I shall therefore return to them in the morning and offer what help I can.'

'That's all very well but these people cannot hope to hold against thirty Viking warriors,' I reasoned.

'So what's to be done?' asked Aelred.

Brother Benedict had a very simple plan. 'As is my wont, I'll put all my trust in God. Surely he will deliver me safely – or at least stand ready to receive my soul if I should fall.'

'I think we can do better than that,' I offered. 'Brother Benedict, you must go down at first light and try to persuade the farmers to get as far from here as they can. Given that you're a man of God they may at least heed what you say and that way will have a better chance of surviving the raid. But it means they must abandon everything except that which they can carry with them.'

'Then what will you do?' asked Brother Benedict.

'Nothing unless I have to,' I said solemnly. 'If the farmers are safe we'll let the raiders do what they will. Only if they're discovered will we be forced to attack.'

'Attack!' said Aelred, clearly shocked. 'To what end? We'll be hopelessly outnumbered!'

'We might be able to buy enough time for at least some of these good people to escape.' Even as I spoke I realised that there might yet be another option. 'Mind you, if these farmers could be persuaded to join us, we could wait until the Vikings reach the farmstead then all attack them from behind. They won't be expecting that, so we might prevail.'

Aelred immediately dismissed the idea. 'As things are I doubt you could persuade them to even speak to you, never mind fight alongside you.'

I knew he was right. It would take a lot for them to overcome their fear of what I was supposed to be and, to their simple logic, anything they did to help me would tarnish their souls. 'Then we can only do what we can,' I said. 'That means we have to get them away from the farmstead before the raiders arrive or they'll all be butchered like sheep. The question now is how long have we got before the Vikings get here?'

'From what I could glean from the man I spoke to it won't be long,' suggested Brother Benedict. 'They could be here at any time so we'd best prepare ourselves.'

With that Brother Benedict settled down to pray whilst Aelred and I checked our weapons. I honed my sword on a stone whilst Aelred ensured that the blade to his spear was keen and well mounted. He also checked the shield he'd picked up from one of the slavers. It was not a particularly strong one and I reckoned that even at best it wouldn't survive more than a few strokes from a battleaxe. Still, it was better than nothing and I began to wish that I had one as well. As we completed our preparations I was also forced to confront the stark reality that I was about to go into battle having not practised or trained with the sword for many months. I was far from battle ready and, restricted by my wound, could not hope to prevail against such overwhelming odds. Yet somehow the thought of dying to save others offered a sort of penance for having led my men to their deaths that day in the forest. It also occurred to me that perhaps I'd begun to believe the rumours about myself. Was I indeed a man returned from the dead? And if so, did that mean I could not be killed again? As so often seemed to be the way of it in my short life, I had more questions than answers. In the end I dismissed the thought knowing that it was a sin to even think upon something which was so obviously blasphemous – there was only one person truly capable of resurrection and it wasn't a boy who was once a novice monk and was now a would-be warrior, and a failed one at that. With that thought in mind, I knelt and, for the first time in many weeks, actually offered prayers that we might survive the battle, ignoring all that Brother Benedict had counselled about praying only to give thanks to God for his great bounty. Instead, I admit that my prayers that day were uttered from fear of what we were about to confront.

Chapter Nine

None of us slept well that night for thinking of the fate which awaited us. As if to make matters worse, a fireball appeared in the sky which Aelred took to be an omen and was so disturbed by it that Brother Benedict and I both tried to quell his fears.

'There's nothing to be afraid of,' Brother Benedict assured him. 'It's just a restless star, that's all.'

'Aye,' said Aelred. 'As restless as we are and therefore not unconnected to our fate.'

I recalled all that Edwin had said that morning on our way back to Chippenham when he and I saw the sun and moon in the sky together. 'There's no such thing as omens,' I assured him. Then I remembered how some men had feared what they said was an omen the night before the battle at Edington. 'The sky turned red and some said it heralded all the blood that would be shed the next day,' I told him.

'And did it?' asked Aelred.

'Perhaps,' I admitted. 'It's true that many died in that battle but most of the blood was that of our enemies. No, if it is our fate to die tomorrow then die we shall. But if we do it'll be because God wills it so, not because of some sign in the sky.'

'Amen,' said Brother Benedict.

'Aye,' said Aelred. 'Amen indeed. But if you're planning on saying any more prayers tonight you might at least ask God to have mercy on our souls for, restless star or not, I have a very bad feeling about all this.'

* * * * *

Having slept so little we were all awake well before dawn. I watched as Brother Benedict knelt for a long while in silent prayer as he always did each day. When he'd finished he got up and, with nothing more than a cursory word of farewell, walked down to join those at the farmstead.

'He's a braver soul than I took him for,' said Aelred as we watched him go. Aelred then began to sharpen the tip of his spear even though it was already honed to perfection.

'That must by now be the sharpest spear in Wessex!' I joked, trying to lighten our mood.

'The sharper the better,' retorted Aelred. 'For a properly sharpened spear saves lives.'

I looked at him curiously. 'How can that be?' I asked.

'Well, for one thing it might save mine,' he said grinning.

As at that point we'd seen no sign of the raiders we assumed there would be ample time for Brother Benedict to persuade the people at the farmstead to leave. But that was the first of several mistakes I made that day for no sooner had the goodly Brother reached the stockade than we heard the unmistakable sound of a Lur – the deep, booming note of the Vikings' battle horn sounding like a roar in the early morning air. Almost at once we could see the raiders approaching, but they were not creeping stealthily towards the farmstead as if to surprise it; they were marching openly, their banner flying and their warriors spread out in a line, armed and ready.

Aelred nudged my arm. 'What the hell is that all about?' he asked.

I could make no sense of it either. They seemed to have given themselves away deliberately, thereby forgoing the element of surprise.

All those in the farmstead had heard the Lur as well but, far from fleeing for their lives as I hoped they would, they looked set upon making a fight of it.

'They'll all be slaughtered,' muttered Aelred mournfully.

There was no denying the truth of that as they could never hope to match what was set against them.

Even as we spoke the Vikings came on, their rank still brazenly open as they advanced. Meanwhile those at the farmstead were busy taking up positions behind the fence, perhaps hoping that the raiders would think twice about attacking a farmstead where the men were armed and ready. That was all very well but I knew that would not deter fully fledged warriors even for a moment. They would like nothing more than the chance to make a real fight of it and would no doubt savour the prospect of the slaughter they knew would follow.

I counted at least thirty Vikings and there were doubtless others I couldn't see. What's more, they were, as I feared, not slavers like those who had taken Ingar and myself but almost certainly men who'd escaped during their retreat after the battle at Edington all those months before. Their leader was a man who stood tall and straight and was obviously very sure of himself. I could see him clearly from where I lay, his yellow hair shaved at the sides but worn long at the back, like the mane of a wild horse. His war gear was equally impressive. He carried a bright sword and was dressed in a mail vest that was so well polished that it glinted in the early morning sun. I could see at once that he was a man to be reckoned with.

Those who came with him were also well armed, mainly carrying axes but with a few having spears or other fearful weapons – though curiously only three of them were armed with bows. It was whilst assessing the warband that I noticed a small boy among them. It was only as he drew closer that I recognised him as Edmund, the Viking boy I'd sought to adopt but who I feared had been taken when we were attacked that day in the forest!

If it was indeed Edmund then it confirmed my fear that those he was with were the ones who'd brutally slain my escort. If so, why was he so at ease with them and— Suddenly I realised what a fool I'd been! Of course he was at ease with them, he was of Viking blood! Not only that but in drawing his sword that day the boy had not been intent on defending us, he was rushing to join our attackers! The ungrateful little runt had betrayed us – and it was therefore his treachery which had cost the lives of my men, not my incompetence!

That dreadful realisation stirred within me a rage so strong that it swept through my entire body. I shuddered, barely able to believe that what I was thinking could be true. Then, when I realised it was, I craved vengeance as others might crave the very air they need to breathe.

Sensing that something was amiss, Aelred put his hand on my shoulder then looked at me, his eyes desperately trying to fathom what I'd seen that so disturbed me.

'It's them!' I hissed. 'It's the bastards who killed my men!'

Aelred stared at me. 'It can't be,' he said. 'That was months ago. They'd be long gone by now!'

'It is!' I insisted, my mind by then already lost to thoughts of vengeance. In that moment I realised the real reason for the given years Ingar had told me about; the true meaning of all those tormented dreams I'd endured about Edmund's fate and, most important of all, the reason I alone had been spared that day. It was so I could avenge the others!

Driven by that thought, I started to my feet but Aelred stopped me, grabbing me and pinning me to the ground. 'Wait!' he insisted. 'Don't show yourself too soon!'

He was right of course. We were the only hope those at the farmstead had of surviving the raid and for their sakes alone we needed to time our attack so as to strike only once the Vikings committed to their bloody work. That way we could hit them from behind and try to even out the odds by taking them out one by one.

Though itching to join the fray, I was persuaded to bide my time for what seemed like the longest wait I can ever recall.

As the Vikings continued to advance I noted that Edmund was kept towards the rear of their line, presumably so he would not be too much at risk. Even so I vowed to kill him if I got the chance, but that would have to wait as there were others who needed to feel the edge of my sword even before he did if I was to help those at the farmstead.

Then, quite suddenly, the leader of the Viking warband stopped and put on his helmet. Thrusting his sword into the air, he then let out a cry so shrill as to hurt the ears. That was the signal for the raiders to attack and with it they all rushed towards the farmstead as one, screaming and howling their abuse.

The Saxons were not to be so easily taken in as I'd thought. Several men appeared almost at once, stepping in front of the fence armed with bows. Even as they started loosing their arrows I saw one Viking reel back in pain.

I still willed them to run if they could, or at least to send the women and children to a place of safety, but, in truth, it was much too late for that. Instead, they all stood their ground, men and women together, hopelessly outnumbered and armed with nothing which could be described as proper war gear or even weapons.

As the Vikings closed on the farmstead, Brother Benedict ventured towards them with his arms outstretched as if imploring them to turn back by sheer force of will – or perhaps expecting some sort of divine intervention. Needless to say he was cut down by the first of them to reach him, knocked to the ground by a single blow from the flat edge of an axe. They could have so easily killed him at a stroke but, given he was a monk, they clearly meant to save that pleasure for later.

It was that which caused me to make my second mistake that day. Incensed by Brother Benedict's cruel fate, I could contain my rage no longer. I grabbed a spear and, with Aelred at my side, attacked too soon.

As we charged forward to join the fray I hurled the spear at the first raider I came to but missed my mark. I drew my sword instead and slammed into him so hard that he had no time to defend himself. I'm not sure whether I killed him or not but even as he fell, I turned to face the next man who dared to confront me. I fancy that he could see the anger blazing in my eyes and hesitated for just a moment longer than he should before thrusting with his spear, hoping to catch me off guard. Instinctively, I caught the shaft of it with my hand and jerked him forward with such force that he was pulled towards me and impaled on my sword. As he fell, I placed my foot on his chest and withdrew the blade then turned to face another man who was coming towards me with an axe. I nimbly dodged his blow and cut him down with a cruel stroke across his back, my sword scything through so deeply that he died almost where he stood. I wasted no more time with him but, as I turned and readied myself once more, someone barged into me with his shield so hard that I was sent reeling and breathless to the ground.

As I lay there winded and all but helpless, I looked up and saw Aelred locked in combat with the man who had barged into me, desperately fending him off with his spear. My friend gave a good account of himself, felling his opponent but then falling victim to another who struck him whilst his back was turned.

I didn't actually see Aelred as he fell but was sure that he could not have survived the blow. Although I did try to get up to help him, my heart was beating so fast within my breast that I could scarcely move. All I could do was to watch in horror as the Vikings who, with such numbers in their favour, seemed assured of victory and therefore took their time to complete their slaughter. After that I remember nothing more of the raid itself.

* * * * *

By the time I came round the fighting was over. I lay very still hoping the Vikings would think me killed, though I knew that ruse wouldn't last for long. I also knew that when they did discover me they'd relish the chance of wringing what life I had left from my body.

Carefully, I raised my head a little to see what was going on. I half hoped there might be some chance of escape whilst they were busy with their spoil or torturing the others who were wounded, but all I could see was the usual debris of a raid – burning buildings and things strewn and discarded on the ground. The latter included many bodies so I guessed that most of the Saxons had been killed. Not having actually seen either Aelred or Brother Benedict slain, I scanned the battlefield for any sign of them. I couldn't see Aelred anywhere but there was a long scrawny body which I was certain was that of Brother Benedict hanging bloody and naked from a tree. I could only hope that the blow which felled him had either killed him outright or had at least left him unconscious so he didn't have to fully endure their torments.

Somewhere in the distance I could hear a woman screaming. When I looked in that direction I could see that she was being passed between three warriors who were taking turns to abuse her. Using her dreadful fate as a distraction, I tried to make good my own escape.

I managed to raise myself up a little further and could then see the full carnage of the raid. Many buildings were still on fire and the raiders were busy pulling what they could from the flames or stripping anything of value from the bodies. One thing was also clear, they had not forgotten about me.

Still on the ground, I groped around for my sword thinking that I would at least die fighting but, before I could grasp it, two of them came across to where I lay. I saw them coming so remained very still, but it was all to no avail as they kicked me so hard in the ribs that I couldn't avoid flinching. I heard them laugh then, taking me by the arms, they roughly turned me over. I struggled as best I could but lacked the strength to free myself as they continued kicking me and shouting. Of course I could understand nothing of what they were saying but then I didn't need to – it was plain enough what they had in mind. One of them then started to strip off my leather jerkin, presumably thinking it worth having and not wanting it spoiled with blood. As he did so, my undershirt gaped open and he saw my scar.

For a moment they both just stared at me, then stepped back as if stunned by what they'd seen. One of them called others to come and look as well. This included the tall warrior I'd seen earlier and who I'd taken to be their chieftain.

'So, are you the famous warrior with the pierced heart I have heard so much about?' said the chieftain. He seemed to speak our tongue well with barely any trace of an accent, yet was clearly not a Saxon. 'Now perhaps we shall see whether it's true that you can cheat death at will.' With that he ripped open my undershirt so that my scar was fully exposed.

I also glanced down at it and could see that it was red and livid, having not fared well from so much exertion. I cursed myself for not doing as Ingar had advised and rested long enough for it to heal fully. But none of that mattered. If they were indeed the ones who'd attacked my escort then I was quite prepared to die if it meant that I could take a few of the bastards with me and thus avenge my men.

Satisfied with what he saw, the chieftain called others to look at the scar as well. As they gathered round many of them seemed so in awe of it that they were almost afraid to get too close.

'Is it true that the arrowhead is still inside?' asked the chieftain, seeming intrigued.

'No,' I said as defiantly as I could. 'I pulled it out with my teeth!'

He looked surprised. 'Then is it not true that you died and then returned from the underworld?'

'Of course it is,' I boasted. 'My God told me that I had to return and slay even more of you heathen bastards before I would be allowed to rest in Paradise.'

The man nodded. 'I am told by Arne, who I believe you have met before, that even though you are so young you are a famed warrior, known to Lord Alfred himself. So what are you really called?'

I glanced across and could see that he was referring to young Edmund who it seemed could not recall my name. I decided to tell them nothing. 'So is that the little runt's name?' I asked instead. 'We called him Edmund after my older brother. Perhaps we should have called him Judas.'

The chieftain looked puzzled and I realised that he didn't understand my reference to the man who had betrayed Christ. 'I am told that you killed the boy's father,' he said.

'That was my brother,' I boasted, resisting the temptation to name Edwin lest he guess who I was from that.

'You are both of you warriors? Then no doubt your father is very proud, though I fear he will soon have one less son to boast about,' he said ruefully.

'My father is dead, as are both my older brothers. Though like me, each of them accounted for many dozens of your kind – and not by shooting arrows at them from behind a tree either. Our way is to look a man in the eyes when we slay him.'

He nodded as though accepting the truth of that. 'So what is your name?' he pressed again.

'As you said yourself, I am called the warrior with the pierced heart. That's all you need to know.'

'Well, warrior with pierced heart and no other name, know that I am called Torstein and that I am Jarl to these men. And as for you, we shall soon see whether you can be killed or not. But for now we shall leave you to think upon your fate. There are things I would know of you before I kill you.'

'I'll tell you nothing,' I said sounding braver than I felt given that I was all too well aware of how cruel they could be when it came to torturing prisoners.

'We'll see about that,' he said. With that two men came to bind my hands.

I realised that he wasn't anxious to kill me, perhaps because, like the slavers, he feared that to do so would bring misfortune upon him. 'So how come you speak my tongue?' I asked as he turned to leave.

'My mother was a Saxon,' he explained. 'She was taken by my father on a raid and kept as his whore. His wife bore him four daughters but no sons, so he favoured me.'

'That makes you a bastard,' I said, half hoping it would rile him enough to finish me and get it over with, thereby avoiding whatever other dreadful torments he had in mind.

'We Vikings are not so fussy about such things,' he said, perhaps guessing what I was trying to do. 'Blood is blood and marriage means little to those of us who spend so much of our time away.'

It was then that I noticed that one of the raiders carried my father's sword – the one also used by my brother Edwin and stolen from me when I was struck by the arrow.

'That sword is rightfully mine,' I challenged, hoping I might at least be given the chance to fight him for it. 'If he wants the right to carry it he should have taken it in battle, not scrabbled around in the bushes to find it whilst I lay wounded.'

The man recognised the challenge when Torstein told him what I'd said and so came over to me and said something I couldn't understand. Torstein translated for me.

'He says that if you value the sword so much you should have taken more care of it. You were sleeping when he took it, thus he spared your life so accepts the sword as a token of your thanks.'

'I wasn't sleeping; I was wounded. He would not have had the guts to take it from me in equal combat.'

Torstein repeated this to the man and they both laughed.

'You Saxons and your precious honour! Do you not know that a life of honour is always a short one?'

'Perhaps, but it got us victory at Edington,' I said, knowing that any reminder of their defeat there would be like scratching at an open sore.

For a moment Torstein stared at me so hard that I thought the death blow would surely follow in an instant. Thinking those were my final moments, I readied myself to die, but nothing happened. Instead, he knelt beside me. 'That was surely a great victory and we are with much respect for Lord Alfred. We are not cowards,' he added. 'We are warriors who honour courage, though, unlike you, we see honour in death, particularly if it's death in battle. My warriors would all gladly die so long as they can do so bravely. I wonder how you will face it when the time comes for me to put you to the sword?'

'What's that to me?' I shrugged. 'I've faced death often enough and even succumbed to it once, as well you know.'

'How would I know that?' he asked, looking curious.

'It was you and your band of thieves who attacked me. You then butchered all my men and stripped our bodies of all we owned.'

Torstein was clearly thinking back, trying to recall the incident which was probably just one of many. 'You mean when we rescued Arne!' he said sounding surprised. 'You were there then?'

'Rescued him? Rescued him from what? He was set for a life of ease as part of a noble Saxon family. I'd even offered to adopt him as my brother!'

Torstein shook his head. 'He would have rather died a thousand times than endure such an insult! His father was a much-respected warrior, a friend to Lord Guthrum himself.'

'And that's why you rescued him?'

'Of course. Why else? Was that when you were struck by the arrow?' asked Torstein.

I nodded. 'And as I died I watched you butcher all my men, one by one.'

One of the other men standing beside Torstein then said something which again I couldn't understand.

'He says that we checked all the bodies,' explained Torstein. 'He assures me that no one there was left alive. Yet here you are and with a scar above your heart to prove you were indeed killed that day.'

'Exactly,' I said. 'I died and was sent back to kill as many of you heathens as I can.'

Torstein turned to look at the man who carried my father's sword. 'Do you see any sign of fear in these young eyes?' he asked loudly, pointing straight at me.

I doubt the man understood enough of our tongue to know what he was being asked so I was not surprised when he didn't answer, but that didn't deter Torstein. He just shook his head. 'No, nor do I. All I see is defiance. He lays here, ready to die but has no fear of doing so. Which is why I shall let him live, but only for now.' With that he looked at me again. 'No one will touch you, boy. Your life belongs to me now and I shall take it only when I'm ready.'

'My life belongs to me,' I said defiantly. 'If you deign to steal it from me know that I shall die with a curse upon my lips that will hang over you like a cloud for all the days of your life.'

The prospect of such a curse from a man whom he believed had returned from the dead seemed to trouble him greatly. He nodded as though to acknowledge the words but was then silent for a moment. 'I shall still kill you,' he said at last. 'Be assured of that. But like I say, only when best it pleases me.' With that he turned and walked away, leaving me to contemplate my fate.

* * * * *

After that I was left to myself as the Vikings continued searching for yet more spoil. Naturally, I looked for any chance to escape but my hands were tied and I was watched constantly. The pain in my chest had passed by then but had left me desperately tired, so I settled myself beside a tree and lay back against the trunk to rest.

Having finished their business of thieving and pillaging from the dead, several Vikings found the livestock which had been hidden in the small wood and drove it back to be slaughtered. Whilst they were doing this, others began to tend their wounds or clean their weapons. Apart from those we'd slain, none of them seemed to have been seriously hurt but at least one of them needed to have his arm bound to stem the bleeding and another had a cut to his shoulder.

Their next concern was to strip their own dead and then cremate the bodies on a funeral pyre. There seemed to be no special ceremony for that, they just shared out the men's belongings then watched as the bodies were consumed by the fire. As they burned, those watching drank to the dead men's journey to Valhalla and recounted what I assumed were stories of their lives.

Even before the fire had died down, one of the men mounted up and, having been given orders from Jarl Torstein, rode off towards the north. I assumed he was simply going to scout ahead for yet more farmsteads to plunder but that assumption was my third mistake. I regret to say that even that was not to be my last.

* * * * *

It occurred to me that it was strange that the raiders had been allowed to pillage so freely. The local fyrd should have intercepted them but presumably either couldn't find them or didn't want to. I could well understand if it was the latter. Torstein's men were warriors of some merit, not just a ragged band of thieves or slavers. They were also well trained and used to moving quickly as, by the following day, they were ready to set off again, all the food they'd taken from the farmstead having been placed on a cart they'd found and hurriedly repaired. They'd also found the mule Aelred, Brother Benedict and I had used to carry our supplies and set that to pull the cart. With my hands still bound and secured by a long rope to the mule's harness, I was made to follow as, at Torstein's command, the whole group then moved off.

'You could at least cut him down,' I shouted, looking at the body of poor Brother Benedict which still hung from the tree.

Torstein, who was one of only three men on horseback, came across to speak with me, riding alongside me as we spoke. 'He's a priest and I hate priests,' he said venomously.

I knew the truth of that. The Vikings relished the chance to torture monks and priests almost as much as they loved to rape any women they could take alive. They even took pleasure in despoiling their bodies once slain. 'He was a monk, not a priest. A Holy man of peace and learning.'

Torstein just sneered. 'What difference is that to me?'

'Then at least bury the others,' I pleaded. 'They did you no harm.' Even as I spoke I was looking round for Aelred's body but could see no sign of it. I could only assume that he'd been taken whilst still alive and then dragged off to be butchered elsewhere. If so, I regretted it with all my heart for he was a brave man and had proved a true and loyal friend. I was also filled with remorse for the fact that both he and Brother Benedict had died on my account. It seemed unfair that once again I should be the only one to survive and that their names should be added to the already long list of those whose death would weigh heavy on my conscience.

'I haven't the time or the mind to bury them,' replied Torstein. 'I've ensured they're dead and thereby ended their suffering. I could have just left them all to bleed out where they lay but was merciful enough to at least hasten their end. What more would you have me do?'

'Bury them,' I said again. 'You could at least do that.'

'Pah! Let your precious God take care of them. Besides, there's no hurry. There are people in the far north of my land who leave their dead unburied for many weeks, freezing the corpse in ice as they then compete in races and contests of strength to see who shall inherit items from the dead man's possessions. Only when all is spoken for do they burn the man's body and scatter his ashes to the wind.'

Scarcely able to believe that anyone could be so callous, I looked back at the ruined farmstead. 'Then at least tell me why you attacked so brazenly?' I asked. 'Surely you should have taken the farmstead by surprise?'

Torstein laughed. 'You Saxons have never understood our ways,' he said simply. 'You think we come just to whet our swords in Christian blood, but there's no profit in that. I have over thirty men to feed so need food and provisions. We sounded the Lur and marched down upon them openly in the hope that any of the fools who lived there would run. That way there would be fewer of them to fight us.'

I suddenly realised what he was saying. 'You wanted them to run away!'

'Of course! We could then simply pick up what we need and be gone to seek more profitable raids. Poor farmsteads have nothing worth stealing except for food so why risk my men being wounded or slain for that?'

'You killed them for a few cattle and a couple of swine?' I said. 'Is that all their lives were worth?'

'I killed them because they resisted. We have no choice but to live off the land as we go, scavenging for food and anything else we need.'

I looked at the cart which contained the carcasses of the stock they'd butchered and the few things they'd deemed worth stealing. 'So much blood shed for so little profit,' I said sorrowfully.

'Why do you pretend to be so coy about the shedding of a little blood?' he asked. 'You did your share of the killing back there. I'm told that at least three of my men are dead on your account alone.'

'I would have killed you all but for my wound,' I boasted.

'It seems you do a lot of killing,' he observed. 'And what difference did it make to the outcome, except to shed even more blood?'

'I'm a warrior and I did my duty.'

'Ah, a warrior is it? And you scarce pulled from your mother's tit. What are you? Sixteen? Seventeen years of age?'

'Did my age make any difference when I had a sword in my hand?'

'You fought well enough,' he agreed. 'I'll grant you that. But you've forfeited your life for nothing. That is unless Lord Alfred thinks well enough of you to pay your ransom.'

'What do you mean?'

'I've sent a rider to demand payment in return for sparing your hide. From what I hear of it he'll pay willingly enough to see you safely restored. Though looking at that wound of yours he'll be wasting his precious silver. I doubt you'll live long even if I spare you.'

I was suddenly shocked. 'But how will he know it's me?' I demanded.

'The rider will tell him that you're the warrior with the pierced heart. That should be enough.'

'He won't know that's me,' I moaned.

Torstein shrugged. 'Well then, so be it. I can't spare another rider now.'

It was then I realised that by not telling him my real name I had made yet another mistake. Because of it, I'd be denied any hope of being ransomed and thereby returned to Alfred and to Emelda. 'So what then will become of me?' I asked, ruing having been so foolish. I should have realised they'd seek ransom for a captured warrior.

Torstein looked down at me. 'Half my men expect me to kill you whilst the other half fear we'll be cursed if I do. Thus they would rather ensure that you died of your own accord.'

'I'd never take my own life,' I challenged.

'I somehow doubt you'll be quite so sure of that once they start to torture your feeble hide. I've never yet seen a man who would not readily open his own veins to avoid dying thus.'

I needed no elaboration on the means at their disposal, so fell silent to contemplate my fate.

'Or perhaps I'll take you with us,' he added.

I looked up at him, not sure whether that was good news or not.

'With that wound you won't be worth much as a slave as I doubt you'd survive the hardship of a life in bondage for more than a week. But some might regard a man who has returned from the dead as a talisman or perhaps…'

'Perhaps what?'

'A rich man who has lost a son or a brother on a raid might pay for the privilege of exacting his revenge on you. I pity you if that's the case but for me the decision is simple.

I'll take the best price I can manage and let the Gods decree your fate from there.'

'Bastard!' I said. 'Have you no mercy in your soul?'

'Ah, if it's mercy you want I'll tell you what I'll do. If I can't sell you I'll kill you myself using your father's sword. Is that not the merciful thing to do?'

Chapter Ten

Learning of Arne's treachery had helped to salve my conscience about the loss of my escort, but I still felt responsible for the death of both Brother Benedict and Aelred. Whether I was guilty on that account or not I cannot say, but either way I had little option but to accept my own fate and face it with as much courage as I could manage. The best I could hope for from Torstein was a quick death, something which the Vikings were more likely to bestow on a man who faced his end bravely. Therefore I knew that I needed to keep up the pretence of being unafraid of dying as best I could. Yet hiding my fear was easier said than done. I had seen so much of death in my short life that the prospect of actually dying didn't concern me unduly; it was the manner of my death which worried me – and not only because of the pain. My pride required that I neither begged for mercy nor died pissing myself from fear as I'd seen many others do before me.

The strange thing was that although I hated Torstein for what he'd done to my escort, I also quite admired him. In some ways he reminded me of Sweyn, the merchant I'd met on my way back from spying on Guthrum's camp at Chippenham. It was true that they both lived very different lives; Torstein was a warrior who commanded such respect from his men that they seemed never to question his leadership whereas

Sweyn worked alone and lived in the shadows. Yet both used their guile and cunning to good effect and neither seemed to fear anything, despite the dangers they each faced every day.

As a fellow warrior, I would have liked to discuss this with Torstein more fully but, as it turned out, he didn't speak to me again for the rest of that day. Instead, he concentrated on keeping his men moving, presumably anxious to avoid meeting the fyrd if they had indeed been mustered. With no prisoners other than me to guard, the Vikings marched in no particular formation, albeit they kept up a good pace and were ever watchful for an ambush or for the chance of further pillage. During this time Arne kept his distance. He seemed to struggle to keep pace with the column as he insisted on carrying his father's sword which was much too big for him to manage but which he wore tucked into his belt. I knew Red Viper to be a very fine weapon and recalled Edwin showing his prize to Alfred during our retreat from Chippenham. Thus I regretted having returned it to the boy as it deserved to be better treated than having the tip of the blade dragged along the ground, but neither Torstein nor any of the others seemed inclined to help the boy with his burden.

Naturally, as we went I began to think of ways I might delay the Vikings to give the fyrd more time to reach us but, bound as I was, there was little I could do. Even as we settled down to make camp that night I was simply tied to a tree then left to my own devices. I was not offered food or even water as none seemed inclined to squander their supplies on a prisoner, especially one who'd killed some of their comrades and, in their eyes at least, was simply waiting to be slain.

The next morning we were roused early and I was given water but nothing to eat. There was clearly great excitement in the camp and I watched as they began to prepare for something which I could only assume meant yet another raid. Men were busy cleaning and sharpening their weapons and all seemed eager for whatever it was that lay ahead.

Torstein came across to speak with me. 'My men think I should kill you now and be done with it,' he said simply. 'They fear that a man who has returned from the dead will bring us nothing but ill fortune.'

I said nothing.

'You are prepared to die?'

I shrugged. 'You'll kill me sooner or later,' I said. 'Better to get it over with so I can return to be with my God in heaven. He'll no doubt be pleased with me now that I've killed a few more heathens.'

He drew his sword and studied the freshly sharpened blade.

'I thought you were going to let me die by my father's sword?' I said.

He shook his head in disbelief. 'You truly have no fear of dying, do you, boy? It'll be a pity to kill you but if I were to let you live you'd have to swear to do exactly as I say and make no attempt to escape. We've much work for our blades to do this day and I can ill afford to have you getting in our way.'

'Why, what are you planning?'

He knelt down beside me. 'There's an Abbey less than an hour's march from here,' he said as though that told me all I needed to know.

In truth he was right; I needed no elaboration on what they would do when they reached the Abbey. It would be an easy target and would amount to wholesale slaughter with the monks who lived there having little with which to defend themselves. Even if they could conjure up some form of weaponry, it was unlikely that many of them would know how to fight or even have the will to do so, being more concerned for their souls than for their lives. 'I'll not give my word to watch as you butcher defenceless men, so do your worst and be done with it.'

Torstein looked at his still drawn weapon. 'I have never before met a Saxon who didn't beg for mercy rather than feel the edge of my sword,' he said, fingering the blade.

'Why should I fear death?' I said sounding braver than I felt. 'I've died before, remember? All I hope is that your sword is sharp enough to get it over with without too much pain.'

He looked at me long and hard and, at that point, I truly believed he would kill me – not out of anger, but in the manner of a cold-blooded execution. Once more I prepared to meet my fate by crossing myself and uttering a short prayer, though it was said more for my spiritual comfort than as an attempt to secure redemption.

'This nailed God you worship must be a powerful God if you are so anxious to meet him again,' he mused, clearly unnerved by my steadfast refusal to plead for my life. 'I should like to know more about him.'

'Well, for a start, the one we nailed to a cross wasn't our God, that was his only son; a man we call Jesus.'

'And this God you worship let you do that? He let you nail his son to a cross and watch him die? That doesn't sound like much of a God to me.'

'He died that we might live,' I explained.

'How is that? How did this son of your God secure the lives of you all simply by dying himself?'

'Because he didn't die. Or at least he did, but he rose from the dead and then went to sit beside his father in heaven. As Christians we believe we can do the same if we do enough to please him.'

'Like you?' said Torstein. 'Did you not also rise from the dead?'

I shook my head. 'No, not like me. As I told you, if I've returned from the dead it's only to kill a few more of the likes of you. Obviously I didn't do enough of that in my first life.'

With that he laughed, got up and then sheathed the sword, clearly having decided to let me live – at least for the time being. 'Such courage deserves better than to be cut down whilst still bound to a tree and unable to defend yourself,' he said respectfully. 'Instead, you will come with us. I want to show you just how inventive my warriors can be when it comes to slaughter. Maybe then you won't be quite so keen on dying again.'

As they finished their preparations I looked at the other warriors more closely. They were indeed a ragged band, many of them carrying wounds that had only part healed or were marked from their previous battles in other ways. Several had fingers missing, which was a common injury in battle, and almost all of them bore terrible scars. Apart from that, they still seemed eager for yet more fighting as they donned their war gear. It was mainly mail vests or leather jerkins like the one I'd taken from the dead slaver but no longer owned. Most also had helmets or leather caps and they all carried an array of weapons. For many of them that was a battleaxe which I knew to be a dreadful weapon to come against, but others carried spears and all had a seax or shortened single-edged sword tucked within their belts. Some of them didn't even bother with a shield as it was not their way to form up for a raid on a settlement or an Abbey as they might for a battle, preferring instead to remain free from any encumbrance as they charged headlong into the fray, hitting hard and fast then hacking their way through any defences. Once engaged it would be every man for himself, though I doubted they would keep anything they seized as personal plunder. Spoil would be shared out by their Jarl afterwards according to merit and seniority.

They were ready to leave almost before I knew it. I was therefore dragged to my feet and had a rope looped around my neck, the other end of which was held securely by one of the warriors so that I had little option but to try to keep up. That wasn't easy with my hands still bound and all I could do was stumble along behind them. Arne was left to lead the horses and the cart so that the others could move swiftly and quietly, all of them anxious to reach the Abbey.

After a while they left the road and began working their way across country, by then moving more slowly so as not to make more noise than could be helped. Soon we crested a ridge with a steep escarpment beyond it that led down to a vale of rich pastures where we could see their objective.

* * * * *

The Abbey was not one I recognised nor, I think, one I had ever visited before. It was a roughly square building, probably originally a large Roman villa or possibly a garrison, with rendered walls and a red-tiled roof, part of which had been replaced with thatch. In fact time had not been kind to the building, most of it having been repaired, extended or improved, though its original form could still be seen. For the most part it was a single storey high and fully enclosed by a wall to the front and sides and by a wide river to the rear. There was a gateway to the front which had a tower to one side of it and was secured by two heavy oak doors, each braced with iron. The doors, I assumed, would lead directly to a large courtyard which would contain various stores and workshops, perhaps a kitchen with a refectory and at least one chapel, all secure within the fortifications. The layout and facilities of an Abbey didn't always follow a pattern that was common to all, therefore I could only guess how that particular enclave had been arranged. Being at the centre of the courtyard, I assumed that the main building housed the offices for the abbot and more senior brethren who would thus be afforded the privacy of a cell to themselves, as would any visitors. The more junior monks and novices would no doubt share one of several dormitories where utter silence would be the rule to allow for quiet prayer and contemplation. Some Abbeys included a nunnery but that one was too small to accommodate both sexes.

Beyond its immediate precincts, the Abbey was surrounded by fields which were needed to provide the monks who lived there with food and anything else they required. Indeed, I could see one or two of the good brothers toiling at the soil and, had we been closer, I might have been tempted to call out to warn them. As it was, I doubted whether any of them would hear me at such a distance and I knew what to expect if I did. There were also some other outbuildings which were probably barns and possibly a brewhouse, plus a dovecot, a number of coops and various pens containing livestock, together with a large pond that was no doubt stocked with fish. All this I noted carefully in the hope that it might prove useful if I did get the chance to escape whilst the Vikings were busy with their raid.

The hardest part for Torstein would be to breach the huge doors in order to secure the courtyard. Once that was taken, they would torch all the buildings there in case anyone was inside who might be able to mount some sort of rearguard assault. Then, with the courtyard secure, it would just be a question of working their way through the various rooms and cells in the main building until they'd completed their slaughter and pillaged all they could find.

'You'll never break them down,' I mused as Torstein surveyed the doors.

He said nothing but must have known I was right. He would also have known that if they tried to rush them, many of his men would be easy targets for anyone armed with even a hunting bow mounted in the tower beside the doorway. Although most monks were men of peace, some of them might have sought to retreat to the monastic life as self-imposed penance for lives spent as a warrior or worse, thus those few might not be averse to defending themselves and their Holy Brothers, even though poorly armed.

'So how will you get past the doors?' I taunted him. 'Will you simply stroll up to them and ask to be admitted?'

He grinned, clearly having already formed his plan. 'No, I won't do that,' he said. 'But you will.'

I was stunned for a moment. 'Why in God's name would I help in the slaughter of innocent monks?' I protested.

'Because if you don't I'll slit your gizzard and pull out your guts with my bare hands, that's why.'

I was scarce able to believe that after all we'd spoken of he could still imagine that I wouldn't readily trade my life for that of so many innocent people. 'I might betray you and raise the alarm,' I said coldly.

'You might. There's only one way to find out and that way we'll also see how brave you really are.'

With that he outlined his plan to his men and then to me. It seemed that this time they would wait for the cover of night and then creep as close as they dared before waiting to make their attack at first light. Those were the tactics I was more familiar with but knew there was a flaw. The monks would be at prayer for Matins well before dawn and therefore unlikely to be taken by surprise. In fact for most of them the day would be well underway by then, meaning they would not be caught whilst still abed as Torstein seemed to expect. Needless to say I said nothing of this. As far as I could tell the plan was for Torstein and me to go forward to pound upon the doors and ask for shelter. As the doors were opened, he would barge through, kill whoever was on the other side of them then wait for his men to follow him into the courtyard.

'One false move,' he warned. 'One word out of turn and I'll cut you down where you stand. Do you hear me?'

I nodded, though of course I had every intention of warning the monks, even if it cost me my life to do so.

* * * * *

Just before dawn Torstein's men moved down the escarpment to take cover as close to the Abbey as they could without being seen.

Torstein looked around one last time to ensure none of his men were visible, then he and I walked towards the

Abbey. He held a knife to my back the whole way and kept it pressed hard against my spine as he pounded on the doors. After only a few moments we heard the sound of footsteps beyond and I knew that whoever they belonged to would open the small viewing hatch in one of the doors to see who was knocking. That was to be my chance – but Torstein was one step ahead of me. He struck me hard across the back of the head with the handle of the knife, so hard that I was knocked almost senseless. As he did so he stopped me from falling by tucking his arm under mine. Then, as the small hatch was opened, I half heard someone ask who was there and Torstein reply that he had found me injured. 'This good Christian needs your care,' he said. 'I think he's been set upon by robbers.'

I wanted desperately to call out but Torstein gagged me with his hand. Then, as one of the doors was opened, he thrust me forward on to the man who stood there before striking the fellow down with his sword. That done, he kicked the other door wide open and gave his signal for the rest of his horde to attack.

The raiding party swarmed towards the gateway with lighted torches, screaming and shouting like fiends as they advanced. Once past the doors the slaughter began in earnest. There would have been at least forty men residing there, all of them men of God. As they scurried for cover, some of them were looking to hide treasured artefacts and relics, others simply trying to hide themselves or flee from their impending doom. All were cut down as the Vikings relished the slaughter they inflicted upon them.

I did what I could to delay matters but no sooner had we entered the courtyard than I was tied to a post and left to watch the terror from there. I saw men cut down with axes or run through with spears and I saw several tossed into the flames of the burning buildings whilst still alive.

Most shocking of all was that the Vikings seemed to revel in all that, jeering and shouting as they did their worst. Gradually, men would appear bearing items they'd found and deemed worth stealing. Silver cups, gold crosses and all manner of precious relics were brought forth from the buildings and thrown into a heap on the ground.

Several monks and one I took to be their abbot were taken captive and they too were brought into the courtyard to await their fate. One of them saw me and looked at me questioningly, though whether he took me for a spy who had betrayed them or was simply curious to know how I came to be there I cannot say. Either way the slaughter seemed to be over for which I at once gave thanks. But once again I was mistaken.

The Vikings built up a huge fire in the centre of the courtyard on to which they threw all the books they could find, having first prised the precious stones from the covers and torn out any pages they thought pretty enough to be worth something. What I couldn't understand was why they needed another fire. All around us parts of the main building were burning fiercely by then as were most of the lesser buildings in the courtyard, but I soon learned what they had in mind.

Once they'd built the fire high enough, the monks they'd taken prisoner were dragged towards it one at a time. A rope was secured to each arm and then stretched out to the sides so that as these were tightened, the poor soul could be dragged closer and closer to the flames. Restrained from behind by a further rope, the luckless victim was prevented from throwing himself into the flames and thereby ending the torture. In this way they were held in place and virtually roasted alive by the intense heat. The Vikings seemed to love that particular torture which they called boiling the blood, and all stood and chanted as the helpless victims died in excruciating pain. The abbot, who was made to watch all this, could do nothing but kneel in prayer, his hands clasped together and raised to God. When it came to his turn he was dragged towards the gates then pressed back hard against one of the doors. A rope was then looped around his chest and he was hoisted up so that his feet no longer touched the ground. Helpless to resist, his arms and legs were then spread wide like wings and a third man brought a large hammer and some brutal nails and, between them, they then set about nailing him to the door. The goodly abbot screamed in terror and agony as the nails were driven home, first through his outstretched hands and then his feet.

Mercifully, the poor man soon lost consciousness and his body hung limply from the door, blood streaming from his wounds. He was left there until God chose to take his soul, though it seemed that the good Lord was in no hurry to receive him for it took a long time for him to die.

Even Torstein seemed shocked by the sheer brutality of the abbot's death. 'And that's what you did to the son of your God?' he said to me quietly. 'You nailed him up to die like that? If so, all I can say is that he's either a very weak God or a very forgiving one.'

'It wasn't like that,' I said defensively. 'As I told you, his son died to save us all.'

I had no words with which to defend my faith beyond that so said nothing more. Instead, I sunk to my knees having at last found the strength I needed to pray in earnest. But it was not for my own life that I prayed; instead I was imploring God to receive the innocent souls of those who had been so cruelly slain for doing nothing more than devote their lives to Him.

Chapter Eleven

That night it rained so hard that I began to think it was God's plan for washing away so much evil. If so, it also served to rinse away the blood from the ground and douse the flames which had engulfed every building. The Vikings cowered from the downpour in whatever shelter they could find within the courtyard – but that didn't amount to much as even though some of the walls of the Abbey still stood, the tiled roofs had collapsed once the timbers supporting them had burned through. Almost all the other buildings were reduced to not much more than charred and blackened ruins and even the perimeter walls and the doors had been scorched and damaged by the flames. The Vikings posted two men to stand guard in the tower overnight whilst the rest of them slept as best they could, all no doubt cursing as the rain soaked them to the skin. I was still tied to the post where I was left to endure the longest, wettest night I could remember, huddled into a ball like a sleeping dog to keep myself as dry as possible given that I had no shelter of any kind.

The dawn brought better weather but also a new problem for Torstein. As we roused ourselves from sleep we looked out on what appeared to be a small army which had taken up a position on the ridge above the Abbey, the one from which we had first seen the Holy enclave. I knew at once it was the fyrd come at last to set matters right. The protection of an Abbey within the Shire was a solemn duty and I couldn't understand why they'd not come sooner. However, whilst their arrival was too late for the goodly abbot and the monks, it did at least mean there was a chance that I might be rescued at last.

The members of the fyrd had lined up in single file on the ridge and looked to be armed and ready. They numbered perhaps seventy men all told and were clearly ready to exact their revenge. Even as we shook ourselves from sleep, three men waited halfway down the slope to speak with Torstein, presumably intending to entreat him to surrender.

Torstein calmly donned his war gear before riding out to meet them, taking two of his senior warriors with him.

I cannot say what passed between the two parties but whatever it was amounted to no more than a few words before they returned to their respective ranks.

Torstein looked angry when he got back, though not unduly concerned by the fact that, by my reckoning, he was outnumbered by at least two or possibly three to one. Not only that, but whilst he'd lost no men taking the Abbey, a few were still injured from the previous raid and barely fit for battle.

As his men prepared themselves, Torstein was shouting his orders, all of which the men seemed to receive readily enough.

'Not so sure of yourself now!' I chided as Torstein walked past me.

The Viking just sneered then inclined his head towards those on the hill. 'Don't get your hopes up, boy. I shall swat those fools like flies.'

'You'll be slaughtered,' I said looking again at the numbers set against him. It was true that the Saxons would have marched through the night to get there but the Vikings were already battle weary and in no fit state to fight again so soon.

Torstein seemed unperturbed. 'Slaughtered by what?' he challenged. 'A few farmers armed with nothing more than pitchforks and rusty spears? They're thinking of their cattle or of screwing their fat little wives, not fighting. Hence they'll flee as soon as we attack.'

'Don't be so sure of yourself,' I warned. 'They still have the advantage of the slope. That was the way of it at Edington as I recall.'

He stopped for a moment as if to consider what I'd said. 'I can deal with that. The man who commands them is a fool and he's followed by nothing but sheep. I've shorn him and his flock before and shall do so again, you mark my words.'

'You've come against him before? If so who is he?' I asked anxious to know his name.

'Pah! I can't remember all the pathetic sods I've fought!' he protested. 'But what does it matter? If he was any sort of a warrior he'd have taken us by surprise this morning and been done with it. Instead of that he has his men line up to be slaughtered.'

'But surely you won't attack? You'll wait for them to come to you?'

He looked around at the ruined Abbey. 'What good would that do? The walls are scorched and weakened and the doors so badly damaged that they can no longer be properly secured. What's more, I have barely a score of men who are fully fit for battle which means no more than half a dozen to each wall at best, so we couldn't defend this place for long. I'm more worried that your Saxon friend will try to starve us out. Although we have all the supplies from the Abbey, we can't afford a siege as that would allow him time to send for reinforcements.'

'So what have you told your men?' I asked wondering how he'd managed to persuade them to face such odds.

'I told them the truth,' he said laughing. 'I've told them that I'm bound for Valhalla and that the road there lies through those fools on the hill. If we die with our blades steeped in their blood the Valkyries will surely carry us all to the Great Hall of Dead Warriors.'

With that he left me, still secured against the post with my hands tied but also under the watchful eye of Arne. Presumably he was considered too young to join the fray and I assumed his orders were to kill me if the battle didn't go well. He therefore sat some way away from me with his drawn sword on his lap, fingering the blade as though he would relish the chance to use it. With my hands tied I would be helpless to resist if he did, which seemed a strange irony given how little time had passed since Alfred had spared his life when I offered to adopt him as my brother.

As Torstein went to join his men it seemed that they were no more concerned at being outnumbered than he was. Certainly there was no sign of panic or fear in their ranks. Instead, they kept the Saxons waiting as they prepared themselves and only when they were good and ready did they walk out through the gates towards the base of the slope.

* * * * *

The Saxons had been kept waiting long enough. As soon as the Vikings started moving up the slope towards them they began beating the backs of their shields impatiently, voicing their war cry of 'OUT! OUT! OUT!' Then, when the Vikings were close enough, they did what they always did when an attack was imminent, they hastily formed their shield wall. I noticed that this was only two rows deep and therefore would struggle to absorb the impact if the Vikings formed into a wedge and hit them hard. I wondered whether perhaps whoever commanded them planned for his men to break rank and swarm down the slope to meet the Vikings head on, thereby using his numbers to good effect. If so, I just hoped he knew what he was doing.

Meanwhile the Vikings saw no cause to tire themselves by rushing up the slope. In fact only when the Saxons loosed a volley of arrows into the air did they trouble to form their rank and then only so they could share the cover of those who had shields. Fortunately for them, it was not a well-directed volley and nothing like the hail of arrows I'd witnessed at Combwich which had so devastated Ubba and his band of berserkers, but it was enough. Unwilling to stand and endure more arrows, the Vikings surged forwards and slammed into the Saxon rank with such force that it surely shuddered under the impact.

What followed was utter carnage. Those on both sides were hacking, cutting or stabbing with their weapons, trying to bring men down and thereby secure whatever advantage could be gained. It was bloody work but, as I feared, the Vikings were clearly having the better of it. They seemed to suffer few losses whilst the Saxon shield wall was all but breached, several men having fallen when their legs were cut from under them. The Saxons were slow to step into the gaps and I could barely watch as the Vikings prepared to push through them, knowing the slaughter which would follow once they did. At that point it seemed that Torstein had been right: they were not well-trained warriors he was facing but men pressed reluctantly into battle. But then, quite suddenly, everything changed.

I could make no sense of it at first. Just as it looked as if the Vikings would secure their victory they turned and retreated down the slope! The Saxons could not believe their luck and, like fools, followed intending to exact their revenge. Their Ealdorman was screaming at them not to break rank but either they couldn't hear him or they were too incensed by their lust for blood to hold themselves back. Thus almost every man broke free and charged after the retreating Vikings, spoiling for their share of the slaughter.

The Vikings kept running until they reached the foot of the slope. There they stopped, turned and hurriedly formed a defensive line of their own. Almost at once the Saxons realised their mistake. A few could not help but run headlong on to the Viking's wall, but others managed to turn in time and began running back up to where their Ealdorman still waited. Many were caught as the Vikings then advanced once more and all were cut down and brutally slain, being no match for Torstein's blood-crazed warriors when it came to fighting one to one.

As always, the Vikings showed no mercy and by the time they'd finished hacking and slashing at the terrified Saxons, over half of the members of the fyrd lay dead or dying. Those farmers and merchants knew then what it was to face trained warriors.

Whoever the Saxon Ealdorman was he was surely no coward but then neither did he seem to know much about battle craft. Instead of standing his ground, he marched down the slope to gather up what he could of his depleted force. As he did so, the Vikings simply moved back as if inviting him to join them again in combat. In fact Torstein even let him reform his shield wall at the bottom of the slope but, once it was set, the Vikings put into effect the next part of their fearful plan.

As the Saxons reformed their line, several of Torstein's men took up a large beam taken from one of the ruined buildings and, between them, lugged it to where their comrades waited. With the beam in hand, they advanced quickly, using it like a battering ram which they slammed into the shield wall. The result was obvious. The wall was immediately breached as men were simply knocked aside and, with that, the rest of the Vikings swarmed into the gap to wreak their havoc.

The fighting which followed could never be described as epic; it was more like a rout. I recall Edwin telling me that in battle a man is beaten from the moment he fears he'll lose and so it was with the members of the fyrd. Having lost heart, they were easy targets for the Vikings and most were cut down where they stood. Those who did survive formed up into a single group clustered around their Lord, crying out for mercy as they waited for their turn to die.

To my surprise, Torstein ordered his men to cease their butchery then went across to speak with the Ealdorman, calling on him to surrender.

'Why should we? You'll kill us anyway!' came the reply.

'There's no profit in blood,' replied Torstein. 'Be it yours or mine. Give me tribute and you can live.'

The Ealdorman seemed pleased at that. 'How much silver would it take for you to spare us and then leave this Shire?'

Torstein looked back at the scorched doors of the Abbey to which the body of the poor abbot was still nailed. 'I demand the abbot's weight in silver,' he said, at which the other Vikings all roared with laughter when he repeated his demands to them.

I looked around at what was left of Torstein's horde, trying to decide whether they were still a viable threat. They had taken losses as well and, as far as I could see, were down to just a dozen men plus some who were wounded but probably still able to wield a weapon if needed.

'I can't find so much silver just like that!' pleaded the Ealdorman. 'You'll have to give me time!'

I think Torstein had not truly expected him to agree to pay so much tribute, but he wasn't about to pass up the chance of such a great haul. One of his men seemed to feel differently and began reasoning with him, perhaps pointing out that the battle had gone their way and given them the chance to make good their escape with all the booty they'd plundered from the Abbey. If that was so, Torstein's greed quickly overcame any qualms he had about remaining. 'I'll give you two days,' he replied. 'No more.'

'Then you'll have to let me go to raise it,' said the Ealdorman, clearly seeing a chance for him and his remaining men to escape.

Torstein knew the answer to that. 'Who is your second in command?' he demanded.

'My son, Caelin,' replied the Ealdorman proudly but without thinking.

'Then we shall hold Caelin until you return. He will be well treated but shall be held as a hostage and as surety for your pledge. If you don't return to make payment in full I shall kill him and nail his carcass up beside that of the abbot. Is that not fair?'

The Ealdorman could now see his mistake, but he didn't seem to have much choice. He therefore agreed to the terms.

'But your men must leave their weapons here,' added Torstein. When the Ealdorman agreed, Caelin was sent forward from their ranks and went to stand beside Torstein looking petrified and probably half expecting to be killed anyway. With that the Vikings lowered their own weapons to allow the Saxons to leave.

The Ealdorman and his few remaining men departed having failed to fight off even a modest band of Vikings. They went as quickly as they could, glad to have escaped what must have seemed to them like the very shadow of death, even leaving those of their wounded who couldn't walk to bleed out on the field where they lay. With their heads lowered and unarmed, they presented little in the way of a threat, but I knew what Torstein was thinking. They could just as easily return with reinforcements and, with his numbers depleted and his warriors so weary, he could not expect to fight a second battle in as many days and win.

* * * * *

When they'd gone, Caelin was also bound and made to stand beside me, his hands clasped together in front of him and his head bowed. He was a lusty lad of about my age, not tall but strongly built. However, looking at his clothes I was certain that he wasn't the son of an Ealdorman, not least because he had no mail vest nor even a proper helmet. The Vikings pushed and shoved him a bit and no doubt he received the odd kick or punch, but he was otherwise not harmed.

'I have a feeling that I'm going to be putting you to the sword in two days' time,' said Torstein as he came to inspect his new prisoner. 'I don't think your friends will be coming back for you, do you?' I think he hoped that in answering, Caelin would reveal whether or not the Ealdorman was likely to return in force, but the lad made no reply. Instead he just looked at me with terror in his eyes.

'What's the matter, boy? Don't you think your father will consider you to be worth a few sacks of silver?'

Still Caelin said nothing.

'What kind of warriors were they anyway?' mused Torstein, looking at me. 'They were so keen to be gone from here they willingly surrendered their weapons and didn't trouble to recover their wounded or even ask to bury their dead.'

I had to admit he had a point. Whatever I thought of the Vikings, the Saxons on that day had shown neither discipline nor skill in battle. Their tactics had been woefully lacking and their Ealdorman was, as Torstein had said, a fool.

Caelin and I then watched the Vikings strip the bodies of the fallen of anything which was of value. It didn't amount to very much as the members of the fyrd were mostly poor farmers. Even their weapons were not worth taking and anything which might be deemed to be worth something had been left behind in the hope that if they were slain it would help to sustain their families in time of need.

At one point during the battle I thought I'd seen Aelred, though I knew that could have been wishful thinking on my part. Even so, I needed to know. 'Tell me,' I asked Caelin once we'd been left to ourselves. 'Was there a man among your ranks by the name of Aelred? And if so, do you know if he survived?'

'Perhaps,' said Caelin. 'Though I cannot say for certain.'

'But you do know him?'

'Aye. I think so. He came to us a few days ago. He said he knew which way the Vikings were headed and could find them. He also said it would be easy pickings as they were so few in number, yet it seems that even then we bit off more than we could chew.'

'But why did he help you? Surely it was no concern of his?'

Caelin looked at me curiously. 'He said he had a friend who was being held captive. A man who is great warrior and can cheat death. I assume he meant you?'

I nodded to affirm the point. 'But why did he come back for me; he owes me nothing?'

'Are you not his master?'

'No, as far as I know Aelred has no master; at least not one he answers to. He's neither freeman nor slave, but then we are none of us what we seem, are we? You, for example, you're not the Ealdorman's son are you?'

Caelin looked down at his feet. 'No, but then neither is that fool an Ealdorman. He's a thane sent by his Lord to see off these raiders.'

Suddenly it all made sense. 'Not an Ealdorman?'

'No,' said Caelin shaking his head. 'Lord Sigbert governs here but he leaves matters to one of his thanes, a man named Eadred.'

'And that was Eadred? The one who made such a hash of the battle?'

'It was. He's supposed to have a way in matters of war so was given command in preference to the other nobles but... well, you saw how poorly we fared against even such a small band of Vikings.'

I was astonished that such an important task as defending the Shire had been entrusted to a man so incompetent. 'And you're what? Their scapegoat? The one they've sacrificed to save their own precious skins?'

'I had no choice,' he managed at last. 'I owe my Lord taxes and Eadred promised me my dues would be forgotten if I pretended to be his son. If I hadn't agreed my mother and father would have been driven out and forced to become beggars in their dotage. This way at least my family can keep our small farmstead.'

'That was a costly debt!' I noted.

'All I hope is that they kill me quickly when they realise they've been duped,' he said. 'I've heard how cruel they can be.'

I looked around at all the dead both on the battlefield and within the remains of the Abbey. 'A quick death is something the Vikings only bestow on enemies they respect and there's not much chance of that given all that's happened here.'

'How will they do it?' he asked, clearly very frightened.

I shrugged. 'That depends on what they can think of at the time. Just remember that the braver you are the quicker it'll be over.' This didn't seem to be of much comfort to him.

'But they haven't killed you?' he said.

'No, not yet. But they will. At present they don't seem to know what to do with me but they'll kill me in time, of that I'm certain. Unless of course your Lord comes back with reinforcements in time to save us both. Either that or with a chest full of silver.'

'Not much chance of that either,' explained Caelin. 'It's my guess he's now sitting by his fire drinking and whoring, knowing that his Lord will be grateful to have avoided paying tribute and got away with it.'

'Then they're all cowards,' I said sternly. 'An Ealdorman should be looking out for those within his Shire, not sending them to their certain death under the command of an incompetent fool.'

'It's always the way,' agreed Caelin. 'We pay for their excess; first with our sweat and then with our blood.'

'Well, if I do get out of here Lord Alfred shall hear of this idiot's treachery,' I said. 'I know him well enough to be sure that he'll not permit his subjects to be treated thus.'

For a moment Caelin stared at me. 'So who are you that you can speak to Lord Alfred in person?' he asked.

'That's a long story and I suspect that neither of us has time enough for me to tell it. Suffice you should know that I'm called Matthew but was christened Edward. My father was Lord Edwulf and I was on a mission for Lord Alfred when I was wounded and ended up here, a prisoner like you.'

He hesitated, clearly surprised that I was of such noble birth given how wretched I must have looked. Then he glanced at my torn shirt and must have seen my scar. 'But are you...?'

'The warrior with the pierced heart? Yes, I am he. But don't believe all the stories you've heard. I'm as mortal as any other man and was just lucky that the wound was not fatal,' I explained. 'How I escaped death I cannot say but I fear I may not fare quite so well the next time.'

Chapter Twelve

Once the last of the Saxons had fled, the Vikings passed the time by tending to their wounds, mending their weapons and resting. Ironically, the monks they'd slain at the Abbey were most likely the people who could have best helped them heal the deep cuts and arrow wounds some of them had suffered, but such is the futility of war – for no clemency is ever shown to those with skills or ability any more than it is for the pious and the righteous.

After a while, those Vikings who had avoided injury prepared fires on which to cremate their dead. They ignored the bodies of the monks and the Saxons, leaving them to the mercy of the crows and wild beasts which would no doubt see in them the chance for easy pickings.

'How long will you wait?' I asked Torstein, certain that whenever he chose to kill Caelin my own life would be forfeit as well. I was not sure why, but Caelin had been taken away by then and secured in another part of the ruined Abbey.

Torstein just laughed. 'Don't worry, I've time enough to kill you both. Then he seemed more serious. 'That's assuming this boy is who we're told he is, not just some poor wretch sent to die in place of the others.'

I realised then that Torstein had seen through the ruse all along. 'So why did you let them go if you feared that to be the case?'

'There was no profit in killing more of them,' he reasoned. 'Besides, I've lost near half my men and even those remaining are tired or wounded. I need to buy them a few days to rest.'

'What if the Ealdorman comes back with reinforcements?' I asked. 'You said yourself that you can't defend these ruins.'

'It'll take time for him to levy enough men to challenge me again and I'll be gone long before he does.'

'But surely you'll wait to see if he returns with the silver he's promised you?' I asked in the hope of persuading him to stay long enough for help to arrive and thereby improve my chances of being rescued, but Torstein wasn't so easily taken in.

'What do you take me for? Some kind of fool? He won't be back to pay what's due as even he's not that stupid. And don't think me battle shy. As I've said, my men are weary and need to rest. I've bought them two days' respite, that's all. Besides, we already have enough booty with all we've taken from this Abbey and we couldn't carry any more even if we had it.'

'Then what about Caelin or whatever his real name is?'

Torstein pointed to the door from which the abbot's body still hung. 'There's room enough on there for him,' he said. 'And for you as well if the mood so takes me.'

* * * * *

On the second morning Torstein sent two men to ride up the escarpment to see if there was any sign of the Saxons coming to pay the promised tribute, though I suspect he would have been surprised if there was. As the riders returned they stopped having spotted something of interest. One of them dismounted and went across to a small clump of bushes and, as he approached it, a man rose up from his hiding place and started to make a run for it. He didn't get far before they rode him down and rather than put up a fight, he raised his hands to surrender. He stood there for a moment before being roughly ushered down the hill at spear point to where we all waited. I could hardly believe my eyes when I realised it was Aelred.

Though I tried not to show it, Torstein could see that I recognised the new prisoner. 'Do you know this man?' he demanded.

I shrugged. 'He's my servant and I'll curse any man who harms him,' I answered fearing I might draw Aelred into my troubles.

Aelred looked confused at first but was sensible enough to go along with what I'd said. It looked as though he'd taken something of a beating during the battle as he limped slightly to favour his left leg and had several cuts to his arms, though none of them serious.

Torstein went across and grasped Aelred by the chin, tipping his head back so he could stare straight into his eyes. 'Looks like your servant shares your love of dying,' he said. 'All the other fools who survived the battle were wise enough to flee when they had the chance. Or perhaps like you this one can return from the dead at will?'

For a moment I thought Torstein would put that to the test by killing Aelred there and then. He had no reason not to despite my threatened curse, but instead he stepped back as if checking Aelred over, much as a man might inspect a horse he was thinking of buying.

'We'll take him with us,' he announced. 'He looks strong enough to be worth something where we're going and, if nothing else, he can help us carry our spoil.' He then had Caelin dragged across to join us. 'As for you, all I can say is that your father lied,' he said bluntly. 'He promised silver but has delivered none. Your life is therefore forfeit to my sword.'

'He may yet come!' pleaded Caelin, having seemingly forgotten or chosen to ignore all I'd said about dying bravely. 'It would take time to raise so much silver for it's the third time in as many summers he's had to pay tribute.'

Torstein clearly found that amusing. 'I know, it was me he gave it to the last time,' he bellowed, turning and repeating it to his men so they could share the joke. With that, two of them stepped forward to cut Caelin's bonds and, as soon as they released him, he fell to his knees.

'Pah! Kneeling is all you miserable Saxons seem to know – whether it's in prayer or to beg for mercy!' said Torstein. With that he drew his sword. 'Well, let's see how you like the edge of my sword. That should stop your snivelling.'

Caelin raised his hands as he implored him to be merciful. It was a pitiful and futile effort as even I could see that as no tribute had arrived, Torstein had no choice but to keep his word as his men would not respect him if he didn't.

I think Caelin realised that as well and so, still on his knees, he started to pray, beseeching God to receive his soul. Without waiting for him to finish, two men seized him by the arms and half carried, half dragged him back towards the doors where the abbot still hung, by then a wretched and decaying corpse, half blackened by the fires and already beginning to reek.

For a moment I thought they were going to crucify Caelin as well, but it was all part of their cruel torment. He was still screaming as, having shown him the abbot's fate, they hauled him over to the fire. It had been relit after the rain and although not as big as the one used to torture the monks, it burned brightly enough. I assumed they were going to boil his blood as they held him there, so close to the flames that the heat scorched his face. Yet it seemed they'd already grown tired of that game. Instead, they lifted him bodily between them and tossed him, still screaming, into the flames.

All this I watched in horror, surprised and grateful that I was still alive but wondering what they would do when my turn came. I hoped I would make a braver fist of it but having seen poor Caelin's fate and that of the abbot and all the monks at the Abbey, I was not sure I would endure it any better than they had.

'So, not so sure of yourself now, are you?' said Torstein.

I thought back to what it had been like to face the prospect of being tortured that night at Guthrum's camp in Chippenham. There I'd prayed in earnest as I waited to die but, although the prospect of my death then was terrifying enough, all I had just witnessed seemed to sap whatever resolve I had left.

'Ah, for once it seems you've nothing to say for yourself,' teased Torstein. 'Then let's say that that poor wretch died to save you, just like your precious God. What do you think of that?'

I looked across to where Caelin's body still burned and shook my head. 'I say it was a dreadful thing to do. You should have just killed both him and the abbot with your sword and been done with it. You didn't have to be so cruel.'

'Don't worry, boy. I'll think of something special when your turn comes,' he promised. 'In fact I've half a mind to let you fight one of my warriors who is too badly harmed to march from here. Either he'll perish at the edge of your sword and thereby be assured of his place in Valhalla or he'll kill you thus saving me the trouble.'

'Is that because you fear to kill me yourself?' I challenged angrily.

He shook his head. 'I've no fear of drawing my blade across your throat,' he assured me. 'But I do fear what the fates might then bring down upon us if I do. So for now I shall spare you so that I may learn more about this nailed God of yours. What puzzles me is how he can give you so much strength when you did him so much wrong. But make no mistake, once safely returned with our spoil I may well cut out your so-called pierced heart and see it for myself, for that intrigues me as well.'

* * * * *

Aelred was bound to me so that neither of us could move without the other.

'I haven't thanked you for saving my life in that skirmish,' I said to him quietly. 'That man who knocked me down would surely have finished me but for you.'

'I thought you killed,' he said. 'I did what I could, but as we feared, there were just too many of the bastards.'

I acknowledged the truth of that. 'So how did you manage to survive? The last thing I remember is seeing you fall as well.'

'I was lucky. The fools were distracted by a woman they saw making a run for it. They left me long enough for me to roll away into the bushes where I hid until the slaughter was done. Later, when they'd gone, I made my way across country but was met by some of the locals and taken to their Ealdorman to be questioned, a man named Lord Sigbert. It seems he'd been unable to find this band of butchers but once I told him where the last attack had taken place he insisted I go with the fyrd, if only to prove I wasn't lying. After the battle I had no mind to stay with them so hid just beyond the rise in the hope that I might help you to escape. This morning I drew closer when I sensed they were about to pack up and leave and…well, the rest of it you know.'

'I wish you hadn't as I somehow doubt your luck will hold much longer. These are murderous bastards as you can see. Have you any idea what happened to Brother Benedict?'

Aelred looked down at the ground. 'Mercifully, the poor bastard was knocked half senseless when they struck him as they advanced. When the battle was done they stripped him naked then hung his wriggling carcass from a tree and flayed him alive, peeling the skin from his body and then leaving him to bleed out in agony, though I doubt he suffered long.'

I crossed myself at the news, for it was indeed a terrible way to die.

'So what's to become of us?' asked Aelred.

'I don't know. For now they seem afraid of killing me but that won't hold for ever. Once they get over all their qualms God only knows what they'll do to us. You saw what happened to young Caelin.'

At that point it seemed as though Torstein was anxious to leave, probably because he couldn't be certain whether or not the Ealdorman would return bringing reinforcements and, worse still, a more able commander to lead them. As he'd said himself, his depleted force was in no position to fight again so soon.

He had his men begin to prepare themselves to march out but, before they could leave, there was still one man who lingered on the threshold of death, being too badly injured to move and with little hope of life. His left arm had been severed during the battle just above the elbow and although the wound had been cauterised and sealed with a heated blade, there was no guarantee that it would ever heal fully. He was clearly too weak and fevered to march so Torstein needed to decide his fate. As was their way, they mixed a strong broth of leeks and herbs which had such a pungent smell it positively reeked. They'd given that to the man to drink the day before and had a crude and simple test which they could use to determine whether or not he was likely to recover. If later they could smell any trace of the leeks emanating from the wound it meant that the seal had failed and therefore there was little more that could be done for him.

Once satisfied that the man was indeed dying, Torstein went to speak with him and although I cannot say what passed between them, I imagine he offered the man a choice of either being put to the knife or being left to die fighting if and when the Saxon reinforcements arrived.

It may seem strange to ask a wounded man how he wished to die but the wretch was clearly in a great deal of pain so if the Saxons didn't return he would face a long, slow death as the wound festered. On the other hand, if they did return he would get the chance to die fighting and so earn his place in Valhalla. I half wondered whether Torstein would carry out his threat and have me do battle with the man but, as far as I know, that option was never mentioned.

In the end the man chose to die there and then. Having thus decided, his comrades went to him one by one to say their farewells and, as they did so, he gave away his war gear and other possessions, clasping their hands firmly to seal the bargain. That done and without any further ceremony, he was given his trusty battleaxe to hold and then plied with mead. Drunk and roaring his defiance, he didn't notice as one of the men crept up behind him and, whilst he was distracted, deftly slit his throat.

His funeral was like those I had seen before insomuch as they cremated his body, feasting and drinking as they watched it burn. Aelred confirmed that they also recounted stories of his life as they raised their drinking horns to wish him well on his journey to the afterlife.

The next morning, having by then disposed of the remains of all their dead, Torstein ordered the other survivors to gather up their things and prepare to leave. As the group set off, two of the horses and the cart were needed just to carry all the supplies and provisions they'd secured from the Abbey, including four very large sacks, each brimful of booty.

By the end of the first day we'd made very little progress before we needed to stop and rest, setting up a makeshift camp beside a river, though I've no idea exactly where we were.

I'd also forgotten about the rider who'd been sent to negotiate a ransom for my release. He returned during that first night but, as expected, the news he brought was not good.

'It seems Alfred doesn't want a warrior with a pierced heart,' said Torstein.

'That's because he doesn't know it's me,' I said, glancing at Aelred.

Torstein shrugged as though it mattered not to him one way or the other. 'Well, it's too late now,' he said. 'Our raids have been well rewarded, especially with all we took from those pious monks at the Abbey and my men are now keen to be on our way with what they have.'

'Why not let me go to Alfred and persuade him to pay what's due? I give you my word that I'll return, either with the silver or without it.'

'Your word?' queried Torstein. 'What would that be worth to me?'

'It could be worth a great deal of silver if you trust me.'

'I trust no one,' he said. 'Especially not some Christian boy who has tricked the Gods and now wants to trick me as well.'

'It's not a trick. Alfred would pay well to see me safe and what have you got to lose, you're only going to kill me anyway?'

Torstein seemed to consider that for a moment, then looked around him. 'I'll tell you what I have to lose,' he said at last. 'The trust of all these men who would follow me to the very gates of Valhalla if I ask them. What would they think of me if they saw I'd been duped by a mere boy?'

I could see what he meant. Jarl or not, just like the Saxon Ealdormen, Torstein needed his men to believe in him. 'So what's to become of me if I add no value to your purse?' I asked, realising that the reason I was still alive was not just because they feared killing me, it was also because they'd hoped for a large ransom.

He thought for a moment. 'I recall that I promised to kill you with that sword you said had once belonged to your father,' he replied at last. 'Would that not be a fitting way for you to die?'

'From all I've seen of death it doesn't make much difference so long as the blade is sharp and the stroke is quick and clean.'

'Ah, now there's a thing,' he said. 'A quick death is something all of us wish for, but I think my men would rather roast your bones or skin you alive. They're even suggesting that we let the horses trample you to death so that the consequences of killing a man who has returned from the dead will not trouble our fate as the beasts will take the blame.'

I tried to imply that it was all the same to me. 'I'd prefer the sword, but you'll do what you will,' I managed. 'Though remember that my God is all seeing and all knowing. Whatever vengeance he chooses to inflict upon those who harm me will not be settled on a few horses but on those who set them to it. And as you know, he's a powerful and dreadful God, fiercely resentful of any who harm those he's chosen to spare.'

Torstein seemed to find that worrying. 'Then it's as well I'm minded to spare you,' he said. 'But not because I fear you or your precious God.'

'Why then?' I asked.

'Because I need you and your friend. I have much work for you both where we're going.'

'So where are we going?'

'South, towards the coast,' he said. 'I have a boat there, well hidden from view. It's not large but it will carry us and all our booty as far as the great river which flows through the settlement you call London. You and your friend will be needed to help man the oars as all my men are weary or wounded. Have you ever been to London?'

I shook my head.

'Ah, then you have much to learn. It is, as I say, a very large settlement built in the shadow of what was once a Roman garrison. One of Guthrum's most trusted and senior Jarls has summoned all who would join him to assemble there.'

'What for?' I asked.

Torstein just grinned. 'All you need to know is that he is called Hakon the Bonebreaker and that he is much feared as a warrior.'

'Is he to disperse lands to those who served Lord Guthrum?'

'Perhaps,' he said. 'Or perhaps he'll launch a fresh offensive of his own once he has an army assembled.'

'But Guthrum has pledged himself to peace,' I said. 'That was the condition which Alfred imposed and which Guthrum swore to uphold. It was a Holy vow which he offered to swear on his ring dipped in blood.'

'Oaths are like women,' he said dismissively. 'You promise anything to keep them in bed when you're horny and then forget them when you're not. Besides, Guthrum won't be there. And anyway, he's probably now given that ring to someone else as payment for some service or other. So what does that make his oath worth?'

'He was also baptised,' I said contritely.

I was surprised when Torstein seemed to take that more seriously. 'Was he?' said the Viking. 'That is a matter of some weight. It would greatly displease our Gods if they think he has forsaken them.'

'Well, it was surely no ploy. Guthrum came to admire the strength of the Christian warriors and the trust we place in our one true God.'

'Are you saying that even he now worships the nailed God?'

'He seemed sincere in that belief from all that I could tell,' I assured him.

Torstein looked doubtful. 'I can't believe that someone as powerful as Lord Guthrum would convert so readily.'

'Well, I cannot say whether he has remained devout, but he and other Jarls of senior rank did agree to convert to our faith after the battle at Edington. Perhaps he did so to ensure his life was spared but somehow I don't think so…'

Torstein turned away for a moment as if to consider all I'd said. 'If it was a ploy then Guthrum is a fool,' he said at last. 'Our Gods would not countenance the worship of another, even as a ruse to gain some advantage.'

'Oh I see,' I said. 'You can rape and pillage. You can murder and you can lie and even break a solemn oath, but if you even pretend to worship another God all the wrath of the heavens will come down upon you? Is that what you're saying?'

I could see I'd touched a nerve as Torstein didn't deign to reply at first. Like all Vikings, he took such matters very seriously. They lived and died in fear of their own Gods, believing their fate to rest solely in the hands of such beings. To forsake them was to take a terrible risk and was not something to be done lightly. 'The Gods do not look kindly upon a man who worships falsely,' he managed.

'But Guthrum is not the first of your kind to see that there is but one true God, nor will he be the last,' I said sternly.

'How do you know all this?' demanded Torstein who clearly still doubted that Guthrum had indeed converted.

'I was there,' I replied. 'I was not one of those who was taken to witness Guthrum's baptism but I was present when it was agreed. Ask young Arne if you don't believe me. He was there as well.'

Torstein looked impressed. 'You were actually there when Guthrum surrendered?'

I nodded to affirm the point. 'I also commanded one part of Alfred's army at Edington,' I boasted.

For a moment he looked as though he could hardly believe what I was saying, then seemed to accept it. 'You have achieved much for one so young. Perhaps I should kill you now before you grow any older and then defeat us all single handed!'

'Well, make up your mind,' I said as boldly as I dared. 'If you are going to kill me I'd rather we got it over with. I'm getting very tired of being bound and dragged around like some sort of slave.'

* * * * *

It took two more days for us to reach the coast. Both Aelred and I found the journey long and tiresome as there were only a few stops at which to rest and refresh ourselves. Aelred made no complaint, but I could see that he was still in some pain from his wounds so did what I could to help him. I even suggested he take Ingar's advice and drink his own piss.

He told some of the Vikings about this when they saw him collecting some in a horn. I gather they thought it very funny saying they would one day tell the tale of the strangest captives they'd ever taken – one with no heart and the other who drank his own piss!

Eventually we arrived at the edge of a large marsh where the reeds stood taller than any man and were so dense that it was all but impossible to find a path through them.

But path there was; a narrow track that ensured we had to walk in single file, leading the horses and the mule which were laden with the supplies and all the booty, the cart having been abandoned at that point because the ground was too soft. As we followed the track it was clear it led somewhere but with no sign of any settlement, I had no idea where. Eventually Torstein signalled for the group to stop, then sent a man on ahead to ensure the way was clear whilst the others crouched down low amid the reeds. After a while we heard a low whistle which I assumed was the signal that it was safe to proceed. We then travelled a little further until Torstein parted the reeds and we found ourselves on the banks of a wide, muddy river where, to our amazement, a boat was indeed moored and waiting.

Two men were guarding the boat though I doubted they were needed given how well the vessel had been hidden.

'So have either of you miserable Saxons ever been to sea?' asked Torstein.

I shook my head but Aelred admitted that when he lived by the coast he had put to sea once or twice, but always against his better judgement.

'Then you've both much to learn,' he said. 'It's not a sturdy craft but it should suffice to see us safely as far as London if we keep close to the shore.'

'So is it as simple as that?' I asked.

'Oh, the sea is never simple,' warned Torstein. 'The coast here is rough and treacherous and there are now Saxon boats set to intercept anyone approaching the shore. Seeing us so close in they'll hopefully think us to be fishermen or traders and leave us be but if they see we're laden with men that ruse won't last for long.'

'You mean there'll be a battle at sea!'

'Perhaps. With luck we can simply slip past them but if not…'

As I dreaded even the thought of putting to sea, the prospect of actually fighting a battle there worried me greatly.

'Why not leave us here?' I suggested. 'We'll only hinder you as neither of us is fit enough to help row.'

'Oh, you'll help right enough. You'll take your turn at the oars and if that kills you both then so be it. I can afford to lose you if I must whereas I'm bound to give my men every chance I can to reach London safely.'

Chapter Thirteen

y fears about putting to sea were not helped when I looked at Torstein's boat more closely. It was a far cry from the sleek longships I'd seen at Combwich, being shaped more like a rounded tub. It was a type we used for fishing and for ferrying stock and supplies from one coastal settlement to another, or for use on rivers. Certainly it was not a craft we would have thought of ever taking much beyond the sight of land.

Having said that, it looked to be large enough to carry us all. It was powered by just six oars – three on either side – and had a mast which, once raised, would support a large square sail secured and controlled by ropes. My real concern was that the vessel looked to have suffered greatly from being hidden in the marsh for some time and, whilst there, much neglected.

The Vikings started by adding their booty to a pile of other treasure. It seemed they'd been busy in the months since they attacked my escort in the forest, raiding and then returning to their boat to stash their booty in the rough camp they'd formed beside the river. It was indeed an impressive haul, enough to make all of them very wealthy men indeed.

Having made themselves comfortable, they set about restoring the boat, first bailing out the large amount of water which had collected in the hull. When that was done, two of them lifted out a large leather bag in which the sail had been stored to protect it from vermin and the weather whilst others began making some repairs to the hull itself, replacing several boards and sealing any gaps with a thick coat of pitch. The oars simply rested in metal clamps rather than being pushed through ports in the side of the hull and these were greased until they moved freely. Torstein personally checked all the repairs as if to satisfy himself that the vessel was indeed being rendered seaworthy and, when their works were judged by him to be complete, he instructed others to raise the mast and secure it. That was a more difficult task which required a number of men, including Aelred and myself, to heave it up on ropes and pulleys until it was upright. The base of it was then securely wedged and braced before a spar was fitted and hauled to the top of the mast with the sail already attached, albeit that remained furled having first been checked for any rents or tears. Finally, whereas I was used to seeing Viking ships bedecked with the shields of those who laboured at the oars, Torstein ordered that all weapons should be stowed out of sight for fear they might arouse suspicion if seen by anyone on the shore.

In all, the repairs took two days to complete and, once done, the booty and supplies were passed aboard and stored in sacks or crates which were stowed around the base of the mast and then lashed securely into place. Personal items were placed in the locker beneath each of the benches used for rowing, though that space was mainly used for some of the more valuable items of plunder.

Aelred and I were required to assist in all this and actually found the work to our liking as everyone involved seemed to relish the prospect of putting to sea. Thus they worked willingly, often singing cheerily as they set about their toil.

'So my Saxon friends,' said Torstein once the work was fully completed, 'now we shall make seamen of you both. You'll man the oars nearest the prow from where you can best see the others and thereby keep time with them. But be ready for a hard journey. We travel quietly but will make all possible speed where we can regardless of the weather. You'll sweat like pigs and your hands will blister as you labour at the oars, but I warn you, we've no room for any but those who work with us against the sea. If you shirk even once my men will simply pitch you overboard.'

Aelred looked at me, clearly worried. 'I've rowed once or twice before but never on a journey as long as this. What about you?' he asked quietly.

I shook my head. 'I've never sailed anything except a raft whilst at Athelney and even that wasn't like rowing,' I admitted. 'But I have a feeling we're both about to learn the way of it.' Even as I said it I feared I would not be best suited to the task because of my wound whereas Aelred, who seemed to have fully recovered from the injuries he'd received in the battle, had the build which I was certain would render him strong enough for the task.

Even with everything stowed on board Torstein was not quite ready to leave. As his men waited, anxious to set sail, he spent time just staring at the sky and, in particular, the stars. He had already planned our voyage but could not tell us how long we would be at sea as so much depended on the weather and, more importantly, the wind and the tides. He seemed to understand those elements instinctively and eventually announced that we were to leave that evening on the ebb tide and under the cover of night, hopefully slipping past any Saxons set to guard the river estuary. As they would be looking out to sea for any sign of raiders it was unlikely they'd pay much mind to a small trading vessel sailing downriver on the tide.

Once the final preparations had been made, the Vikings began to clamber aboard. In all we numbered just a dozen men who planned to sail to London, including Torstein. Aelred and I were shown to our benches near the prow and manacled to them with chains in case we tried to escape by swimming ashore once the boat was underway.

Four of the others also took up places at the oars whilst Arne and one other positioned themselves at the prow to act as lookouts – not just for Saxon ships but also for sandbanks and shallow water that might otherwise ground the small boat as the tide receded. Torstein would doubtless steer the boat using a steering board, a large oar which was positioned at the stern. The three remaining men stood with him, ready to unfurl the sail once it was needed.

Once settled, Torstein's crew waited patiently for word to be given. The remaining men had been left ashore with orders to meet us in London with the horses and the mule. Having bid them farewell, the ropes securing the booty and supplies were given one last check as Torstein readied the boat to leave.

For my part, whilst still dreading the prospect of putting to sea, I was also strangely excited. I was seeing a very different side to the Vikings. No longer warriors and merchants of death, they'd become skilled seamen who joked and sang as they laboured and who actually treated both Aelred and me quite well, perhaps by then regarding us as one of them rather than as prisoners, though we remained in chains, manacled like slaves to our benches.

* * * * *

Launching the boat in the river was easy. We had only to push off with the oars then leave Torstein to steer us into mid-stream where we could take advantage of the flow and the outgoing tide to carry us towards the estuary under the cover of night. Once there, all torches on board were snuffed out and those not needed to work the boat were ordered to keep low lest anyone on the shore should see them. Then, once a little way from land, we took up the oars in earnest and rowed quickly out to sea.

At first both Aelred and I found it difficult to keep proper time with the others as we rowed, struggling to ensure that every stroke would bite into the water as they were supposed to. Seeing what a poor fist we were making of it and with nothing more pressing to do, one of the men came across and stood between us. Beating the time with his foot, he helped us to muster some sort of rhythm and thus we soon had the way of it, but it was indeed very hard work. So much so that I was forced to wonder how long I could endure the pace that was needed without a rest.

Taking full advantage of the dark, we made good progress, anxious not to be seen by the Saxon ships set to intercept raiders whilst still at sea. This was all part of Alfred's great plan to improve the defences of his realm and Aelred and I were the only men on board pleased to note that he'd begun to put that into place. Even so, I knew it was unlikely they'd come out to us as they would be few in number and launched only in response to a Viking ship being spotted somewhere on the horizon. Our small trading boat would not arouse suspicion given they would have received no reports of a raiding party patrolling that part of the coast.

I was too busy straining at the oars to think any more on the matter as I knew that with every stroke there was a danger of disturbing the wound to my chest. I consoled myself by thinking that was probably a better way to die than being slain by Torstein, even if he did keep his word and use my father's sword to do it.

We quickly gained sufficient distance from the shore to be clear of rocks and the risk of being seen. Then, with a favourable wind, we turned to follow the shoreline and two men stepped forward and began to unfurl the sail. As it set with a loud crack, Aelred and I at last got a chance to rest.

From that point on the sailing was easy as we rode the waves with an almost effortless grace, gathering speed as we went. We continued through the remainder of the night and much of the next day, always following the line of the coast but keeping far enough out to sea to ensure we did not alarm those ashore who otherwise might fear a raid. I discounted any idea of being rescued as I realised that if we were attacked by the Saxon boats and our craft set on fire, my chances of survival would be no better than any of the others on board, or worse if I was still in chains at the time.

Whilst we made good progress, life on board was painfully cramped. Aelred and I were not allowed to leave the bench on which we sat but at least, being too far from shore to escape, we were released from the manacles. Even then it was very uncomfortable as every so often a wave would break over the bow so that we got soaked from the spray. Also, the salt from the sea stung our eyes and the wind seemed to chill us to the very core.

There was little to do for those not taking their turn to row, steer or trim the sail except to sleep. Some men played dice but as the boat rocked and heaved on the waves even that wasn't easy. Sometimes one of the men might sing or start to tell a tale but as I understood nothing of what was said, all I could do was rest and rely on Aelred to translate for me as best he could.

'I don't think I'm well suited to life at sea,' complained Aelred at one point. 'My stomach wants to retch as every wave is broached.'

When I looked at him I could see that he did indeed look very pale. Several times he turned to vomit over the side then scooped up a handful of seawater with which to wash his face and mouth. I didn't feel much better myself but seemed to settle to the movements of the boat more readily than he. Far worse than the feeling of sickness was that whenever the wind shifted or died away we were made to row once more, often for longer than we felt able to endure. Not only were we both soon exhausted, but our hands became blistered and sore. One of the men gave us strips of softened leather to wrap around them to help protect them but I realised that was only because if either Aelred or I was not up to the task, he or one of the others would have to take our place. Yet even with our hands wrapped it soon became difficult and painful to row any further, but neither that nor the prospect of my heart bursting within my breast was sufficient cause for us to complain, fearing that if we could no longer do our allotted share of the work we would be tossed overboard.

It was on the third day that I realised that all was not well. Those hardened seafarers were well attuned to any changes in the weather and all had sensed that a storm was brewing.

As the sea began to swell and the waves grew higher, so they began to take in some of the sail. Soon after that they took it down completely and Aelred and I were put back to the oars once more.

As we strained hard against the wind and waves, the little boat seemed barely able to cope. It rocked and wallowed as the storm tore into us and was tossed about so much that I was sure it would soon capsize and we would all be lost. Aelred and I were both terrified, but those men were all well used to a sea that complained and grumbled and they seemed unperturbed until, eventually, even they judged the storm to be too bad for us to remain at sea. Thus we turned and headed towards a large cluster of rocks which lay just off the mainland. The tallest of the rocks there rose so steeply from the water that it looked impossible to climb. Yet atop of it were the remnants of a brazier which had presumably been set there to act as a lighthouse in Roman times, intended to guide ships past that particularly treacherous part of the coastline. It had long since been abandoned and the metal rungs set into the rock to form a ladder by which to reach it were so rusted as to be unsafe.

It was indeed a dangerous coast, but Torstein seemed to know the position of every rock or sandbank. He also seemed to know that behind the rocks was a beach and skilfully steered us towards it. That offered a measure of shelter so, having landed, we dragged the boat clear of the water and hid it as best we could, then prepared ourselves to wait out the weather.

We stayed on the beach for two full days, sheltered but open to the risk of being attacked from the mainland which was closer than felt safe. Because of that we were not allowed to start a fire and were all ordered to remain close to the boat in case we needed to set off in haste.

This respite gave Aelred and me time to rest and our hands a chance to harden. I also noticed that the wound in my chest had not been unduly affected by so much exertion, suggesting that it had indeed healed at last.

Whilst we rested, some of the men clambered across the rocks at low tide to collect mussels whilst others dug up lugworms to use as bait for fishing, casting their lines from the beach and pulling in an abundance of striped blue and silver fish which seemed almost too easy to catch. With no fire, all this fare was eaten raw and, to vary our diet, two men ventured further afield to find and butcher a seal, spearing it and then bludgeoning the poor creature with the flat of an axe blade. Once killed, the seal was skinned and the flesh cut into strips then hung up to be dried in the wind. The Vikings apparently regarded that as a delicacy – one which was also eaten raw.

* * * * *

As soon as the storm abated we gathered up our things and set off again. We rowed clear of the rocks until the sail could be set once more and from there began to make good progress.

As we continued along the coast I noticed smoke rising from various beacons placed on the higher ground, presumably to pass word from one settlement to another of our presence. Torstein had seen the signals as well but seemed unperturbed. When I asked him about it he told me that he knew we'd been seen whilst sheltering from the storm and that it didn't matter, for all the time we remained at sea such a small boat was unlikely to be judged a threat. I could see that was probably true – or at least it was until, as we rowed past a large open bay, two ships could be seen sailing directly towards us with the wind behind them.

Torstein immediately turned our boat towards the open sea and ordered the sail to be raised, clearly meaning to avoid the prospect of a battle rather than confront them. As he did so, we were all made to continue rowing as hard as we could, with Torstein shouting his instructions above the noise of the wind as it filled the sail.

'I think he means to outrun them,' said Aelred who could understand at least some of what was being said.

I looked back at the two ships and could see that they were bigger craft than ours, each manned by twenty men and therefore making better speed than we were. When Torstein saw this he changed his mind. He ordered us to stop rowing, to ship the oars and to take down the sail so that we drifted whilst he skilfully kept us in position.

The rest of the Vikings gathered on the rail, spears and axes in hand as if ready to fend off any attack.

'What the hell is he doing now?' I asked Aelred.

'He's letting them get closer, banking on the fact that they won't risk an attack when so far from land.'

'But they're still coming straight at us!' I said. 'This could be our chance to be rescued!'

'I wouldn't get your hopes up,' warned Aelred. 'These Vikings know far more about fighting at sea than our friends over there ever will.'

Even as he spoke it was clear that the Vikings lined up along the side of our boat were not actually expecting to fight. In fact concealed behind them were three men with bows. They'd lit a torch and were intending to set fire to their arrows then shoot them into the Saxon ships as soon as they came within range. I realised at once what would happen if they did.

'I can see no way to warn them!' I said to Aelred.

He agreed so all we could do was watch as the two ships sailed towards us and to almost certain ruin.

It took no time at all for the Saxons to sail close enough for us to hear the voices of the men on board, though with so much shouting, making sense of what they said was impossible. Yet they seemed ready and willing to fight us as they crowded on to the bow, armed and intent on boarding us.

Torstein waited, biding his time until they came well within bow range. It was then that the fate of the Saxons was sealed. Their huge sails straining in the wind made an easy target for the arrows which ignited them as soon as they struck home. As the oiled sailcloths went up like a torch, all those on board both vessels looked up in horror. Screaming and shouting to each other, those on one of the ships managed to cut down the burning sail and cast it over the side but were then left helpless, with nothing but their oars to power them. That meant that most of their crew had to abandon any thought of fighting, leaving them so desperately vulnerable that they had no option but to turn away and make for the safety of the shore. The other ship was less fortunate. Fragments of the burning sail fell down into the hull and, even though they tried to damp those down, the fire quickly took hold and spread, helped by yet more lighted arrows that Torstein had his men loose upon it.

The panic of those on the stricken vessel was obvious, the crew having no option but to leap over the side to escape the flames. Those wearing mail struggled to stay afloat and were quickly lost whilst those who could swim made for the shore – but it was soon clear that none of them would make it that far. We watched as the ship, once fully engulfed in flames, slowly turned on to its side and sank.

The second ship was, by then, pulling away, not even stopping to pick up any survivors from the water. It was obvious they were terrified, knowing that if Torstein chose to attack them they would all be slain as they floundered there, unable to fight back without abandoning their oars.

But Torstein saw no value in completing the slaughter. He simply watched as the remaining ship struggled away then ordered us back to the oars. From there we continued on our way as though nothing had happened.

* * * * *

For several days after that we made our way along the coast where the shoreline seemed to change from sandy beaches to pebbles, then eventually to tall white-faced cliffs that rose up directly from the sea. Once past those there was very little wind, so we took turns to row hard until we came to a wide, muddy estuary with swamps and marshes on either side. Torstein seemed pleased as we turned into the estuary and prepared to make our way towards the settlement called London.

With the river running against us, we were obliged to wait until the tide turned enough to carry us upstream, thereby giving us all a chance to rest. Holding the boat in the mouth of the estuary required great skill but Torstein was more than a match for that. He steered it towards the northern shore where he beached it on one of the many mudflats there, then settled back to wait for the tide to rise.

Aelred and I were no longer manacled at that point, the chains having been removed whilst at sea and not replaced. Thus we were tempted to risk making a run for it but, in such thick mud, it would have been impossible to walk, never mind run – and we realised that a man caught in the open would be an easy target for one of the Viking bowmen.

When at last the tide began to turn, Torstein ordered us to man the oars once more. It was slow hard work at first but eventually the sail was also hoisted to take advantage of a stiff east wind which helped to carry us upstream. At that point Torstein allowed one of the others to take the helm whilst he joined Arne at the prow from where they could pick out areas of turbulent or shallow water which we needed to avoid. In fact the river seemed a treacherous place, like a long twisting snake with currents and eddies that were each enough to cause the small boat to flounder, but, at last, the settlement at London came into view. Whilst all the others on board were thinking of what it would mean to be ashore – a dry bed of fresh straw, hot food and strong mead, not to mention a woman or two – I was thinking of something else altogether, realising that it might be my last chance to escape. What's more, I had already formed a plan on how to do it.

* * * * *

At first sight, the Saxon settlement at London looked to be one of the largest I'd ever seen, being easily as large as Chippenham and bigger even than Winchester. Only as we drew closer could I see why it appeared to be so large for it was, in fact, two settlements, both straddling the wide river. The one on the northern bank was clearly a Saxon settlement and looked to be both prosperous and busy. It was established just to the west of what remained of the walls to an old Roman garrison and boasted many wharfs and warehouses, all with good moorings for the traders who used the river to navigate their boats that far upstream. There were even the remnants of a bridge which must have originally spanned the river, but which had long since fallen into disrepair and had large sections of the walkway missing.

What surprised me most was that on the southern bank there was a large Viking encampment which seemed to reside quite peaceably even though so close to the local Saxons. The calm acceptance of each other's presence was presumably based on trade and mutual advantage as I could see no sign of any guards on either bank and there were many small boats ferrying passengers and goods from one side to the other.

Given how close they were, the settlements seemed to me to be the embodiment of Lord Alfred's dream of Vikings and Saxons living in peace together, side by side. As if to refute that, I noticed a yard for building longships on the southern bank which looked to be much too big for any normal commercial purpose. They'd already fashioned a dozen hulls all of which were moored either side of a wide pier, ready to be fitted out. When completed, it would mean that the ships could be sailed directly into the river rather than be manhandled from the shore in order to be launched only when the tide allowed. I could only guess why so many longships might be needed but knew it was something Alfred should be told about given that a fleet of ships could mean the prospect of a coastal invasion.

No one made any comment about the vessels being built or, at least, they said nothing I could understand, but I think all were as surprised as I was to see the two settlements existing side by side. As a warband, Torstein's men, like many other Vikings who still sought plunder or slaves, probably regarded any treaty between Alfred and Guthrum as nothing more than a convenient ruse. Similarly, although I had been there when the truce was declared, I was far from convinced that the terms, even once finally agreed, could actually work, particularly after all I'd seen and endured since then. Either way I was not about to miss my opportunity to escape on the slim chance that I would be received well when we landed on the Viking shore.

* * * * *

I saw my opportunity as we sailed closer to the southern bank where, although the moorings were more basic, Torstein could be sure of a welcome from his own kind. We approached with the sail straining in the breeze which was deemed strong enough to carry us home. Those of us at the oars were therefore relieved of our labour and most of the men took to gazing at the shore to see what awaited them. Whilst they were thus distracted, I knew it was my chance to act.

I leaned across to Aelred to tell him of my plan. 'Can you swim?' I whispered.

He nodded. 'Aye, like a fish,' he said simply.

'Then be ready,' I said. 'Get up when I do and follow me. I plan to upset the boat and when I do, strike anyone near enough to stop you then dive overboard and make for the northern shore.' He looked surprised and made as though to protest that it was further than it looked, but I gave him no chance to say anything more. Judging the time to be right, I stood up and went to the rail as if intending to relieve myself over the side, standing close to the man who was handling the steering board. Torstein was still positioned close to the prow at that time, staring at the Viking settlement and clearly feeling very pleased with himself, not realising that he'd relaxed his guard too soon. I smiled at the helmsman then, when he least expected it, struck him full in the face with my fist, then gave him a hard shove so that he stumbled then fell headlong overboard. Even as he hit the water I grabbed an axe which was stored near the stern and used it to cut the rigging. As I did so, the spar which carried the sail dropped like a stone on to the Vikings standing or seated either side of it, enveloping them all like a shroud. Two of them were free in an instant and came straight at me, but Aelred was also on his feet by then and quickly had the measure of them. As he struck them one after the other, both were sent reeling into the water.

With no sail to power it and no one at the helm, the boat was at the mercy of the wind and the river. It seemed to wallow for a moment before listing over to one side. Several men fell in at that stage, but I had no time to see what became of them. Instead, I simply dived over the side and started swimming towards the northern shore hoping to reach the safety of the Saxon settlement.

Once clear of the boat, I looked back and could see that it had, by then, fully capsized, tipping everyone into the water along with their trove of plunder and everything else they'd stowed on board. A few men seemed to be struggling for the shore, but several had already drowned in the rough water, either because they couldn't swim or because they'd become entangled in the ropes trailing in the water and dragged under.

I looked for Aelred and could see that he was making better progress towards the northern bank than I was. I tried to reach him but had never tackled anything like that which confronted me. The rough waters seemed icily cold and swamped me with every stroke so that I struggled even to keep my head above the waves. I soon realised that I was making no headway – in fact I seemed to be getting further and further from the Saxon settlement as I was carried away by the vicious current. I was soon too exhausted to do anything more than concentrate on staying afloat so had no choice but to allow myself to drift with the flow.

I eventually made it ashore a good way from the ruined bridge but, even though I knew I was still in danger, I was too exhausted to do more than drag myself up on to the muddy bank, desperately trying to gulp air into my lungs.

The bank where I came ashore was bordered by tall reeds and rushes which I hoped might provide some measure of cover, so I crawled towards them. I had not the strength to do more than roll myself out of sight then lie there shivering with the cold, desperately trying to recover from so much exertion.

As I began to feel better I looked for any sign of Aelred but couldn't see him. I hoped he'd made it to the other side or, failing that, had at least survived the river even if like me he was on the wrong bank. I checked the wound to my chest and found that it was none the worse for wear. Grateful for that, I crawled back to the water's edge to drink but found that the water tasted gritty and salty, probably because the tide had carried with it the muddy seawater from the estuary. As such it was all but undrinkable so instead I used it just to refresh myself, then lay back to decide what best to do.

In terms of my position, the Viking settlement lay some way upstream of me and all I had to do was wait until dark, walk back towards it and seek help from one of the ferrymen in order to cross the river to the Saxon side. Whilst I waited, I wanted desperately to light a fire to dry my sodden clothes and warm myself but knew the risk of it being seen would be too great. Besides, I was too exhausted and so just lay there and allowed myself to sleep. I can't say how long I slept but it was already light when I was rudely awakened by two Viking warriors who, I'm ashamed to say, had caught me completely off my guard.

Chapter Fourteen

I'd been a fool not to think that those at the Viking camp would do other than send out men to look for survivors from the capsized boat. Having found me, it didn't take them long to realise that I was not one of them. They began by shouting at me and prodding me with their spears, trying to force me to my feet. When I resisted one of them struck me hard across the face then held me down whilst the other tied my hands together in front. That done, they hauled me to my feet then made it clear that I was to go with them. Being outnumbered and unarmed, I had no choice but to comply, so allowed myself to be marched at spear point back to their encampment. I had no idea what to expect there except that I knew it was unlikely I'd be treated well. I even half hoped that Torstein had survived the river so he could confirm that I'd been his prisoner, but realised it was more likely that he, like many of the others, had drowned.

The Viking encampment was set just beyond the bleak marshland to the south of London, surrounded by pools of brackish water most of which were bounded by reeds. It was clearly not a permanent settlement, most of the shelters and huts having been hastily and somewhat crudely put together from whatever came to hand. Nor was it as large as it had appeared from the river but, by my simple reckoning, there were at least three hundred people there, many of them living in tents which were packed so close together they might just as well have been covered by a single awning. There were also numerous workshops and trading stalls, most with little more than a canopy to keep out the weather and separated only by a maze of muddy paths. Apart from the traders and the merchants, there were also many slaves, but by far the largest group was that of what seemed to be fully fledged warriors, many of them openly bearing arms. Surprisingly, there were also a lot of Saxon women in the camp who, having been raped or widowed and having nowhere else to go, had taken to becoming whores.

I couldn't help but be reminded of when I visited Guthrum's camp at Chippenham and I began to fear that what I was seeing was, in fact, an army. My fears were compounded when I noticed that there were virtually no defences. I wasn't sure whether that meant they felt secure after having accepted Lord Alfred's offer of peace or whether they were about to embark on some sort of invasion and therefore saw no need to fortify a temporary encampment. The latter seemed the more likely, particularly given all the longships I'd seen being built beside the river. Either way, they didn't seem to be expecting an attack – or perhaps they thought the marsh offered protection enough. I had no time to look any closer as I was taken directly to a crude hovel where I was pushed inside and the door closed and barred behind me.

It was as dark as night in there and reeked of sweat, piss and vomit, but I was not alone. There was another prisoner who sat huddled in one corner, gently rocking back and forth on his heels and muttering aimlessly to himself. When I introduced myself he just looked up at me, then turned away.

'So who are you?' I pressed.

He looked at me again then said in a voice which I could barely hear that he was called Cenric.

'So Cenric, why are you here?' I asked, trying not to sound too harsh as he was clearly very frightened.

He told me that he'd killed a Viking whilst stealing a sheep to feed his family. 'It was a fair fight, yet I now stand accused of murder!' he moaned, sounding almost incredulous at his fate. 'What sort of justice is that?'

'They'll hang you just for stealing the sheep, never mind killing one of their own,' I said.

He shrugged as if he already knew the truth of that.

I asked after Aelred but he shook his head saying that as far as he knew he and I were the only prisoners, though there were many Saxon men and women held as slaves plus other people brought in from places far across the sea. If true, that meant Aelred might have made it to the other shore or at least evaded capture. Unless of course he'd drowned.

I glanced around the hovel and realised it might be possible to break out – not through the door but through the walls which were nothing more than flimsy boards crudely nailed into place.

'It'll do you no good,' warned Cenric as he watched me try several panels looking for one which was loose or poorly fitted. 'Once outside it'll be like walking through a nest of vipers as we're right in the middle of their camp here with the bastards all around us.'

'But we have to warn Lord Alfred,' I insisted. 'This is not just a settlement, it's an encampment full of Viking warriors!' With that I managed to lift back part of one panel only to realise that from all I could see, Cenric was right; escape was all but impossible. I therefore settled down in one corner of the hovel and tried to rest as best I could.

As I sat there I began to contemplate my fate and the more I did so the more dejected I became. Had I really survived so much only to be executed alongside a man who was both a murderer and a common thief? Was that the great purpose God had in mind for me and for which he'd spared my life so often?

After a little while the door was opened and two of the guards indicated that Cenric was to follow them. I didn't know then where he was being taken to but, if he had indeed killed one of their number, it didn't bode well for him. He was shaking as they pulled him to his feet then started to forcibly drag him from the hovel. He struggled and managed to stop long enough to look at me, his eyes almost pleading for me to help him – but there was nothing I could do.

I was kept there for several hours after that, desperately trying to stay warm given that my undershirt and leggings were still wet. Eventually I too was fetched and led to a large area which had been cleared and where burned a blazing fire. Cenric was there already, stripped naked and suspended by his arms from a makeshift scaffold so that his feet barely touched the ground. I could see that he was in great pain and had many cuts to his face and body, some of which oozed blood. He had clearly suffered a brutal beating and looked to be only partly conscious. All around him were men and women who were presumably there to witness his chastisement.

A number of benches had been set around the fire, one of them covered in furs on which was sat a man I recognised. He had been seated next to Guthrum and Ubba that night I ventured into the Viking camp to spy on them. He had been the least terrifying of the trio, but I remembered his long copper-coloured hair which was still tied back with a silver ring. I also recalled his sallow complexion and little amber eyes which were set too close together. He didn't look much like a great leader of men, not like Guthrum or even Ubba, but nonetheless all there seemed to be in awe of him.

I was pushed towards the fire and made to stand before this man whose name I didn't know but now guessed to be Jarl Hakon himself – Hakon the Bonebreaker Torstein had called him and I soon realised why. Next to him was a huge club with nails and studs protruding from the head. It was surely a brutal weapon, designed to inflict some terrible wounds. I should have been scared witless at that point but, if truth be told, I was long past feeling anything and was actually just grateful to be so close to the fire so that I could warm my bones and give my still damp clothes a chance to dry.

One of his guards tried to force me to my knees in homage but I was in no mood to be bullied. I shrugged him off and glared at him, looking as threatening as I could given that my hands were still tied.

Jarl Hakon said nothing but instead summoned another man to step closer. As he hobbled towards me on crutches I recognised yet another familiar face, that of Ulf, the old warrior who had served as interpreter during Alfred's negotiations with Guthrum after the battle at Edington.

'My Lord Hakon says that you may stand,' he said, not unkindly.

I nodded my thanks. 'Then ask him what he wants of me,' I demanded boldly, though still shivering despite the warmth of the fire.

'First he would know who you are,' said Ulf.

I hesitated for a moment before lifting up my undershirt so they could see my scar. A gasp went up when all there saw and seemed to recognise it. 'I think you know full well who I am. I'm called the warrior with the pierced heart.'

Hakon seemed to find that amusing. He turned and said something to Ulf who immediately translated. 'My Lord says that he does not believe in men rising from the dead. It is true you have suffered a terrible wound, but he says you were lucky that it healed, that's all. He has seen men recover from such wounds before.'

It was my turn to smile. 'Then Jarl Hakon is a wise man. Wiser than most at any rate. But you and I have met before.'

Ulf peered at me then seemed to recognise me. 'Were you not at Alfred's side when we spoke with him?' he recalled. 'Did you not return a sword to the boy Arne and offer him protection?'

'That's all true. Except that I offered to adopt Arne as my brother as a gesture of peace between our peoples. As it turns out he was a treacherous little toad who repaid me by betraying me to Jarl Torstein.'

Both men looked bemused.

'Lord Alfred was magnanimous that day despite his great victory,' I explained. 'He deemed that enough blood had been spilled, both Saxon and Viking.'

Hakon nodded, clearly understanding some of what I'd said. I remembered how Alfred had pretended not to understand the Viking tongue when Guthrum came to negotiate his surrender. It seemed that the Vikings had learned much from that particular ploy.

'So why has Lord Alfred sent you here to spy on us?' Ulf demanded.

'I'm no spy. Neither was I sent here by Lord Alfred. I was taken captive, first by miserable slavers and then by Jarl Torstein. I escaped when the boat bringing us here capsized but I couldn't make it to the Saxon shore.'

'How can we know this to be true?' said Ulf. 'Your reputation has reached us even here and we can have no doubt about your loyalty to Lord Alfred.'

'And what would I tell him? That you have an army and that you mean to invade? There are what, barely two hundred warriors here? Even if you had twice that number he would defeat you in an instant as he did at Edington. And at Combwich for that matter.'

'This is not an army,' Ulf assured me. 'It is simply a place for our people to gather to await the arrival of Lord Guthrum in person who will then dispense lands to those who served him well. It was decreed by Alfred himself as part of the peace between them that Guthrum may govern here in Alfred's stead.'

'I know for I was there if you remember. But Guthrum is to govern in Alfred's name, not in his stead,' I corrected.

Ulf shrugged as though it made no difference.

'This is not the first time I've visited a Viking camp either,' I said.

Both men looked at me, clearly surprised.

'Have you forgotten my singing so soon?' I asked, teasing them.

Still they seemed not to recognise me.

'On Alfred's orders I entered Guthrum's camp at Chippenham and pretended to sing and dance for food,' I reminded them. 'Though I cannot say that I was offered much in the way of hospitality.'

Suddenly Hakon roared with laughter.

'My Lord says that he does indeed remember that day. He says that he much admires your courage, though thought your singing was an offence to his ears.'

I laughed and thanked him, then pressed my luck. 'So what's to become of me? Am I your prisoner or will you let me return to Lord Alfred as is my right? If this is truly not an army you've gathered here, then you've nothing to fear from me – or from him.'

The two men conferred for a moment then Ulf announced their decision. 'Jarl Hakon says that your friend here must die. He stole from a man and then took his life as well. As for you, whilst he hates spies, he will overlook that you entered Guthrum's camp that night as much has happened since. However, there are other charges against you that must be answered.'

'Such as?' I demanded.

'His loyal Jarl, Torstein, is even now recovering from the river. Jarl Torstein says you upset the boat on purpose which cost him all his plunder and the lives of five of his men. He demands vengeance for this.'

'I'm glad Torstein survived for I much respect him as a warrior. But the treasure he lost was plundered from Saxon homes and churches so was never rightfully his in the first place. How can he claim to have lost what he never owned? As to his men, they were warriors so took their chances. I've no cause to answer for them.'

As this was translated Hakon nodded to acknowledge each point without saying a word to indicate whether he accepted my argument or not. When Ulf had finished, the Viking seemed to consider the matter.

'Torstein has been summoned and will speak for himself,' said Ulf. 'According to our law you have taken the lives of many and for that you must forfeit your own, just as Cenric here must do. As we wait for Jarl Torstein to arrive, my Lord Hakon has ordered that you be given dry clothes and some food.'

I thanked them and asked whether Cenric might at least be cut down as well. This was denied so instead I tried to explain my position. 'As I've said, I've been a prisoner since soon after I left Chippenham. During all that time I've been forced to watch the slaughter at several Saxon settlements and a Holy Abbey. For those acts I also demand vengeance as they were clearly in breach of Alfred's treaty with Lord Guthrum.'

Ulf nodded. 'It is true that there is fault on both sides, but my Lord insists that he hears Torstein's argument as well.'

'And if he finds against me?'

'Then you will be put to the sword but, as a warrior, you will be allowed to die with honour.'

With that my hands were untied and I was given a clean tunic to wear and a warm woollen cloak to wrap around my shoulders. I was also offered a bowl of hot broth which I drank gratefully. I asked for some water to be given to Cenric who still hung from the scaffold in great pain, but that request was refused. Then, even as I considered my options, Torstein arrived looking none the worse for his dunking in the river.

He bowed to Jarl Hakon then kissed his ring before addressing me. 'So either you can swim like a fish or you've returned from the dead yet again.'

'I can swim,' I said simply. 'As it seems can you.'

'We were lucky that men brought a boat to save us,' he said. 'Otherwise we might all have drowned.'

'So tell me, did my servant Aelred survive?'

Torstein said he didn't know, but that they'd found no trace of him.

'And what about Arne?'

'He did, unlike many of the others. Also, all my booty and belongings were lost to the river for which you must pay with your blood.'

'You can hardly blame me for your incompetence,' I said.

Ulf seemed interested in this and demanded to know what I meant.

'The man at the helm was drunk as were many others. He fell over the side and, as I was nearest, I seized the steering oar and tried to steady the boat,' I lied, making up the story as I went along.

'That's not so!' exclaimed Torstein.

I shrugged. 'I was closer than you. Unfortunately, as I told you, I've no knowledge of sailing so turned the boat about and she floundered when she went across the wind. The ropes securing the sail could not hold and gave way, causing the gear to collapse on to those nearest the mast.'

'You cut the ropes on purpose!' accused Torstein.

I feigned a look to appear incredulous. 'How could I do that?' I said. 'I was a prisoner. You let a drunken fool take your place at the helm so must take the blame for his mistake.'

Ulf looked at Torstein for a reply.

'This is nonsense. You set about to sink the boat so you and your friend could escape!' pressed Torstein.

I spread my hands wide. 'Had I known anything about boats I might have tried that, but if that was my intent would I not first have steered it closer to the Saxon shore? Only a fool would have done so when so close to the wrong bank of such a wide river.'

Ulf repeated all this to Hakon who nodded wisely. Although none of what I said was true, I had to admit it did sound convincing.

'My Lord says that you should both have drowned in the river, but that fate brought you here instead. It should therefore now decide this matter.'

'How can that be done?' I asked.

'The matter will be determined by combat between you at dawn tomorrow,' announced Ulf as though that was an obvious decision.

I could see at once what Hakon was trying to do. Given that I'd seen his army gathering there on the banks of the river and all the longships which were being built, I could not be allowed to live. Yet if he killed me and Lord Alfred heard of it, which he surely would given how close we were to the Saxon settlement just across the river, he'd certainly seek reprisals. If on the other hand I was slain in combat over some personal grievance, no criticism could be levied against anyone.

My concern was that if Torstein and I did fight, I would almost certainly lose as, after all I'd endured, I was in no fit state to take on a warrior like him even once rested. Yet it seemed I didn't have much choice. My only consolation was that I would get the chance to die avenging my men whom he'd so brutally butchered on that fateful day in the forest. 'I accept the proposal,' I managed as boldly as I could. 'But on two conditions. I must be allowed to fight with my father's sword, assuming that also survived the river. If I win the contest, then the sword remains mine and I am free to return to Lord Alfred unharmed.'

'Agreed. And the second?' asked Ulf.

'That Cenric here will be freed as well.'

Ulf explained that to Hakon who seemed to find it amusing. 'My Lord decrees that only one may live. Therefore if you prevail then this man will die. If you are slain, he will be spared from execution.'

It was not much of a bargain but I was in no position to argue. Not sure what I would do at that point, I looked towards Cenric who had clearly heard what was said.

'J-just d-do it,' he said, barely managing to speak. 'Forget m-me, my f-fate is s-sealed.'

It was a brave thing to say but I suspect he was in such pain that death would have come as a welcome relief. Still I hesitated but, in the end, I realised I had no choice. I was certain I would not survive the fight with Torstein, not just because I doubted my fitness to fight but also because it was likely that he was almost as skilled with the sword as was my brother Edwin. Though I had often practised with Edwin I had never come close to bettering him. 'All right, I agree,' I said reluctantly. 'But I would have your word on this as a bargain between us. Also, if I fall my body must not be spoiled and will be given to the Saxons for a Christian burial.'

'You can demand nothing,' said Torstein who, by then, seemed to be growing weary of the haggling.

Ulf looked to Hakon then raised his arm. 'He has spoken well and given an account of his position. He therefore stands on an even footing as yourself,' he said. 'Like you, he can choose what becomes of his body. Though from all I've heard of him as a warrior you may want to consider what you want for your own remains should the contest not go well for you.'

* * * * *

'So, what is your true name?' asked Ulf as Torstein and I stood before Hakon the next morning prior to fighting.

Certain that I would be killed, I had already decided to tell them who I was as at least that way both Alfred and Emelda would learn of my fate. 'I am called Matthew but was christened Edward. I am the third born son of Edwulf who was an Ealdorman and friend to Lord Alfred. My brother was a warrior you may have heard of. His name was Lord Edwin.'

Hakon looked surprised to say the least.

'My Lord has indeed heard of your brother and regarded him well,' said Ulf.

Torstein also looked impressed. 'I never fought your brother, but I have heard tell of him. As for you, I'll take no pleasure in killing you, boy, but you have cost me the lives of many of my men, all my booty and my boat, therefore I have no choice but to fight you.'

'It will also enhance your reputation if you are the one brave enough to slay the warrior with the pierced heart,' I pointed out. 'But know this, my God will surely avenge me if you do kill me before he's ready to take me back and I wouldn't want to stand in your shoes if he does.'

He looked a little uncertain at that and was, I'm sure, considering his own fate. For my part I had spent the night trying to decide what best to do. Fighting Torstein was not going to be easy. Even though I'd lost count of the men I'd killed by then, almost all of them had been slain by guile or chance. Apart from in the general melee of battle, I had not stood toe to toe with a trained warrior and traded blows with him in a contest such as the one I was about to face.

'My Lord would know whether you wish to borrow a mail vest and helmet?' said Ulf.

I was tempted to accept the offer but whilst trying to form my plan the previous night, I'd remembered the story Aelred had told us after we'd escaped from the slavers; the one about the small man in the land of giants. Hereric had overcome and slain his much bigger and stronger opponent by tiring him and by allowing himself to move more freely. I'd realised that might well be my only chance and I therefore declined Ulf's offer. 'My sword and a shield will suffice,' I said. 'I need no mail vest for as you know I've died before so have nothing to fear from a mere mortal such as Jarl Torstein.'

'You really do have no fear of death, do you, boy?' said Torstein.

I smiled at him. The truth was that I was all but quaking with fear and struggling not to show it by shivering in the cold morning air. Yet I knew that death in combat was better and quicker than whatever other ways they could find to torture me so tried to appear as bold as I could. 'If my God should choose to call me back to him I'll go willingly,' I said. 'But if so, I would have you tell Lord Alfred of my fate. He should know what has become of me and will be consoled to hear that I rest with God.'

Chapter Fifteen

It was as I prepared myself for the contest that the doubts began to grow ever more vivid in my mind. Not only did I fear that I was no match for Torstein, I was also worried that being still weary from all my exertions, the wound to my chest would make me tire too easily and thereby prevent me from giving a good account of myself. Yet I knew he was equally concerned about the prospect of killing me, fearing what might come of slaying a man who he believed had returned from the dead. Strange that the wound which should have killed me in the first place was now my best chance of survival – and had actually prevented me from being slain several times at least. But I sensed all that had changed as Torstein seemed not only desperate to avenge the loss of all that which I'd cost him when I capsized his boat, he also needed to repair his own reputation as a warrior after having lost so many men during his raids and having nothing to show for it.

As we prepared ourselves, I was given my father's sword which, as agreed, I was to be allowed to use and which I was told had survived the river when the man who'd taken it from me was also rescued. He looked less than pleased at giving it up and I was worried lest he challenge me as well. Any qualms I had on that account were quickly quelled when it became obvious that he, like others, was not keen to fight a man with my reputation.

As soon as I held the sword again it felt as if it somehow belonged in my hand. The Vikings believed that a sword embodied the reputation not only of the man who owned it, but also that of all those whose blood had soiled its blade. Strangely enough, from the moment I picked it up I felt the strength and courage of both Edwin and my father, both of whom had wielded it with such pride. It was almost as though they were suddenly there in spirit to guide me and protect me. Emboldened by that, I tried a few strokes and felt again the perfect weight and balance that only such a fine weapon could bestow. With that I began to feel that at least I had a chance.

Through all of this Torstein remained unusually quiet. He was fully armed, resplendent in a mail vest, helmet and shield. His own war gear had been lost to the river, but he'd borrowed what he was wearing from another warrior. He also carried a seax tucked into his belt and a smaller blade lodged in a sheath bound tight against the lower part of his leg. As I looked at him I tried to recall all that Edwin had taught me about fighting and began looking for any weakness I might be able to exploit. I had already worked out one way the warrior might be beaten and that stemmed from the fact that despite many opportunities, he had always seemed reluctant to kill me, fearing it would bring him ill fortune if he did. If those doubts still troubled him, that might well help to stay his hand at the crucial moment – and that hesitation allow me vital moments to prevail. I therefore resolved to play upon his concerns as fully as I could. I started by stripping off my tunic to stand before him bare chested so that he could clearly see the scar on my chest. I could tell from the look in his eyes that my ploy had worked well enough.

Before fighting, we each turned to acknowledge Jarl Hakon. Torstein knelt before him and kissed his ring again whereas I allowed him nothing more than a respectful nod of my head.

That done, I turned away then made great play of falling to my knees and praying with my hands clasped together and raised towards God, recalling again that Torstein was intrigued and more than a little afraid of the one he called the nailed God. I remained at prayer for longer than was needed then, just when Torstein seemed to be losing patience, I made him wait a little longer before getting up and borrowing a shield and a seax which were offered by one of the other Vikings. I then drew my sword and tried a few more short strokes with it before standing ready for the contest to begin.

* * * * *

As I expected, Torstein was tired of waiting. He lurched towards me like a dog springing to the attack. He clearly intended to finish the fight quickly but moved less freely than me so all I had to do was step aside, making no attempt to strike him.

Surprised, Torstein turned to face me then came at me again, this time swinging his sword as though to cut my head from my shoulders. I well remembered how Edwin had taught me to deal with such an assault by leaning back and letting the blade sweep past me but, I confess, when it came to it I lacked the nerve to stand my ground. Instead, I simply raised my shield to counter the blow then ducked beneath it. Torstein looked at me smugly, knowing that avoiding him thus betrayed a lack of sword craft on my part.

We circled each other for a few moments before he came at me again, this time charging straight at me, ramming his shield into mine and catching me off balance. I stumbled yet managed to keep my feet but then he struck my shield again with his, this time so hard that I was sent sprawling to the ground. To my relief he didn't close in for the kill. Instead, he paraded himself before all those who watched, roaring loudly and urging them to acknowledge his skill.

As I got up I realised that my lip was bleeding freely from where I'd caught it, probably on the edge of my own shield. I wiped my mouth with my hand and stared at the blood. Perhaps that's what it took for me to realise just how close I was to being slain. More likely the sight of the blood reminded me that I still needed to avenge all my men who'd been butchered on Torstein's orders. Either way it was enough to stir me into action. I ran straight at Torstein who barely had time to turn and face me as I crashed headlong into him. Somehow he managed to remain on his feet but he seemed stunned as I struck him again and again with my shield, ramming it into his and driving him back.

As soon as I relented he looked at me and smiled. 'So there's yet enough life left in you to make a fight of it!' he challenged.

With that we closed on each other again. This time I stood my ground and countered his strokes with my sword and shield. As I did so, I felt the power of his arm as our weapons clashed together, something which I knew my brother Edwin would not have approved of lest the blades were spoiled. The strange thing was that after all my exertions whilst rowing, my arm felt stronger than ever and I found I was able to match Torstein, blow for blow. Yet I knew that if I continued to trade strokes with such a skilled warrior he would surely get the better of me in the end; thus I caught his shield on mine then heaved him back with all my might to give myself some respite from the fray. No sooner had I done so than I realised that my own shield had split and was therefore all but useless.

As I tossed the broken shield aside Torstein must have sensed victory. He lowered his weapon and smiled at me again. 'It seems your nailed God wants you back after all,' he said, then raised his own shield once more and started towards me, by then confident of victory.

There was nothing I could do without a shield except to get in close enough to at least impede his strokes, but even that wouldn't protect me for long. Already I was tiring just as I feared I would and knew I had to finish it. Then I recalled something I had once seen Osric do – as head of Alfred's personal guard he favoured combat at close quarters and I knew that to copy his move might be my only chance.

As Torstein closed on me I made no attempt to avoid him. Instead, I held myself ready and, as he thrust his shield forward meaning to follow it with a swift stroke from his sword, I grabbed the top edge of it with my free hand and gripped it tightly. Quickly stepping to one side of him, I then jerked the shield down before driving my sword hard into his exposed shoulder. His mail vest saved him, but I knew that at least the point of my blade had pierced his flesh. Sure enough, as he reeled away I could see he'd felt the blow keenly enough and that blood was oozing from the wound.

For a moment we faced each other once more. He looked unnerved by what had happened and more than a little surprised. I doubt that the wound troubled him greatly, but it made him realise that the fight was far from over. If nothing else, it made it difficult for him to hold his shield properly so that it looked heavy in his hand, though he wouldn't release it altogether. Also, with the weight of his mail vest and with his sword feeling heavier with every stroke, he looked to be almost as weary as me. Then, as he managed to compose himself, I knew what was coming next, just as I knew he'd toyed with me long enough. Edwin's words rang in my ears. '*Strike and prevail*,' he always advised me, '*strike and prevail*'. Surely that would now be Torstein's plan as well?

He came at me hard and fast, crouching low beneath his shield to protect his already wounded shoulder, then heaved his sword towards me with all his might. All I had to do was lean back to avoid his blade then hack at his legs as he went past me, scything the blade into the back of his knee. He stumbled and then fell heavily to the ground where he lay as if not quite sure what had happened.

The wound to his leg was not serious but, impeded by his heavy mail vest and desperate not to let go of either his sword or his shield, he struggled to gain his feet. Yet even on the ground he was far from helpless. As I moved in closer he lashed out with his sword to keep me at bay but must have known then that the contest was mine – he couldn't keep that up for ever and I certainly wasn't about to give him any chance to get up!

Even though I now had the advantage, I knew I had to time my next move well. As he swiped at my legs again and again with his sword I simply stayed out of reach and waited for his arm to tire. When it did, his strokes became slow and laboured so, seizing my chance, I moved in closer and hacked at the lower part of his outstretched leg with my sword.

This time my blow was delivered with all the force needed to all but sever his foot at the ankle. He roared with pain, dropping his weapons as he reached out to nurse his wound. As he did so, I quickly stepped in behind him and pressed the blade of my seax hard against his throat.

He was powerless to resist. Even if he could escape my blade there was no hope of him fighting on as he couldn't possibly stand with his foot so badly injured. I smiled to myself remembering Aelred's story about the little man in the land of giants. It had proved a meaningful tale as Torstein, a bigger and more accomplished warrior than I, was at my mercy.

'Argh!' he groaned. 'S-so your G-God has n-no need of you?'

I smiled. 'So it seems,' I said, then looked to Hakon to see whether he was inclined to have me show any mercy. He just looked away so I knew that Torstein's fate was sealed.

Given all his wounds and that he had a blade pressed hard against his throat, Torstein must have known it as well. 'I'm d-done,' he said bravely, his voice rasped with pain. Clearly accepting his lot, he removed his helmet and, as he did so, I picked up his sword and returned it to him, knowing that if he died whilst still holding it his path to Valhalla was assured. As he weighed the weapon in his hand he gave a wry smile and nodded as if to thank me for the courtesy.

'D-do it!' he insisted without showing even the slightest sign of fear.

Strangely, though I still craved vengeance, I found I had no deep-seated wish to kill him. I therefore hesitated for a moment as though inclined to let him live.

'K-kill me!' he demanded. 'D-don't leave me to live like a h-hobbled cr-cripple!'

I knew then I had no choice so turned to Hakon. 'I'll finish him if you spare Cenric as well,' I insisted. 'I offer Jarl Torstein a clean and honourable death in return for the life of your prisoner and freedom for myself.'

Torstein looked at Hakon making it clear what he wanted.

Still Hakon hesitated. He had the option of killing Torstein himself, or rather having one of his men do it for him, but that way Torstein would be denied his place in Valhalla. After a few moments he agreed that he would stay the execution, the plight of Cenric being of little consequence to him.

As soon as he'd made his decision I had to act. 'May your Gods have mercy on your soul,' I whispered, then drew the blade across his throat.

Torstein died without complaint and, although still not at ease with killing anyone, I reasoned that I'd now killed so many that one more would not make much difference. In any event, he had deserved to die. How else was I to avenge my men? Yet, having taken his life, I felt no great satisfaction from it – though I confess I was secretly proud that my skills as a warrior remained intact in spite of all I'd endured.

* * * * *

As two of his men carried off Torstein's body, they glowered at me as though thirsting for revenge. Jarl Hakon seemed more charitable. Even though he made some aside, he stopped Ulf from translating it.

'You have proved your point and earned your freedom,' said Ulf. 'You may go in peace. My Lord will send word to Lord Alfred of your return and will send a man to ride with you under his protection to ensure you travel safely. The man will then need Lord Alfred to grant him safe passage to return to us with the horses.'

I thanked him then sheathed my sword, symbolically securing the peace tie as I did so. 'And what of this man?' I asked, inclining my head towards Cenric who still hung by his arms from the scaffold. Given that he'd been there since the day before I was surprised he was still alive.

Hakon shrugged. 'It will be as was agreed,' said Ulf. 'Though he deserves to die.'

Ulf summoned a man who had been watching the fight and said something to him.

'As my Lord has promised, we will not complete the execution of this wretch, but this man is the brother of the one he killed,' explained Ulf. 'Vengeance is his if he wants it. That is our way.'

'But Cenric is in no fit state to fight this man or any other! He'll scarce be able to stand when you release him!' I said angrily, sensing I'd been duped.

Ulf shrugged. 'He must reap what he has sown, as must we all. That is not a matter for my Lord to determine, but a just and legal issue for these men to settle between them as best they may.'

With that, the man walked across then took the rope to which Cenric's arms were tied. I thought at first that he planned to honour Hakon's word but instead he hoisted

Cenric even higher so that he could no longer rest his feet on the ground. Then he drew his knife and without so much as a word to anyone, thrust it hard into Cenric's belly before twisting the blade.

Cenric looked down at me as he died. In a way I think he realised he'd got off lightly given that the Vikings knew how to make death linger, sometimes even for many days.

'Bastards!' I whispered under my breath. 'You gave me your word!'

'My Lord gave his word to spare Cenric from execution,' said Ulf. 'He has honoured that but this man craved vengeance and had a score of his own to settle, so my Lord's word cannot bind him.'

'This is nothing but trickery!' I stormed accusingly.

Ulf just smiled. 'He killed one of our warriors so was bound to die. Even if we'd set him free the family of the man he killed would have found him. Besides, he was all but dead already.'

For a moment I was silent, not sure what to say. There was nothing I could do to help Cenric and I realised that with such a callous regard for what had been promised, my own life still hung in the balance. Instead, I glared at Jarl Hakon. 'Such treachery is beyond contempt,' I muttered. 'How do I know you'll honour the other part of the bargain and release me?'

'Jarl Hakon's word is good,' said Ulf. 'We would know when it is that you plan to leave?'

'I'll leave at first light tomorrow,' I managed bitterly.

'So soon?' said Ulf.

'I have not seen my woman for many months and am anxious to return to her with all possible speed,' I said.

Ulf smiled knowingly then acknowledged the request but insisted that I dine with Jarl Hakon in person that evening. Although I had no wish to sit at table with a man who had allowed Cenric to be butchered so coldly, I knew I dare not refuse as it was intended to be a great honour. Therefore that evening I sat with him and other Jarls in the chieftain's tent and, through Ulf, discussed many things. In particular, they were all anxious to know how we'd defeated Ubba at Combwich. As we'd left no survivors there they had not heard of how the battle was fought. I said only that we took them by surprise, not mentioning that most of the berserkers died having been ambushed by arrows and slingshot as they tried to cross the ford.

'Lord Alfred has shown himself to be a great warrior,' said Ulf. 'We are all much impressed by him.'

'Lord Alfred is not just a great warrior; he's an even greater King. And a wise one. He seeks only to bring peace to this troubled land.'

One of the servants, or more likely a slave, passed me a plate of boiled mutton. 'When I dined at Lord Guthrum's table I was given only scraps. Now I see what I missed,' I remarked.

It was indeed true. The table was laden with meats and smoked fish, fresh fruits and all manner of honeyed cakes and bread. We also drank our fill from a pitcher of hot spiced wine. When it was done we made our farewells. Hakon said that although he was saddened that it had cost the life of his friend and ally, Jarl Torstein, he wished me no ill as at least Torstein had died well. He also told me that Alfred was now at Winchester, not Chippenham, something I had already guessed might be the case.

'My Lord would have you assure Lord Alfred that the men here mean him no ill. They will soon disperse so he has nothing to fear from us.'

'Is that so?' I said. 'Then I will tell Lord Alfred that when I see him.' Of course I didn't believe a word of it, any more than would Alfred, and the more they tried to convince me the more I suspected that what they said was nothing but lies.

As I left Hakon's tent I was unsure as to whether I could bring myself to shake his hand, but he had no such reservations. My only concern was whether he fully intended for me to reach Winchester alive. I knew he dared not lose face by going back on his word to free me, yet neither could he afford for me to report all I'd seen to Alfred. Therefore I had sense enough to realise that the man sent to escort me might well have orders to kill me along the way. As such I suspected that the most dangerous part of my long journey was yet to come.

Chapter Sixteen

I reckoned that my chances of reaching Winchester alive were slight. The journey would provide my escort with many opportunities to kill me, with my death then being blamed on robbers or vagrants which, in such troubled times, would not give rise to even the slightest suspicion.

The man ordered to accompany me was named Asger who, I was told by Ulf, didn't speak my language but was a fine warrior. However, when I was introduced to him I was shocked to find that he looked to be nothing more than a fat and lazy wastrel – as far from being a warrior as I was from being a saint! That served to convince me that he was indeed a paid assassin. I consoled myself with the thought that at least with him bearing Jarl Hakon's pennant we were unlikely to be attacked by other Vikings so all I had to do was keep my eyes on him at all times.

I decided not to ask further after young Arne – or Edmund as I knew him. Having been told that the boy had survived the river, I knew that if I saw him again I might be tempted to say or do something I would later regret. Although the little runt deserved to die for his treachery, my thirst for vengeance seemed to have been sated by slaying Torstein, though there would have been some satisfaction in knowing that the boy had at least seen me do it.

Having been given some fresh clothes to wear, I prepared to leave the Viking camp early the next morning, anxious to get as far from it as I could. Asger and I were each given a horse and some meagre supplies for the journey, but I noticed that the latter would scarce be enough to sustain us for the time it would take to reach Winchester and then for him to return. That meant that either he didn't expect to have to travel that far or that he was hoping to get fresh supplies when we got there. I had no way of knowing which but, either way, I became convinced that my fears about him having orders to kill me along the way were justified and I therefore resolved to be rid of him as soon as I could.

Our journey would take us south towards a settlement at a place called Leatherhead from where we would cross the river Emele before then turning westwards towards Winchester, a journey which would take perhaps three or four days in all, depending on the weather. We would pass through mainly Saxon held territory where I felt I would be safe enough, though being on the very fringes of Wessex it was not an area I'd ever visited before.

As we rode off I allowed Asger to lead so that I could watch him closely. He seemed to be always eating, delving into a bag strapped to his saddle to produce an apple or a leg of poultry, casually discarding the remnants over his shoulder. Every so often he would turn to look at me, smiling but making no attempt to speak.

It was left to him to carry Hakon's pennant on a cane strapped to his saddle so that it could be clearly seen by all. Yet I began to wonder whether that was for my protection or for his given that it also served to make it clear which of us was the target if someone was detailed to shoot me with an arrow as we passed.

Eventually we came to a shallow river where I ordered him to stop and water the horses. Reluctantly Asger dismounted and, as the horses drank, he also knelt to scoop up a few handfuls of water. It was then that I saw my chance and took it.

Without warning, I placed my foot in the small of his back and pushed him so hard that he was thrust headlong into the river. The water was not deep and almost at once he turned and tried to get up but, being such a fat lump of a man, he struggled to do so. It would have made no difference even if he had found his feet as by then my sword was drawn.

As he sat there, Asger faced a simple choice. He could stay where he was in the river or he could try to make a fight of it. In the end he did the sensible thing and remained where he was, no doubt feeling very foolish but probably grateful I hadn't simply killed him outright.

I noticed that he'd cut his head on a stone as he hit the water and, as always, it bled quite freely once wet. He wiped away some of the blood from his brow then looked up at me anxiously wondering what I would do next.

Despite my suspicions, I couldn't bring myself to kill him. After all, I had no proof as to whether or not his orders had been to harm me, so decided to spare him. Instead, I calmly went across and mounted his horse, the one which carried Hakon's pennant, then rode off, taking my mount with me as well. I heard him protesting as I rode away but without his horse there was nothing he could do to stop me.

I hoped that the pennant would be passport enough and that any would-be assassin would not know which of us had survived – me or my escort. That said, I knew I couldn't risk travelling alone for long whilst wearing Viking clothes and with two valuable horses, each with a Viking saddle. Feelings were still running high in the kingdom at that time and, if mistaken for a Viking travelling alone, I would make a tempting target.

* * * * *

It was dark when I reached Leatherhead, a surprisingly large settlement of perhaps thirty dwellings or more. It was located at the head of a gap in the northern downs through which ran the river Emele, a wide but slow river that flowed from somewhere to the south towards London. I went first to look at the river and water my horses and found that whilst there was no bridge across it, there was a ford which was shallow enough to cross, even on foot. Just beyond the ford and a little way upstream of it was an island, opposite which stood a mill that seemed to struggle in the slow current, together with various stores and sheds. On my way to the river I'd passed by the settlement itself. Most of the dwellings were sited on the higher ground on the northeastern bank of the river, presumably as a defence against the risk of flooding. I decided to ride back there to seek lodgings for the night.

The people in the settlement stared at me as I rode in, no doubt wary of a stranger – particularly one dressed as a Viking. I ignored their gaze knowing that none would openly challenge me as they would no doubt be used to travellers taking advantage of the gap in the hills or to access the Harroway, an old tin-mining trail that led westwards as far as Winchester and beyond. I had already decided that the trail would be the safest route for me to follow as it was used by so many others.

Because I was bearing arms, I had first to see the local Ealdorman and seek his consent to cross his lands but needed no directions to find his Vill – it was a large Hall set amid a cluster of other buildings on the edge of the main settlement. What surprised me was that it was virtually unprotected, having no fortifications to speak of apart from a simple fence and a gate where just two armed sentries had been posted.

'What do you want, boy?' challenged one of the guards as I drew close enough to hear him.

'I'm a Saxon warrior bearing arms and seek your Lord's permission to pass,' I said firmly. 'Also, I need to get word to Lord Alfred with all possible speed.'

The guard seemed unimpressed. 'A Saxon warrior you say? Yet you carry a Viking pennant and have two horses, each with a Viking saddle.'

'I will explain all that but must first speak to your Lord in person.'

'You'll state your name and your business now or I'll have the skin flayed from your bones, you idle wretch!'

I hesitated for a moment before replying. 'My name is Matthew, christened Edward. I am the son of Lord Edwulf and my brother was the warrior Edwin. I serve Lord Alfred and am under his personal orders and thus demand an audience with your betters. And whilst we're waiting, if you would indeed flay the skin from my bones then I invite you to try.' With that I drew my sword. 'I'll warrant I'll have this sword in your guts before you get close enough to smell the sweetness of my breath.'

For a moment the guard looked unsure as to what he should do. 'All right Matthew christened Edward, I'll send word to Lord Werhard and see whether he'll receive you or not. But if this is some Viking ruse you won't be riding away from here with your head on your shoulders, be assured of that!'

I dismounted and led my horses through the gates, then handed the reins to a stable boy. 'Rub them down well and feed them. I've a long journey ahead of me tomorrow,' I ordered, then watched him closely as he led the two horses away. Two men then came across and escorted me towards the Hall which was sited in the centre of the many buildings which together formed the Vill. The Hall was a large and neatly thatched building with elaborately painted fascia boards and two carved pillars to frame the entrance. The design and size of it pointed to considerable wealth which, given how close we were to the Viking encampment at London, I found surprising but assumed that whatever prosperity it enjoyed stemmed from the extensive and very fertile fields I'd seen earlier. Also, because of its position, Leatherhead was probably a wealthy settlement relying on trade from people using the ford to access the gap through the northern downs.

As we approached, one of the doors to the Hall was opened and it was clear that I was expected to step inside. Before doing so, one of the men pointed to my sword. 'I'd best hold that,' he said without any hint of a challenge.

It was not unusual for a stranger to be relieved of his weapon when entering a Saxon Hall so I surrendered it without complaint. The man raised his eyebrows when he saw it, recognising that it was indeed a very fine weapon.

'That sword is worth your life ten times over so mind you take good care of it,' I warned. 'Stay close to me whilst you hold it and don't leave my sight, do you hear me?'

The man understood and entered the Hall a few paces in front of me.

'So, Lord Werhard is Ealdorman here?' I asked, thinking that perhaps I should have known that.

'Aye sir, that he is,' said the guard.

Even as he spoke I could see a man ahead of us seated on a fine chair at the far end of the Hall. The chair was mounted on a platform and between it and the doors a fire big enough to heat such a large room burned brightly. He looked to be a bull of a man, powerfully built but with a huge bloated belly, a vast beard and long black hair, the ends of which he toyed with as though preening himself like a jay. I instinctively disliked him.

I walked around the fire and approached him but made only a token bow, thereby implying that I regarded myself as at least his equal. That seemed to displease him.

'So you say your name is Matthew, christened Edward and that your lineage includes the late Lord Edwulf and the warrior Lord Edwin? If so, that's some pretty potent blood you have flowing through your veins.'

'And you I take it are Lord Werhard, in which case I'm honoured to meet with you and...'

'I'm not Lord Werhard, I'm his son, Oeric. My father is old and leaves all matters to me.' He had a smug look on his face as though he could barely be troubled to speak with me, yet what he'd said changed things completely. As Oeric's name was not derived from that of his father, he was clearly not of high birth. I had no idea why he would be trusted with running the Shire if that was indeed the case, but it seemed I had the advantage.

'Then I would have you send greetings to your father and offer him my regards.'

Oeric nodded then leaned forward in his chair. 'I hear you would also have me send word to Lord Alfred, is that right?'

'Aye. I need him to know that I'm safe and that I have urgent news. I would also have you charge men to escort me to him in haste.'

Oeric feigned surprise at my demands then quickly checked himself. 'You will know that Lord Alfred is at Winchester now where he resides in splendour as we strive to pay for his battles and his grand plans.'

I could suffer Oeric's complacency in speaking to his betters but not his criticism of Alfred. 'To Winchester then, but you're mistaken. Alfred strives only to improve his realm as any King should. As to his battles, he has earned us the right to live as Saxons and the cost of that must be borne by all, including those who didn't deign to stand with us.' The last point was almost an accusation as I was certain that neither Oeric nor his father had fought at Edington, nor sent men to aid us.

'We are far from Chippenham here and word did not reach us in time,' said Oeric defensively. 'Also, it was left for us to protect the rear of Alfred's kingdom from the hordes gathered at London.'

It was a lame excuse and he knew it.

'Be that as it may, I must now make haste if we are not to lose the advantages he bought at the cost of so much honest Saxon blood.'

Oeric shrugged as if to dismiss my point. 'Well, if you tell me what news you bear I'll have a rider despatched at once. You can then rest awhile and I'll provide men to escort you when you are again fit to ride.'

'I thank you, but my news is for Alfred's ears alone.'

'But look at you man! You're dressed like a Viking wastrel and are clearly all but exhausted. Stay here and rest for a few days or at least for tonight that you can make better time tomorrow. Winchester is yet two days' ride from here.'

I could see he was right so agreed. 'Thank you, I'll stay one night but must then be gone so do not judge me rude on that account.'

'Good, I'll have one of my servants attend you and then tonight you shall dine with me and my father. You can then be gone tomorrow as early as is your wont.'

One of his servants showed me to my lodgings which were within the bounds of the Vill. There my sword was returned to me and I was given clean clothes and a basin at which to wash. I was also given a polished mirror into which I could peer at my reflection. When I did, I was horrified to see that I did indeed look very dishevelled – the tonsure I'd been given as a novice monk had grown out and my hair was long and matted. Also, I'd grown the makings of a weak and whiskery beard which I decided to keep as it made me look older than my years. Despite this, my face appeared drawn and hollow after all I'd endured and I realised that I was much thinner, probably for having eaten so little for so much of the time I'd been away. I did what I could to tidy my appearance then went to join Oeric, anxious to meet Lord Werhard in person.

We dined at a well-stocked table set on one side of the Hall, laden with meats and fruit. His father didn't join us but

Oeric had some very pretty girls attend us and it was clear that their duties were not purely domestic.

'So tell me of your adventures,' he asked with one of the girls seated on his knee.

Something told me not to trust him, though I could find no cause for that other than my own inclination to dislike him. I recounted some of what had befallen me then asked after his father, implying that I was surprised he'd not come to a greet me in person as was my due.

'He will be here anon. But you must know that he's old and that his appetites are diminished in all respects,' he explained, inclining his head towards the girls.

I took his point but, with that, an old man was ushered into the Hall, his back bent and his long hair and beard almost as white as snow.

As the old man approached us I stood up respectfully and allowed him to take his rightful seat at the head of the table. I noticed that Oeric didn't bother to stand in his father's presence or even acknowledge him beyond a cursory nod of his head. Instead, he kept eating with one hand whilst toying with the girl with the other.

As Oeric had said, the old man ate little but seemed pleased to speak with me. I had to admit that I liked him far more than I did his son.

'I knew your father,' he told me. 'I was deeply saddened to hear of his death, and regret he should have died as he did.'

'Did you also know my brother, Lord Edwin?' I asked.

The old man shook his head. 'Not personally but by reputation of course. I'm told he was truly a great warrior.'

I acknowledged the point.

'And you Matthew, I've heard much about you. My son tells me you are anxious to return to Lord Alfred in haste?'

'True, my Lord. I have much to report. My journey thus far has been both long and arduous, not to mention eventful, and I've been forced to endure much danger and hardship along the way.'

'These are indeed troubled times,' he agreed.

'Yet your Shire seems peaceful enough and I notice that you've felt no need to protect either your Vill or the settlement with fortifications.'

Werhard looked anxiously at his son before answering. 'We fare well enough given there are so many Vikings gathered in London which, as you well know, is but a full day's ride from here. Being on the very edge of Wessex and a prosperous settlement, we make a tempting target and many of the farmsteads and smaller settlements within the Shire have all too often suffered raids.'

'What about the fyrd? Cannot they protect them?'

Again Werhard hesitated but left the question unanswered. 'I'm tired and you must forgive me,' he said. 'My old bones seem unable to support me for long these days before I need to rest.'

With that he rose from the table and left the Hall, though I sensed even then there was more he wanted to say.

* * * * *

I too was glad of an early night, especially as I needed to be away at first light the next morning in my haste to reach Winchester. Yet even as I prepared to sleep there came a faint knock at the door to my lodgings.

'I would not disturb you,' said Lord Werhard. 'For you must be tired. But there are things you must know, things I dared not speak of earlier.'

I invited him in and allowed him to sit on the only stool whilst I perched on the edge of my cot.

'You mentioned the raids earlier and asked about the fyrd. Well, Oeric trains the fyrd and does what he can, yet they seem always to arrive too late to offer protection and, so far as I know, have not once managed to intercept any raiders. In my day we would have hunted them day and night to teach them a sharp lesson about the consequence of raiding Saxon homes.'

'So what's changed?'

He spread his hands and then gave me a look that implied there was something he could not, or would not, put into words. 'Alas, things are different now and it seems the old ways are past. Alfred would have peace though not all of Guthrum's horde seem to fully understand that such an arrangement needs both sides to agree.'

'Alfred would not protect any Vikings still intent upon raiding Saxon settlements,' I said.

Lord Werhard shrugged. 'Yet still we suffer.'

'Surely the fyrd could do more…'

He looked at me again. 'Perhaps it suits them not to fully engage with the raiders.'

'Do you mean the fyrd is afraid to fight them?'

He shook his head. 'No not afraid. But I sometimes wonder whether it suits them to look the other way.'

Suddenly I realised what he was saying. 'You cannot mean that the fyrd is—' I stopped myself from saying more, for if what he meant was that the fyrd was profiting from the raids in some way that was a very serious prospect indeed, something he, as Ealdorman, was obliged to ensure didn't happen. No wonder he was reluctant to speak of it directly in front of Oeric if it was he who commanded the fyrd in Lord Werhard's stead.

He seemed to sense what I was thinking. 'My son has many qualities,' he said. 'But he's greedy for silver and power. I quell those faults as best I can but I'm old and will not be here much longer to do so. I fear for the good people of this Shire when I'm gone.'

'But he's your son! Surely you…?'

'Not by birth. He's a changeling who came to me by marriage to my wife whom I loved more dearly than life itself but who sadly passed away some years ago.'

That explained why he'd not been named after Werhard. 'So, who was his father?' I asked.

Lord Werhard looked at me mournfully. 'My wife was lowly born and he was conceived following a raid in which she was raped and abused. His blood may be that of any number of heathens. Who can say?'

I thought for a moment of what that meant, recognising that in taking Emelda to wife I would also be marrying beneath my station. Also, having been forced to become a whore, if by chance she was with child I would have to accept the risk that I might not be the father. It was a reminder of Lord Alfred's misgivings about the match, all of which I began to see were not without good cause. With that Lord Werhard rose to leave.

'I tell you this because I knew your father and because someone outside these walls should know,' he said. Then he changed the subject. 'No doubt you will wish to leave long before my old bones can stir themselves on the morrow. I wish you God speed, Matthew, and a safe journey. Pray give my best regards to Lord Alfred. Tell him the way of things here in Leatherhead. I know it will be of concern to him.'

* * * * *

As planned, I left early the next morning accompanied by four men, all of them armed. We carried what we would need for the journey on a sixth horse which was laden with cooked meat and some salted fish, plus various utensils and a bow.

The journey was without too much risk as there were few robbers who would attack an armed band and the Harroway was as safe a route as could be devised given that it was so well used by travellers and merchants. Viking raiders remained a threat but even they would think twice about revealing themselves by engaging a group who were all mounted and thus able to ride away from trouble.

Although it rained for the next two days we made good progress and arrived at Winchester sooner than expected.

Chapter Seventeen

The settlement at Winchester was even bigger than that at Chippenham and not much smaller than the Saxon and Viking settlements at London combined. We approached by crossing a narrow bridge across the river then entered via a gate which formed part of the old Roman walls. Beyond that was a large open square where a market had been established with more stalls than I could count. The place was alive with people and everywhere I looked there seemed to be works underway with teams of men repairing and reinforcing the old Roman fortifications.

Alfred had established his court within the bounds of his Vill close to the centre of the settlement and, as we approached the inner gates, I was not surprised to find that none of the men on duty knew me. Nonetheless, they seemed to recognise Lord Werhard's banner so after a few brief words, let us pass. As we dismounted a man came across to greet us.

'I am Matthew christened Edward, son of the late Lord Edwulf,' I said. 'You will have received word of my coming and I must speak with Lord Alfred at once.'

It seemed I was indeed expected, Lord Werhard having despatched a rider the night before we left. Therefore the man bowed respectfully then turned to lead the way.

'Will you ensure my escort are well looked after?' I asked, then thanked them for their service before being hurried away towards where I was told Alfred was waiting, anxious to see me.

The Vill itself was well protected and fully enclosed with a tall fence. Apart from the usual lodgings and outbuildings, it included a fine stone minster but was dominated by the Great Hall itself, a magnificent building big enough for at least a hundred men to assemble, possibly more. It had two huge carved oak doors to the front, framed by a covered porch and guarded by two armed men, both of whom moved to bar my path even as I mounted the steps. The man who accompanied me spoke to them and I was allowed to pass, though once again I was relieved of my sword before being allowed to enter the Great Hall itself. Even once inside there were more guards and a good many other people who presumably had business with their liege. I recognised one of them at once.

'My Lord Ethelnorth,' I said, half bowing to acknowledge his seniority. Ethelnorth brushed all that aside as he embraced me.

'Matthew it's good to have you back,' he beamed. 'Though a little the worse for wear by the looks of it.'

'I'm well enough,' I said. 'Though it's true that my journey has been both long and arduous.'

With that Alfred himself realised it was me and, ignoring others, summoned us both over to where he was seated at a huge table on which many plans and drawings had been unrolled. Once again my attempts at homage were ignored. 'It's good to see you safe and have you back with us,' said Lord

Alfred. 'Now come, both of you. There is much to discuss but we must speak in private. And Matthew, I would hear of your adventures.'

It seemed a warm greeting from two such important men, but it allowed me no time to prepare myself or rehearse what was going to be a very long story. It seemed not to matter at the time but, looking back on it, to respect my proposed new role as a courtier and adviser I should have been ready to give a more concise and reasoned report. As it was, many of those who had waited patiently for an audience with Alfred looked dismayed as a bedraggled boy seemed to warrant their King's immediate attention. He dismissed them all and led Lord Ethelnorth and me to a small private chamber. As we entered he motioned to the guards to stand beyond the door and ensure that we were not disturbed. Others were told to bring me food and mead, plus a basin of water so I could wash and refresh myself.

'You've grown since last we saw you,' said Alfred, standing back and looking me over. 'You're no longer a boy and remind me of your brother when he was about your age – though I'm bound to say that you don't look much like a young man of noble birth!'

'Sire, I have endured much on my travels and have not yet had time to…'

Alfred laughed good naturedly. 'It's good to have you back in whatever state you're in. We feared you'd been slain or taken when we found what remained of your escort but no sign of either you or that boy you adopted as your brother.'

'I fear I did not acquit myself well in that,' I confessed. 'Because of bad weather we needed to make better time in order to reach Exeter before you, so I took a short cut through the forest where we were ambushed by Vikings who sought to free the boy. It transpires he's the son of a great Viking warrior – the man my brother Edwin tortured and then killed.'

Alfred reached out and put his hand on my shoulder. 'It's all part of the heavy burden of command,' he said consolingly. 'You carry no blame for the loss of your escort though we all of us feel the pain of it when something like that happens.'

'Yet the responsibility rests with me,' I acknowledged.

'One thing you'll learn is that when you command you take decisions that affect many; but you can't always get them right.'

Given how many men had died on my account it was reassuring to hear him say that and, in truth, having learned of Arne's treachery, I had begun to accept that there was nothing more I could have done except perhaps to have taken the longer route and thereby avoided the forest.

'So how did you survive?' asked Lord Ethelnorth.

'I was the first to fall my Lord. I was wounded by an arrow to my chest and then left for dead. There is much I need to tell you of what transpired after that and which I would now report if you have the time.'

'Go on,' said Alfred.

Hardly knowing where to begin, I told them first about Hakon and the forces he was gathering on the southern bank of the river at London because I deemed that to be of most immediate concern.

'How many men did you see there?' he asked, looking worried.

'At least two hundred warriors,' I said, guessing at their number. 'Possibly more. Not as many as were at Chippenham when I went to spy on Guthrum but still a sizeable force. What's more they're building ships which may mean they're planning an invasion, perhaps even along the southern coast of Wessex.'

Lord Ethelnorth shook his head woefully. 'Surely we don't have to fight the bastards again? God knows we beat them soundly enough at Edington!'

'An army of two or even three hundred men is no longer big enough to cause us immediate concern,' reasoned Alfred.

'No, but others may yet join them!' warned Ethelnorth. 'Sire, you should have put them all to the sword when you had the chance. Their lust for blood knows no bounds therefore you can ill afford to allow them any latitude.'

Alfred raised his hand. 'Yet Guthrum has so far kept his word. And we've had no reports of the movement of any large numbers of men who might join with them.'

'But Sire, they're commanded by a warlord named Hakon, not Lord Guthrum,' I warned. 'He was present when I went to spy on Guthrum's camp that day. He was the third man I told you about, the one who sat with Guthrum and Ubba.'

Ethelnorth was clearly worried. 'We have to send an army if only as a show of strength to deter them,' he reasoned.

Alfred considered all this then shook his head. 'No, that would be a clear sign to suggest that I don't trust Lord Guthrum. My negotiations with him are not yet fully agreed and I dare not risk upsetting them at this crucial stage as that still remains our best hope for peace.'

'Pah! When Hakon and his horde start forming up their battle lines your precious treaty won't be worth shit! What's more, you'll need to send an even bigger army then!' warned Ethelnorth.

'Hakon has a large force, I grant you,' said Alfred. 'But as I say, from what Matthew has told us and from other reports

I've received, it's not yet an army. We'll send men to watch the camp and keep us advised in case their numbers grow or they move as if to attack, but I'm in no fit state to fight again so soon if it can be avoided – our men have already spent too long away from their homes and farmsteads. They need time to restore their lives and to gather in the harvest before the winter is upon us.'

'So what will you do?' I asked.

'Watch and wait,' said Alfred. 'We must also ensure that all the Ealdormen are warned so they can prepare to defend their Shires.'

I couldn't help but laugh.

'What's the matter, Matthew?' asked Alfred.

'Sire, I've met one of the local Ealdormen and I fear that fighting is not something he has in mind.'

'What do you mean?'

'I mean, Sire, that I stayed at Lord Werhard's Vill at Leatherhead for a night and was shocked at what I saw there.'

'Lord Werhard is a good and trusted man who has always served me well,' observed Alfred.

"That's as may be, Sire, but he's now old and frail. His stepson Oeric rules the Shire in his place.'

'What? Is he appointed Reeve?'

'Not in name. But by inclination something much more. Indeed, he rules as though he's already Ealdorman in Lord Werhard's place.'

'Does he by God!' said Alfred angrily. 'He has no right except with my consent. This is treachery indeed!'

'Sire, it cuts even deeper than that,' I said, hardly daring to voice my concerns about all I'd seen there. 'I believe Lord

Werhard was trying to warn me that all is not well within his Shire. Being at the very edge of your realm it suffers many raids yet the fyrd cannot seem to prevent them. I suspect that it's ill trained and poorly armed. What's more, it isn't mustered on a regular basis and—'

'What are you saying Matthew?' demanded Alfred.

'Sire, I fear the raids are carried out to secure enough provisions for Hakon's men. The fact that they venture so far to carry them out suggests they find it easier to raid and pillage there rather than closer to their camp.'

'You mean they don't shit on their own threshold?' said Ethelnorth.

'Exactly. Their presence is tolerated in London and the surrounding settlements and rather than disturb that they carry out their raids further south.'

'Then why does the fyrd not stop them?' asked Alfred.

'That's the point my Lord. Anyone else would have ensured that the fyrd is at full strength and fully armed, but not Oeric.'

Alfred and Ethelnorth both considered the point then suddenly realised what I was suggesting.

'Are you implying that they profit from the raids?' asked Alfred.

'Perhaps my Lord. Or at the very least that it suits them not to intervene. Though I cannot say whether they claim a share of any booty or benefit in other ways.'

'Matthew, that's a very serious accusation.'

'But Sire, not one which I make without good cause. Lord Werhard himself implied as much and besides, he and his stepson live safe and well in a Hall almost as grand as this yet it's without fortifications, nor is it fully guarded. Despite this it seems not to have suffered any raids whilst the people in the outlying settlements endure them repeatedly. What other conclusion can you draw?'

Alfred looked shocked. 'It remains the responsibility of all the Ealdormen to protect their people,' he stormed. 'Not screw every ounce of worth from their already diminished lives simply to fill their own coffers! We'll have to find a way to remind Lord Werhard and his son of their duty.'

'Agreed,' said Ethelnorth. 'But first we have to deal with Hakon. That's the most immediate concern.'

'I'm meeting Guthrum soon to further discuss the treaty,' said Alfred. 'I'll raise the matter with him then.'

'Then this treaty of yours had better be good,' warned Ethelnorth.

'What does it say?' I asked, not sure whether I had the right to ask.

'I'm discussing a plan with Guthrum whereby he'll take his men north, drawing a line beyond which he will not raid or attack, thus leaving Wessex in peace. All I'm doing is offering not to intervene in his affairs there provided his people live within their bounds and in peace.'

'And you trust him to honour such a truce?' queried Ethelnorth.

'I've no cause not to. Besides, at the very least it will give me time to secure my realm.'

'It's madness!' said Ethelnorth. 'Like I say, they're treacherous bastards; you can't believe a word they say!'

'Perhaps,' said Alfred. 'But the lands I'm ceding to him are those beyond Wessex which he already controls in one way or another. He'll distribute these to the men who have served him and that may well include some of those camped with

Jarl Hakon. They'll then protect those lands for us, serving as a barrier against others who might invade Wessex. To save what they've been given they'll fight beside us, not against us, and thereby strengthen our position.'

Lord Ethelnorth still looked far from convinced and I had to admit I had my doubts, but Alfred gave no time for more questions. 'We need peace,' he reasoned. 'War has got us nowhere.'

'Yes,' said Ethelnorth. 'But tell that to that bastard Hakon the Bonebreaker. I fear he has other plans in mind.'

* * * * *

So,' said Alfred as we sat at his table waiting to eat, 'tell me more of all that has transpired whilst you've been away.'

I quickly recounted my adventures, including all that had befallen me.

'And so you are the mysterious warrior with the pierced heart?' chuckled Alfred, for it seemed to amuse him.

I undid my shirt ties and showed him my scar.

He looked at it closely and shook his head. 'Dear God, it's a miracle you survived such a wound. Are you yet recovered?'

I said that I was, explaining that Ingar had used her skills to remove the arrow without probing. I omitted to tell him of Ingar's prophecy that the wound would one day kill me. Strictly speaking, the omission was not a lie but then neither was it the full truth. That worried me as I recalled that my abbot had once warned me that the way with lies is such that they always lead to others. 'The healer said she believed I'd

250

actually died and come back to fulfil my destiny on earth in what she called "the given years".'

Alfred, ever wise in such matters, didn't dismiss the idea out of hand. Miracles and such like were, for him as for us all in those days, an integral part of our faith. Indeed, it had been a visitation from St Cuthbert which had guided him through the darkest days at Athelney, so he had cause enough to respect such things. 'We of course had no inkling it was you when they came to demand ransom,' he explained. 'We thought instead that it was a huge sum to pay for a warrior who would, in all likelihood, die within a matter of days if he was indeed so sorely wounded.'

'Would you have paid it had you known it was me?' I asked, perhaps overstepping the degree of respect to which he was entitled.

Alfred hesitated for a moment, then smiled. 'Of course. Indeed, we would have paid ten times as much to see you safe.'

Relieved, I started to thank him.

'Mind, I would have deducted it from what I owe you,' he added.

I was not sure how to take that but then realised he was joking.

'Matthew, what I owe you cannot be measured in silver or land. You above all others, save perhaps your dear brother and Lord Ethelnorth here, served me well in a time of great need. I promised to give you land in return for the treasure you donated to our cause and that will be honoured in full. Also, you shall inherit your family's lands and, if the Witan so agrees, you shall become an Ealdorman and one of my most trusted counsellors, just as we discussed.'

I thanked him and promised to serve him well, but I could see that he was waiting for me to raise the question we both knew needed to be asked.

'How are things with Emelda?' I inquired as easily as I could. During my travels there had been times when I doubted my love and commitment to her, but I longed to at least see her again in the hope that my feelings would then become clear.

For a moment Alfred looked awkward. 'She's as well as might be expected,' he managed. 'But there are things you should know.'

'Such as?' I asked.

Alfred glanced at Lord Ethelnorth before he answered. 'Matthew, she is with child,' he said.

My heart soared when I heard that, but I could tell Alfred had yet more to say on the matter.

'Fearing you lost, I sent her to a nunnery where she could be cared for. This was simply a way to spare her the questions and ill rumours I feared would follow once her condition became known. I knew that the wives of the men who were with us at Athelney would not take kindly to the thought that their husbands might have fathered a child with a woman they think of as a whore.'

'But surely I'm as likely to be the child's father as any?'

'Perhaps,' said Alfred. 'But if you count back the months it's quite possible that she conceived it before the time that you first lay with her. Therefore the child might be anyone's.'

The news hit me hard. 'That can't be so,' I said. 'Besides, if I claim it as my own who will know any different?'

Alfred calmly acknowledged the point. 'That's true and you are free to raise another man's bastard if you wish. But

Matthew, think on this. You are now a wealthy and very important man in this realm. You carry the name of your forebears whom you've honoured by your service to me and by all the sacrifices you've made. Is all that to pass to what might turn out to be the son or daughter of a lesser man?'

'It might even be the spawn of that treacherous bastard Cedric,' added Ethelnorth. 'He took her often enough.'

I could see what he was saying and called to mind how disappointed Werhard was to have adopted a son of whom he could be neither proud nor sure of. I knew also that if I told Alfred about all that had passed between Ingar and myself, it would count against me, but decided I had to mention it. 'There is another issue here,' I said choosing my words carefully. 'It's possible that I've sired another child with Ingar, the pagan healer who saved me. It was not of my own volition, you understand. She drugged me then took advantage of me to sire a daughter who she claims will become a great healer, having a father who has cheated death and a mother already known for her skills and knowledge of the old ways.'

Alfred looked shocked at first.

'As I say, it was not of my own inclination,' I insisted.

It was left to Lord Ethelnorth to lighten the mood. 'I've lain with one or two pagan wenches myself,' he said laughing. 'Though I can't say they made me do it – or even that they were all that willing at the time!'

Alfred ignored the quip, though I recalled that it was rumoured that in his younger days he'd also bedded wenches with an almost legendary zeal, something which was often blamed for the problems he suffered with his stomach, an illness said to have been inflicted as punishment for his misspent youth. 'And are you to provide for this child?' he asked.

I shook my head. 'I offered but she would have none of it. She worships the Earth Mother who she claims will provide all she needs.'

Again Lord Ethelnorth laughed. 'That's until she learns who you are and where you stand within the realm. Or what you're worth!'

'She knows that already, for I told her,' I admitted.

Alfred got up and moved across to stand by a small window. Meanwhile food was brought and placed on the table in front of me. I washed myself then, having said grace and waited for Alfred's consent, began to eat hungrily.

'This is a matter of some weight,' said Alfred at last. 'Two bastard children may one day dispute your estate and cause a rift that only blood will heal,' he warned.

'I'm still minded to wed Emelda,' I said as if that should make a difference.

'I fear that's not now an option,' said Alfred. 'Besides, you must think of her and the child.'

'But I am! I—'

Alfred shook his head. 'No, you're thinking of your duty and whatever pledge you've made to her. But consider this. She believes you killed so will not be surprised if she never hears from you again. She's shed her tears and come to accept her fate and yours. I'll make provision for the child on the basis that the father was one of those who stood with me at Athelney. She and the child will thus be well provided for.'

I thought for a moment then shook my head. 'I can't forsake her,' I said. 'I made no promise of marriage as we agreed but it was understood between us.'

'Then you must honour whatever commitment you feel you've given. But why not just take her as your woman? Treat her as if she is your wife if you will, but don't acknowledge the child as your own.'

What he suggested went against my creed though I was beginning to see that it did make sense.

'Be strong enough to do this for the child's sake, if nothing else,' he continued. 'If you acknowledge it, he or she will one day inherit your estate. Others may then step forward to claim the child as their own, demanding a share of its inheritance. Worse still, the child of this pagan witch may demand her rightful share as well. Either way your heritage will be one of envy, distrust and, as I've said, most likely blood.'

If I looked uncertain at that point it was because I knew that all Alfred had said was true. 'Where is Emelda?' I asked.

'As I said I've sent her to a nunnery and, for your own sake and hers, I'll not tell you where. But know she's safe and well cared for. All there believe her to be a woman whose husband died fighting for his Lord, not a whore bearing the bastard child of a man she cannot name. It's better for her that it remains thus, for that way she has honour and respect. If you would see her, wait until the child is born. Even then you must resolve to pretend you are a friend of her dead husband if only to preserve her reputation.'

'This is wise counsel,' suggested Ethelnorth. 'Surely you owe her that?'

'Aye,' continued Alfred. 'And I believe that when you see the child you'll know in your heart whether or not it is of your blood.'

Reluctantly I agreed. 'And what do I do until then?' I asked.

'Ah, now that's a much easier thing for me to answer. Rest for a few days then come with me and Lord Ethelnorth to meet with Guthrum. After that there is much to be done and I'll need men like you I can trust. Do you recall that when we spoke as we waited for Guthrum to surrender I mentioned forming an army that will fight for peace?'

'Most certainly,' I said. 'And I would be part of that if you'll have me.'

'Of necessity, my plans have changed somewhat but the objectives remain the same. I now intend to fortify key settlements to protect us from attacks, just as I'm doing here at Winchester. From all that you've told me that is now of paramount importance, particularly in places close to the borders or the sea. What I have in mind is charging the Ealdormen to take full responsibility not only for training the fyrd but also for ensuring that the men within their Shire are properly armed. The fyrd will comprise men levied from all the settlements which desire its protection, all serving in rotation so that a force stands armed and ready at all times. Those on the coast will also have ships at their disposal to intercept the Vikings whilst still at sea, attacking them whilst the raiders are still weary from their journey and thus ill prepared to fight.'

'I met with some ships which put to sea in pursuit of Torstein,' I said. 'It did them little good for both were turned back. One of them was actually set afire and sunk with all on board then either drowned or lost.'

Alfred smiled. 'Thus far we've used just fishing and trading boats, or captured longships, but I've commissioned designs for specially built vessels, each manned by as many as sixty oars so they can strike hard and fast regardless of the wind.'

I acknowledged that it was a sound proposal. 'But training is important,' I stressed. 'You must have men able to handle such craft. Likewise with the fyrd. The men need to know how to remain steadfast in the shield wall and how to fight. You recall how readily we trained all those who stood with us at Combwich?'

'I'm sure most men know well enough how to handle themselves,' said Alfred.

'Perhaps Sire, but I saw one Ealdorman, Lord Sigbert, who left it to one of his thanes to fight his battles for him. The man he appointed was a fool who lacked any military skill and thereby led his men to almost certain defeat. Jarl Torstein beat him soundly even though hopelessly outnumbered.'

Ethelnorth nodded. 'I fear there are others like that as well. What's more, the raids are becoming commonplace again.'

'So how will you pay for all that you now propose?' I asked changing the subject slightly. 'Surely the people have been taxed enough?'

Alfred grinned. 'I won't have to trouble them further on that account. Lord Guthrum has provided the means.'

'But how?'

'You'll recall that when we retook Chippenham I demanded that all booty was to be returned to me?'

'Yes. He seemed reluctant but had little choice at the time.'

Ethelnorth seemed to find that amusing. 'It's surprising how men seem not to worry so much about the value of what you take when you hold a sword to their throat!'

'True,' said Alfred. 'And when it came to it we found the Vill was stacked full of loot and plunder. All taken from Saxon homes and Abbeys, but it would now be impossible to return it to its rightful owners, therefore I shall spend it on making my realm secure.'

'Was there really so much plunder there?' I asked incredulous.

It was Ethelnorth who answered. 'More than you could count!' he said. 'There were chests brimming with jewels, silver and fine stones together with chalices and crosses of pure gold and goodness knows what else. Certainly enough to pay for a few extra helmets and spears.'

'Like I said, I intend to provide much more than that,' corrected Alfred. 'But having bled our realm dry, Guthrum has acted more like a collector of taxes than an invader and in so doing, will help us to secure it. What it actually means is that I can proceed with my plans at once and without taking coin from the already empty purses of my people.'

Chapter Eighteen

The following day Alfred summoned both Ethelnorth and me to see him again. We waited patiently in the Great Hall whilst he dealt with various matters of state and where the noisy throng of those demanding his attention seemed to have grown even larger.

'As you can see, much has changed whilst you've been away,' mused Ethelnorth.

'Indeed,' I said. 'I gather the realm is alive with new projects and proposals which is all to the good.'

'Aye, but ships and fortifications take time to build so progress may be slower than Alfred would like.'

'Then what of all these people?' I asked, pointing towards the crowds of men who were clamouring for their King's attention.

Ethelnorth managed a smile. 'They are all greedy merchants and traders vying to sell him what they think he'll need. For that they must speak with him in person because whilst Lord Alfred still consults the Witan, he's no longer bound to have it endorse his every move. His reputation is such that he has a free hand in almost every way.'

'Surely such power is a heavy burden for any man to carry alone?'

'And for anyone but Lord Alfred, one which would be wide open to abuse,' agreed Ethelnorth. 'He always takes a fair hand in everything, but you wonder how much of the strain of it all he can manage and for how long. Like a tree laden with fruit, the bough is wont to bend and break if the wind against it blows too strong.'

'So who will be there to pick up the pieces if he falls?'

'Don't worry, he's all too well aware of how fragile all this becomes when left to him alone and is making provision for others who can oversee some matters – trusted Reeves to act as administrators and governors who will report to him direct. And of course there's us.'

'Are we so important?'

'Of course! We've earned his trust and with so much in hand he needs men like us more than ever now. Not just to carry out his orders but to speak frankly when he goes too far or to point out any flaws in all the plans he's been forced to construe so quickly.'

It was then that I heard a commotion at the entrance to the Great Hall where it seemed a man had foolishly tried to push his way past the guards. He had been detained readily enough and forced back against a wall at spear point.

'Let him pass,' I shouted when I recognised my old friend, Aelred.

Osric, who remained as chief of Alfred's personal guard, intervened and escorted Aelred to where I waited.

'Matthew, do you vouch for this wretch?' asked Osric. 'He claims he has urgent news for the King but is unknown to us and—' He stopped at that, perhaps not wishing to imply that Aelred didn't look to be the sort of man who would normally be admitted to the Great Hall and thereby into the Alfred's presence.

'This rogue is indeed known to me,' I said, laughing as I embraced Aelred warmly then stood back and looked him over as if to check it was really him and not his ghost. 'So tell me, how the hell did you survive the river?' I asked.

'I eventually made it to the Saxon shore though some distance from the settlement. It has taken me all this time to get here,' he explained.

'Well, I'm truly pleased to see you,' I said, then introduced him to Lord Ethelnorth. Aelred was suitably respectful, bowing slightly and not attempting to shake Ethelnorth's hand. I then explained all we'd been through together and the fact that Aelred had saved my life.

'And you came all this way just to tell Lord Alfred what you thought had become of Matthew?' asked Ethelnorth.

'I did my Lord. I would presume to call Matthew my friend and have taken it upon myself to look out for him.'

'Such loyalty is to be commended,' acknowledged Ethelnorth, clearly impressed. 'But I think you need hardly concern yourself with young Matthew's safety; he seems to have a way of getting himself out of trouble.'

Aelred grinned. 'Aye my Lord, so he does. But he then gets himself into even more of it straight afterwards! Out of the pot and into the fire is how I see it.'

I could see that Ethelnorth liked Aelred at once, particularly his way of speaking plainly even if that meant sometimes overstepping the mark. 'Well, then he may have need of you again,' he said. 'For I somehow doubt that Matthew's adventures are yet complete.'

* * * * *

Aelred waited outside whilst Alfred had Ethelnorth and me shown into the small chamber to one side of the Great

Hall once more, then joined us there. Such offices were not normally part of a Saxon Hall, but Alfred had foreseen that he might need somewhere private to talk without first clearing the main Hall itself.

'I'm sorry for keeping you so long and for calling you back so soon,' he said. 'There seems so much to be done and so little time.'

I noticed that as he took his seat his hand clutched his stomach and that he grimaced, clearly still suffering from the inflammation in his gut. He made no mention of it as he sat back and looked at us. 'Despite all I've said, I find I'm yet uneasy about all that transpires in London,' he said. 'And I know Ethelnorth that you have grave doubts about Hakon's intent. So Matthew, tell me more of what you actually saw there.'

I thought carefully before I answered. 'Sire, what surprised me most was that the Saxon settlement which is just across the river seemed to accept the presence of the Vikings so readily. It was as though they had reached an uneasy peace between them.'

Alfred nodded wisely. 'That may be to the good,' he said simply.

'Yes Sire, but what worries me is that the Vikings were there in such numbers. As you said, they are not yet an army but close to it. If they moved from there to attack us—'

Alfred raised his hand. 'I'm certain Hakon will not move against us, at least not yet. Whatever his intentions, he's not building all those longships for nothing so won't make his move until they're ready.'

'But can we truly be sure of that, Sire?'

'I believe we can. And as I said, my plan is for Guthrum to move north where he already has many supporters. Once there, the position will change as Hakon fears him as much as he fears us and knows that if he were to move on either one of us he could be crushed between us and slaughtered. In the meantime, he's helping us by drawing bands of robbers and troublemakers from across our realm to join him, just as a dog gathers fleas.'

'Which may well aid our cause,' observed Ethelnorth who, having slept on it, seemed more at ease with the position – or perhaps he was satisfied that Alfred was at last heeding his concerns.

'How so?' I asked.

'Well,' said Ethelnorth. 'You can either immerse the dog in the river so that all the fleas run to its head for fear of drowning where they're easier to deal with or...' he hesitated for a moment. 'Or you can drown the dog and all its parasites with it,' he managed at last.

I considered this for a moment. 'What happens if Guthrum joins forces with Hakon? Together they'd be a serious threat.'

'But Guthrum has given me his word,' said Alfred.

'Pah!' said Ethelnorth. 'A word he's broken before!'

'He won't this time because he'll have lands of his own to protect,' reasoned Alfred. 'Land is what he came here for, not just booty and blood. Why would he risk crossing me once he has what he wanted in the first place?'

Ethelnorth shook his head. 'So, after all those battles and all that blood we give back the land we fought for to the very man who took it from us in the first place!'

'All the lands I'm ceding to him are already under Viking control,' explained Alfred. 'He gains not one single hide of land which forms part of my realm. All I'm doing is ensuring that he leaves Wessex in peace.'

'But as Lord Ethelnorth has said, they're treacherous bastards,' I warned.

'Which is why I've formed a plan in case I've misjudged Hakon's intent,' announced Alfred. 'And it's one which also suits our purpose well.'

Both Ethelnorth and I were surprised but knowing how adept Alfred was in that respect, waited eagerly to hear what he'd come up with.

'My intention is to strengthen my realm by setting up fortified burghs which will provide protection for all.' He placed a plan of Wessex on the table in front of us and unrolled it. It showed just over thirty settlements which he planned to fortify. 'As you can see, they're close enough to reinforce each other if any one of them comes under attack, being but a day's march apart.'

Lord Ethelnorth and I both agreed that the plan had merit.

'So where will you start?' I asked.

'I have already done so,' he said pointing at the plan. 'It will take time to complete but work is underway here, here, here and also here. Plus some rudimentary defences are being constructed at most of the other major settlements. Given all that Matthew has said about the treachery in Leatherhead...'

'As yet unproved,' I pointed out.

'Yes, as yet unproved. But the settlement there controls a gap through the northern downs and is therefore a place we should strive to protect. If Hakon does recruit more men then moves to attack us, it's my guess that he'll most likely send the ships you saw being built to sail around the coast and have them moor up on one of the beaches or inlets somewhere on the southern shore. He'll then march overland to meet them and use them to support and supply his army.'

Ethelnorth looked shocked. 'With the ships ferrying supplies and reinforcements he would be very difficult to shift,' he warned.

'Exactly,' said Alfred. 'But to reach the ships he'll need to access the pass through the hills at Leatherhead and use the ford there to cross the river. Therefore we should secure that position at all costs.'

'There are other routes he could take,' I ventured. 'Other passes and other fords.'

Alfred acknowledged the point. 'But once he starts to march on us he'll have to move fast. The gap at Leatherhead would be the quickest and therefore the most obvious route for him to take.'

'But if you fortify Leatherhead what of your negotiations with Guthrum?' pressed Ethelnorth.

'Guthrum will see any steps we take as just part of all the other works I'm undertaking within the realm so would have no cause to take offence.'

Whilst certain that Alfred would have already considered every possibility, there were some aspects I was still unsure off. 'But it would be no use improving the fortifications at Leatherhead unless you send more men there as well,' I ventured.

Alfred got up and walked towards a small alcove where he poured mead from a pitcher and drank it. 'Once armed and properly trained, the fyrd should be able to deal with the raiders,' he said as he returned and settled back into his seat. 'As for Hakon's forces, if they do deign to attack all the fyrd would have to do is delay them long enough for me to arrive with reinforcements.'

'Who trains the fyrd now?' asked Ethelnorth.

'Lord Werhard's stepson, Oeric,' I said. 'Not that he does much in the way of training.'

'Perfect,' said Alfred. 'So I have every excuse to send someone there to take on that role. We can then slay four birds with a single stone. The new man can oversee the provision of the fortifications. He can also train the fyrd and use it to see off any raiders. Whilst there he can also discover whether that upstart Oeric does indeed profit from the misfortunes of his people.'

'And if he does?

'Then he shall be severely punished for his treachery. By singling him out I shall send a clear message to any other Ealdormen who are abusing their position.' With that, Alfred got up again and this time stretched his back. Then he continued. 'Ideally we would punish all offenders but that could drive a stake through my realm and thus divide us at a time when I crave and so badly need unity above all else. By making an example of this upstart Oeric I'll show them all that their duty to their King is not something to be taken lightly.'

Both Ethelnorth and I agreed the plan had merit but we both had reservations.

'I agree that having trained the fyrd and fortified the settlement they should be able to deal with any raiders,' reasoned Ethelnorth. 'But you'll need to send more men if you would have them stand against Hakon's army as well.'

'Agreed,' said Alfred.

'So how many men do you have in mind?' I asked.

He hesitated before replying. 'Just two,' he said solemnly.

'Two!' I said, hardly able to believe what I was hearing. 'Who do you have in mind who could achieve such a thing!'

Alfred then looked me straight in the eye. 'Well, you for one,' he said. 'Plus another warrior of your choosing.'

'Sire!' I said, incredulous at what he was saying. 'Surely you can't be serious! This is too much to ask of just two men! It's a huge and perilous undertaking and…'

'Then who better to see it done? I need a man I can trust completely and one who has sufficient authority and is known to be a fine warrior. Someone the members of the fyrd will respect and listen to. Do I ask too much?'

I was too stunned to answer at first. 'Sire, I will follow any order I'm given…but how can it succeed? It is possible to train farmers to fight off raiders but not to see off over two hundred Viking warriors!'

'Delay them,' corrected Ethelnorth. 'The plan is not to beat Hakon, just hold him up long enough for reinforcements to arrive.'

Alfred could clearly see that I was more than a little worried by the prospect of what was being asked of me. 'I have no army to send to Leatherhead,' he explained. All the men I can muster are needed elsewhere and for other projects. Therefore I must seek a diplomatic solution to this problem, not just a military one.'

'Meaning what, my Lord?'

'Meaning that I shall give you letters saying that you are authorised by me in person to take over running and training the fyrd there and fortifying the settlement as you see fit. The warrior you take with you would do the physical training leaving you as my Reeve to provide the necessary authority. Your reputation alone should suffice to inspire the members of the fyrd and may even serve to discourage Hakon. Then, once the fyrd is fully trained and the settlement secure, you can turn your attention to the raids and also discover whether or not this rogue Oeric has a hand in them.'

'And all that with just one man?' I queried.

Alfred nodded. 'There's no one more suited to the task. Select any warrior you like but choose wisely. You need a man you can rely on.'

Ethelnorth looked relieved that he was not being asked to go on such a seemingly impossible mission. 'Matthew, you'll need to choose well,' he warned. 'If there is treachery afoot then all those involved will have much to lose. Your problem will be knowing who is your foe as they may find it suits their purpose to have you quietly disappear. It'll be like prodding a nest of wasps and you can ill afford to be stung.'

'Aye,' said Alfred. 'It is a dangerous role; I make no bones about it. It's perhaps even more dangerous than anything I've ever asked of you before.'

* * * * *

With Alfred's plan settled in principle, Ethelnorth left, anxious to meet with two men who had brought word from Exeter where he'd set up his own Hall and from where he controlled that part of Wessex, acting as overlord in Lord Alfred's absence. Once he'd gone, Alfred made it clear that he and I needed to speak further.

'Is there yet something more I should know?' I asked, almost dreading what else he might have in mind for me to do.

Alfred seemed to choose his words carefully before he answered. 'If Werhard's son is at fault, accusing him of treachery is not something to be undertaken lightly. And remember, as Lord Ethelnorth rightly pointed out, there will be others who support him who may see it as being in their own interests to be rid of you rather than see their benefactor exposed.'

As I feared, even that part of the mission was far from straightforward.

'You'll need to exercise all your skills of tact and diplomacy,' added Alfred. 'But if at any stage you feel you're threatened, you must withdraw and report to me.'

'So am I to actually take on the raiders or not?'

'That will be your decision, but you must be assured of victory if you do.'

I was silent as I considered all he'd said. 'Then I will endeavour to bring those who are at fault to justice.'

Alfred shook his head. 'Ah, no. Unfortunately that's a luxury I can ill afford. A full trial will take time and if the son of an Ealdorman is one of the accused he'll be entitled to be tried by his equals, some of whom may be even more guilty than he is. Therefore you may need to act swiftly and decisively.'

I thought for a moment then realised what he was saying. 'You mean execute him without a trial!'

'No, I mean dispense justice as you see fit.'

That was not an order I relished as I knew that such responsibility would not sit easy on my conscience. Even though I'd killed many men by then, it was always with good cause or in self-defence. What Lord Alfred was asking was close to cold-blooded murder.

'There will be a time when we can look to justice for all,' explained Alfred as though sensing my misgivings. 'Until then I must do what I can to protect the ordinary people from the excessive greed of their betters. That's why I need men like you; men who will not relish the authority I'm bestowing on them and can therefore be trusted to do what's right when the need arises.'

I understood and, though not at ease with what was being asked of me, nodded my agreement. I couldn't help but recall how Edwin and I had been sent back to kill the traitor Goda during the retreat to Athelney. That also had little to do with justice; it was a question of simply ensuring his silence for the safety of all.

'So, when will you leave?' asked Alfred.

'If it pleases you, my Lord, I would come with you to the meeting with Guthrum, for that may tell us more about Hakon's intentions. On the way I should like to find time to visit Edwin's grave which I fear has been long neglected whilst I've been away.'

'The mass grave of all the men who died at Edington has been well tended,' Alfred assured me.

'Even so my Lord, I should like to pay my respects.'

He acknowledged the point.

'In the meantime, I'm minded to see my old abbot to renounce my vows, something I've been remiss in not doing before. I'll then leave for Leatherhead at once. The raids are likely to become less frequent as the winter draws in and so I can use that time to get the training underway and also begin work on the fortifications.'

'Excellent. Have you yet decided who to take with you on this mission?'

'Yes, Sire, I would choose a man named Aelred. He's a ceorl but one who has proved his loyalty to me many times over.'

'A ceorl? Would you not be better choosing a thane or a warrior to go with you? One who can not only properly train the fyrd but also watch your back?'

I shook my head. 'If it comes to a battle there will be warriors enough once the fyrd has been trained. Until then, the man I need should be one who knows my ways and can be trusted even when others fail. But there's something I must ask you first.'

'What is it?'

'I suspect that Aelred has not led an entirely blameless life and I would therefore have you offer him a pardon in recognition of his service at my side. I don't doubt he'll transgress again but he should at least start out on our mission with his slate wiped clean.'

'What has he done?'

'I can't say for certain my Lord, except that I know he's partaken freely of your deer and game and I wouldn't be surprised to find he has other more serious misdeeds to his name as well. He has also never acknowledged any bondage though may well have obligations to someone.'

'He sounds like a wise choice,' acknowledged Alfred. 'Who better to take into a den of thieves and robbers than one who knows their ways? But would you have me pardon him knowing so little of what he's done?'

'You did as much for those who agreed to stand with us at Combwich,' I reminded him. 'You knew nothing of their crimes yet freely pardoned them all.'

Seemingly satisfied at that, Alfred agreed. 'Very well, I'll issue a full pardon to Aelred. But he must first confess his sins before God and then promise to mend his ways.'

I smiled at the thought of Aelred making confession. 'Sire, I'll have him come with me to see my old abbot,' I offered. 'Though as to any promise, I somehow doubt that will bind him for long!'

'You've learned much whilst you've been away. But Matthew, there is one other point. I must ask you whether you are indeed well enough to undertake this mission?'

'I think my wound has now healed,' I said. 'It took longer than I thought and meant that I tended to tire easily, albeit I seemed to then recover readily enough. The exertions of rowing the boat to London seemed not to trouble me and when I fought Torstein I felt only a slight weariness on that account.' All of that was true but it was the second time I'd not been entirely honest with him given that Ingar's prophecy was still ringing in my ears.

'Just remember, the most dangerous scars are the ones you cannot see,' he warned.

I wasn't sure what he meant by that but said nothing.

'And what about Emelda? Have you reached a decision regarding her and the child?'

That was more difficult for me to answer. I was loath to admit it but my feelings towards Emelda were not as strong as they had once been and thus I was ready to accept all that Alfred had counselled about not seeing her until after the child was born. 'I have, Sire,' I said. 'Though my conscience is not at ease with it.'

'So you've decided to leave her be?'

'Yes, though I pray that she never learns that I'm alive and have avoided her.'

'This mission will take you far from here and from her nunnery so there's no reason why word should reach her. By

272

all means go to her when you return. By then the child should be born and you can make your decision based on what you see and what you feel within your heart.'

As always, it was wise counsel. With that it remained only for me to persuade Aelred to come with me on what was perhaps the strangest mission I had ever undertaken – and one that I knew could be even more dangerous than anything I'd ever faced before. Not only that, it seemed it could well fall to me to ensure that the dark clouds of war which still loomed over us would finally be dispelled.

To be continued…

Glossary

Whilst not all universally accepted, the following is an explanation of some of the terms as used in this story:

BERSERKERS Feared Viking warriors who were said to work themselves up into a frenzy prior to fighting, often by imbibing some form of hallucinogen. They sometimes fought bare-chested or wearing a symbolic bear skin and were said not to feel pain or fear anything, even death.

BRETWALDA A mainly honorary title given to a recognised overlord.

CEORL The lowest rank of freemen.

EALDORMAN A high-ranking nobleman usually appointed by the king to oversee a shire or group of shires.

FYRD A group of able-bodied freemen who could be mobilised for military service when required.

LUR A battle horn.

JARL A Viking nobleman or chieftain.

REEVE An official appointed to oversee specific duties on behalf of the King or an Ealdorman. These included administrative and sometimes judicial responssibilities.

SEAX A short single-edged sword.

THANE A freeman holding land granted by the King or by an Ealdorman to whom he owed allegiance and for whom he provided military support when needed.

VILL The fortified estate of the King or an Ealdorman, usually comprising a large Hall plus other buildings to provide accommodation, administrative offices and stabling etc. It was usually supported by extensive holdings in terms of farmland, pastures and hunting grounds.

WITAN An assembly whose duty was to advise the King and with whom he could consult.

Acknowledgements

I should first like to thank all those who have provided such positive feedback following the publication of *Blood & Destiny*, which was the first in this series. Inevitably, writing is a somewhat solitary pursuit and any encouragement is always welcome. To that end, I should particularly like to thank the team at RedDoor – Clare, Heather and Anna – not only for their support but for their belief and confidence in me as a writer.

The Warrior with the Pierced Heart is primarily a work of fiction and most characters, including Matthew himself, have emerged from my own imagination rather than from the pages of history. It is, however, based on a great deal of detailed research for which I must once again thank the many very knowledgeable historians, too numerous to mention, whose work has provided both information and inspiration. Similarly, I am indebted to various re-enactment groups who, through their commitment and attention to detail, share my enthusiasm for bringing history to life.

That said, any mistakes, errors or omissions are all mine, including the many 'liberties' I have taken throughout the story.

Finally, I am, of course, extremely grateful for the support of my wife and family who, as with Book 1, were so often deprived of my full attention whilst I was away with Matthew on his many adventures.

THE SHADOW OF THE RAVEN SERIES
Blood and Destiny
(Book 1)

It's 878 and, with most of his army destroyed following a surprise attack by the Vikings at Chippenham, Alfred, King of Wessex is forced to retreat to the desolate marshes at Athelney. Whilst few believe he could ever hope to restore his kingdom, he remains determined – no matter the cost.

Among Alfred's small band of weary survivors is Matthew, a novice monk who must learn to fight like a warrior if he, along with his brother and fellow Saxons, are to have any chance of defeating the fearsome Vikings.

As an impending battle looms, Matthew is charged with a vital role that means he must face danger and betrayal and undertake a hazardous journey which will test both him and his faith to the limit.

This red-bloodied tale is not just about battles and gory hand-to-hand fighting; it is about victory against the odds as the Saxons fight not just for their freedom and their religion, but for their very existence.

Published by RedDoor £8.99
Also available in audiobook (Audible) and e-book

The Final Reckoning
(Book 3)

Following his triumph at the Battle of Edington, Alfred strives to restore his kingdom. Yet the prospect of further invasion looms large and he is troubled not just by further Viking raids but also by dissent from some of his own nobles who seek to abuse their power. There is only one man who can be trusted to set matters right, but it means Matthew must undertake a perilous and seemingly impossible mission – one which may well cost him his life if he is to dispel the clouds of war which are once more gathering over King Alfred's kingdom of Wessex.

To be released shortly

About the Author

Chris Bishop was born in London in 1951. After a successful career as a chartered surveyor, he retired to concentrate on writing, combining this with his lifelong interest in history. This is the second book in **The Shadow of the Raven** series, the first, *Blood and Destiny*, having been published in 2017.